A POOR MAN'S TRUCE

Titles in the Series

The Reckless Apprentice

A Poor Man's Truce Copyright © 2018 by H.E Scott. All Rights Reserved.

All rights reserved. No part of this book may be reproduced in any form or by any electronic or mechanical means including information storage and retrieval systems, without permission in writing from the author. The only exception is by a reviewer, who may quote short excerpts in a review.

Deranged Doctor Design
derangeddoctordesign.com

This book is a work of fiction. Names, characters, places, and incidents either are products of the author's imagination or are used fictitiously. Any resemblance to actual persons, living or dead, events, or locales is entirely coincidental.

H.E. Scott
Visit my website at www.hescott.ca

Printed in the United States of America

A Poor Man's Truce

Chronicles of Sangan
Book 2

H.E. Scott

For Dale,
Thank you for your never-ending enthusiasm,
encouragement and cheerfulness.
Missing you every day.

CONTENTS

To my friend
Leslie

[illegible]

CHAPTER 1

A cool breeze blew through the clearing, ruffling Elieana's hair, tickling her face. She awoke, startled. She had dreamt Darec caressed her cheek. Blushing with embarrassment, she looked around self-consciously, then became angry, the thought, a distraction, something to keep her from her goal of getting away with Nada. She selfishly did not want to see Nada go back to Belisle and her father. Immediately she berated herself for even thinking of keeping them apart.

Nada had a right to be with her family but Elieana feared the danger facing her. There were many who believed, Nada's father, King Stefan, incapable of ruling, being in very poor health. How much more would they disagree with his young daughter ruling in his stead or perhaps allow it but take advantage of her youth. Elieana shook her head sadly; if it befell Nada, to be crowned queen, as King Stefan's heir, danger would always lick at her heels.

Deciding she should keep busy rather than think of things she could not change she rose and stretched her aching limbs, sore from the day's long ride. She wandered over to the cliff edge. Their ride that morning had climbed quite high into the mountains and from this vantage point she could see the Alati Sea, sparkling in the waning sunlight; and tiny islands no larger than the head of a pin. As she gazed out at the scene before her the sun slowly changed the sky to soft, muted tones of orange, pink and gray. Glorious, she thought, and she breathed deeply of the sweet, fresh air as the sun slowly slipped into the sea.

Darec walked over to where Elieana stood, bringing two mugs of heavily sweetened, Bakla tea. Without a word, he passed a mug to Elieana, who took it from him gratefully. She gripped the mug with both hands, the warmth feeling good on her stiff fingers. Darec's small kindnesses unnerved her, she desperately wanted to dislike the man and again felt embarrassed with the memory of her dream.

"Thank you, Darec," she said, avoiding looking directly at him.

"Consider it a token of peace. I should have warned you my men were meeting us, but I did not expect to meet them so soon."

"No matter, it would probably have kept me in the saddle though," she replied, smiling at him. "I'm sure I surprised your men. I imagine they did not expect an armed attacker throwing herself at their feet."

Their eyes met and for some seconds it seemed as if all movement and sound stopped. A moment later the feeling, replaced by awkwardness, caused them both to stumble in their conversation.

"It's a..."

"Will you..."

As if on cue, the cook clattered a pan, calling them to dinner. With the moment shattered Darec smiled down at her, a half smile, as if he had just had an amusing thought. With a grand bow, he motioned towards the cook fire. "After you," he said and Elieana walked ahead of him towards their dinner.

The men clustered around a very small campfire, the flames very bright, producing little smoke. They nodded at Elieana as she entered the circle to get her plate but said nothing, intent on their food.

The cook had prepared a splendid meal from the surrounding forest: tubers and berries in abundance and the crayfish, succulent and sweet, he found in the pool of water they camped beside. Elieana praised him for his resourcefulness. Beaming with pleasure at her praise the cook gave her an extra helping. When they had eaten their fill, the cook doused the fire and darkness settled upon the campsite. "It's due to how close we are to the trail, my dear," said the cook. "It is a raider's trail and it is often traveled at night. Because we are so high up the fire will be noticed from a long way off, the reason why we used Munga wood for the fire. It burns hot with hardly any smoke, but the flames could be seen at night. Unfortunately, it will be a chilly night for us. If you need another blanket, I have an extra."

"Thank you. You are most kind. I did bring a heavy fleece and leggings, so I hope I won't have to trouble you."

"You have only to ask and I will bring you what you need."

"Some more tea?" she said and held out her mug to him.

The cook nodded and poured more Bakla into Elieana's mug.

"What is your name, sir?"

"Orris."

"You are from the south, it sounds, from your accent," said Elieana.

"I am, but an age ago. The Sangan hoards drove my family out of the mountains. Since that time, we settled in Pelagos, with no desire to return."

"I am finding there are many people in Pelagos who are from other places," said Elieana. "Well, thank you, Orris, for the meal and conversation. I know I will sleep well this night."

"Rest well, we are all here to protect you."

Elieana tried to keep the surprise off her face as she walked back to the tree where she rested earlier. Orris' statement awakened a niggling fear. Surely, they were well away from any danger. Unless the raiders were more of a threat than she realized.

When she reached the tree, she saw someone had taken her blanket, pack and saddle and made a cozy bed in a sheltered spot between two large tree roots, large enough to conceal her presence and keep the wind off, making it cozy and warm. She settled herself comfortably and leaned back against the trunk of the tree, to drink her tea, and gaze up at the night sky. Slowly the murmur of voices died down and the meadow settled into stillness.

Unable to fall asleep Elieana retraced the events of the previous days. As she sat pondering, she heard something move in the bushes nearby and then pandemonium broke out. Men shouted; she heard grunts, the sound of blows of some object on soft body parts. Someone approached where she lay hidden. Her fingers curled around the hardened leather scabbard of her sword. She swung as hard as she could. The scabbard hit something; her hand went numb and she dropped the scabbard. Elieana jumped up and ran towards the campsite. Whoever had attacked had been speedily defeated and Darec's men gave chase through the forest.

Orris, the designated healer for the men, relit the fire, preparing to tend any wounds. Elieana went over to help him and pointed to the tree where she lay only moments before. "There is one by the tree, I think he is unconscious. I hit him quite hard when he ran past. He didn't move after he fell," she said falteringly, feeling very guilty for causing someone injury.

Darec glanced towards where she pointed then he and one of his men went to investigate. They found a man laying splayed out on the ground. He was curiously dressed all in black and had concealed his face with a strip of black fabric wound completely around his head. Limp as a dead man, he still breathed. The blow from Elieana's scabbard broke his arm. The large tree root he struck his head on rendered him unconscious. They grasped the man's legs and unceremoniously dragged him into the light of the fire.

Elieana and Orris worked together, splinting and binding his arm and then the men trussed him up, so he could not escape when he regained consciousness.

Shortly after, Darec's men staggered back to the camp, supporting one of their comrades who bled profusely from a large gash on his head. The man's ghastly white face looked like a death mask in the flickering firelight.

Elieana rushed over and pressed a pad of cloth over the wound to staunch the flow of blood while she waited for Orris to come and stitch the wound.

"Arloff is dead, sir," said one of the men. "He killed his attacker."

Darec nodded to the man who then walked out of the light of the fire, his head hanging low in grief.

Elieana caught Darec's eye, "His uncle," said Darec.

Suddenly an overwhelming feeling of responsibility swept over Elieana. Had they not come in search of the packet these men would not be here tending their wounded and burying another one of their comrades.

But wait, a voice inside her said, wait. Had Nada not been injured by the sword they would not have uncovered someone's plot to kill. The outcome could be even more devastating if they didn't discover who buried the sword on the beach. Another wave of guilt swept over her. Her chest tightened in grief for the dead man. What were they doing here looking for a packet of papers to prove Nada's pedigree, instead of in the city, looking for the person responsible for the buried sword?

In the middle of her self-castigation two of Darec's men dragged another, struggling man, into the campsite. They dropped him in the dirt at Darec's feet. Darec grabbed his hair and yanked his head back. He pulled his blade from the scabbard on his belt and held it to the man's throat. The man's eyes bulged with fear and he slumped down, sinking to his knees.

With a flick of his knife Darec cut the cloth covering the man's face, revealing the smooth, unblemished face of a boy no more than thirteen years. A droplet of sweat trickled down the side of his face and fear shone bright in his eyes.

"Who are you and where do you come from?" snarled Darec.

The boy swallowed, nervously, his skinny throat, bobbing.

"I am Galen, from the village of Sacla, on the River Noor. Raiders have attacked many villages recently. We banded together to ambush the raiders and kill them. They have dragged away our able-bodied men and driven off our herds."

Darec let go the boy's hair to let him fall prostrate on the ground.

"We are not the raiders you are seeking," said Darec. "What colors do these raiders wear, what crest?"

"They wear no colors; they ride disguised. Only one wore a crest." The boy described a crest of mountains, a wall and a golden ring in the foreground.

Darec and Elieana glanced at each other simultaneously. Both knew the crest of Vasilis, the Ambassador from the city of Belenos near the border of Pelagonia and Baltica.

"How is it you saw this crest? The Ambassador's soldiers would not attack villages," said Darec, his tone one of disbelief.

"They disguise themselves when they attack. One of our men slashed at a rider as he passed, cutting him but also hitting the saddle and this came off." He reached into his jerkin and pulled out a leather pouch, the crest of the Ambassador's bodyguard stamped on the flap.

"I kept this as a souvenir. I will not rest until I kill the man whose name is stamped on the inside of this pouch. That night, the man it belongs to, killed my father."

Darec looked at the boy's solemn face, aggrieved this attack caused him to grow old before his time. "I do not know what the Ambassador's soldiers are doing so far from Belenos," said Darec. "Perhaps we can talk further, I believe there is much to learn from you."

"And I from you. What business brings you here?"

"We search for the wreck of a royal carriage. It crashed off the roadway many years ago."

"I know of it. If you wish to salvage from it, you are wasting your time. There remains only a burnt and rusting frame."

"Can your men lead us to where it is?" said Darec.

"We will direct you but not take you the full way. We still hunt the renegade soldiers. If you allow me I will call in our remaining men. We will rest with you this night."

Darec nodded, and the young man trilled like a night rover. Soon other men, dressed all in black, filtered in from the forest; most, small of stature, they were very young.

At first the men of both groups eyed each other suspiciously. Galen jumped up on a nearby boulder, announcing they were not enemies and that they would guide Darec's men to the wreckage of the carriage.

Some of Galen's men laughed at the thought of their search for the wreck. They all knew nothing of value remained, some of them having been to the wreck many times to throw stones at it and set fire to the king's property.

A short time later another man from the villager's group came forward. He nodded to Darec and put his fist to his chest, saluting soldier to soldier.

"I recognize you from battle, sir. We fought during the battle in the Chelan Valley."

Darec looked surprised at this comment. His men retreated that day. He did not recall the man being one of his soldiers.

"I am Christoff," said the man. "You retreated before us. Your men fought bravely and had our reinforcements from the west not arrived the victory would have been yours."

Speechless, Darec nodded at the uncommon honor bestowed by a one-time enemy.

Christoff reached out his hand to Darec.

"I offer you friendship. The battle is over, many good men died and now is the time to forge new bonds."

"You are a most unusual man, Christoff," said Darec as he grasped the other man's outstretched hand.

Christoff laughed good-naturedly. "Now my friend, how can I help you in your search?" said Christoff.

"We search for a royal carriage, wrecked many years ago on the road north of Belisle," said Darec.

"There are many stories about the carriage and how it came to be wrecked."

"What stories, can you tell me?"

"The occupants of the carriage were carried away by Razora panthers. I don't believe it. I believe men attacked it and carried the occupants to a castle in the mountains, built by some long dead bandit. It sat in ruins for many, many years but we believe Vasilis rebuilt it. He had it completed and fortified before the war fully broke out. We believe his plans do not include peace."

"How did you come to this belief?" said Darec.

"Unfortunately, I do not have proof of his intentions. I only know the soldiers from the castle disguise themselves. Under their disguise they wear Vasilis' colors. They venture further and further, stirring up trouble and attacking villages. Men and boys disappear without a trace.

"One village, Delan, has not been attacked with force or frequency. I suspect the headman has an arrangement with someone. Perhaps he passes information to them. This I only know because my sister lives in this village, her dead husband's village. She tried to leave but his family threatened to keep her children. She fears for her safety and has told me so in what messages she has smuggled to me.

"I have not seen or heard from her for some time. I fear something has happened but cannot go to her because the raids have become so frequent."

"Show me where the carriage is, and I will visit Delan and your sister," said Darec.

"I would be in your debt if somehow you could bring her away to safety."

"I cannot promise to bring her away, but if I am able, I will bring her news of you," said Darec.

While the two men sat near the fire talking their men brought the dead and wounded into the campsite. The injured, Orris and Elieana patched up as best they could. One man had a broken leg and another, a large gash on his arm from shoulder to elbow. Elieana and Orris worked through the night. They set the man's broken leg and Elieana, with neat stitches, sewed the gaping wound in the other man's arm.

When they finally finished, Orris gave her some of the large, creamy-colored flowers, growing copiously around the bubbling pool they camped beside. Laroo flowers, he called them.

"Steep the petals in boiling water," he instructed her. "The liquid deadens pain when taken by mouth, the scented steam relaxes and assists with sleep. When applied as a poultice the flowers prevent putrefaction of a wound."

Elieana placed some of the petals in a cup of boiled water and as the petals soaked she breathed in the steam and felt the stress of the previous days vaporize, leaving her relaxed and comfortable.

"They are most potent when picked in the dead of night," said Orris.

"I can feel it," said Elieana, who felt as if she could lay down and go blissfully to sleep. Elieana found in Orris a new friend. Both had a desire to help people. Each had a wealth of knowledge they shared as they worked. Orris instructed Elieana on other uses of the flower and how it could be dried and kept for future use. After their talk, Elieana gathered up as many Laroo flowers she could find and flattened them between some of her clothing, to dry, for future use in her healing practice.

When the sun rose, Darec directed four of his men, Orris and his two injured men to go to the village of Sacla with Christoff and from there return to Pelagos. The other five men rode ahead to Delan, to scout the village and watch for unusual activity. Darec and Elieana would continue to the site of the carriage wreck and they would meet again near the village of Delan. Darec and Elieana rode fast and hard, following behind their young guides, taking time only to stop and water their horses.

CHAPTER 2

With Galen's directions, Darec and Elieana quickly located the site of the carriage wreck. As they were told, all that remained were the metal rims from the wheels and various other bits and pieces. Shrubs and grass grew up through the debris and had they not been looking specifically for it they would have passed it by.

Elieana, gazed around the clearing where the wreckage lay. As she recalled the scene from so many years before she related it to Darec. She showed him where the carriage had tumbled down the embankment. Although she had not seen the accident her memory of the scene played back in in her mind what had likely happened. First the wheels slid over the edge and then the whole carriage slipped over the cliff, pulling the frightened horses with it. Elieana looked around the clearing as if she were a spectator to the event. She could picture the injured horses struggling in their harness; men calling out in pain; a Razora panther attacking; a woman trying to get out of the carriage. She turned slowly in a circle then saw the tree where she buried the package, now standing at least thirty feet tall.

Elieana ran to the base of the tree and falling to her knees she pulled up the shrubbery growing around its base.

"Here, Darec, it is here," she called over her shoulder.

Darec knelt beside her and helped her pull up the brush and grass. They dug down about a foot and found the leather-bound packet covered with roots and dirt but undamaged from seven years of weather falling on its resting place. Elieana looked at it in disbelief. Until she held it in her hands she had not let herself believe it might still exist.

Carefully Elieana dug around the packet to unearth it. The parchment inside smelled musty and old but the ink had not run on the pages and everything Elieana had told Darec remained clearly readable.

The parchment, the queen's journal, told of her reason for leaving her husband, her intended route and the names of her entourage. It listed safe havens where they would stay during the journey. Letters of introduction described her not as the queen but as a highborn lady searching for refuge, a safe place from the specter of war. A separate page listed her wealth and where she hid it. The remaining pages in the journal spoke of Nada, Princess Silanne, her real name, and her pedigree in the event her mother could no longer care for her.

"I changed her name to protect her," said Elieana as she massaged her temples to relieve her tension.

"It is understandable. A thorough search took place after they disappeared. You had luck with you that no one recognized her," said Darec.

"I had great fear in those days, which is why we moved from place to place so often. People asked questions because she did not resemble me. I told them she was my dead husband's daughter. Most people accepted it, and if I encountered more questions I found reason to move on."

"You realize this packet is a dangerous thing?"

"Yes, I do, very much. If I could burn it I would happily do so, but it must be returned to the king and so must Nada be reunited with him." She paused and with a queer look on her face corrected herself, "Princess Silanne, I mean."

Those words, now she had spoken them, somehow helped her bear the thought that Nada would no longer be with her. She knew the King must have been overcome with grief at the loss of both wife and daughter, at the least one of them could be returned to him.

Elieana sat for a moment, looking up at the trees towering overhead, a gentle breeze rustling the leaves, the smell of the forest and the sounds of myriads of birds singing and chirping. The sounds comforted her, and she felt, at that moment, even if she lost Nada, she did right by her. She rose from where she sat, dusted herself off and walked towards her mount. She scratched the animal's ears and under its chin. It nuzzled her with its soft, velvety muzzle. Elieana rested her head on the horse's strong neck, taking comfort from its gentleness.

As Darec watched her, he folded up the parchment and put it carefully back inside the packet then tucked the entire thing inside his jerkin where it would remain until he delivered it to the king. "Right, shall we ride to the village of Delan?" asked Darec.

Elieana looked at him, a sad expression marring her face. "Yes, but should we not also get the packet to the King?" she said, believing the quicker she could get the deed over with the sooner she could start to heal from the anguish she already felt at the loss of Nada.

"We should, but if Ambassador Vasilis is involved in some conspiracy we must find out what it is before the wedding. He has much to gain from this wedding and much to lose if Silanne takes her rightful place. He is one of the guests, a high-ranking guest, considering that he is the natural father of the groom. I am sure he will depart for Pelagos shortly. Have no fears with regards to the packet, Elieana, I will guard it with my life."

"I will follow your lead," said Elieana, then she mounted her horse and waited for him to ride in front of her on their way to the village of Delan.

They followed the bandit trail south until they came to a lookout giving a view of the roadway below. At this point the road to Magra's village forked to the east. When they came to a small trail leading north again they followed it until they came to the outskirts of Magra's village. On one side of the road Christoff had marked a path with slashes on trees, so he could sneak into the village without being seen. Just before nightfall they arrived at the road to the village and as they approached, one of Darec's men, who watched for them, stepped out of the trees.

"Sir," he said, saluting Darec. "Our camp is through the bush near the outcropping of rock, to the south. The trail is marked for you."

"Have you met anyone else on the road?" asked Darec.

"No, Sir," said the guard as he stepped aside to let them pass.

Darec and Elieana followed the trail towards the camp, leaving the guard, concealed by the thick undergrowth, to watch the road.

Philen sat with two men of their group who had traveled ahead to the outskirts of the village. When they entered the camp his face split into a huge grin. "Darec, Elieana, we've got some supper here. It is cold, but it will fill you up," said Philen as he cleared a spot for Elieana to sit down.

"You are having quite an adventure, Philen. You have changed much since the day of Nada's injury."

Philen grinned at Elieana and then just as quickly he hid the grin with a more serious expression.

"Yes, Elieana, you are right, I am having an adventure, but I am also in search of whoever did this terrible thing. Anyone from Pelagos or the fishing village could have been the one injured by the sword. Had you or Darec not been there anyone cut by the sword would have died. We may not have discovered the sword and with no warning perhaps we would be surprised by something even more terrible."

"I have a terrible feeling of foreboding," said Elieana, "As if there is something just at the edge of our lives that will change everything in an instant. It troubles me deeply."

"We will find what it is Elieana and we will overcome it," said Philen as he patted her shoulder, reassuringly.

Before Darec sat down beside them he handed the packet of papers to Elieana.

"What is this? Why are you giving me the packet?" asked Elieana.

"If anything happens and we do not come back, I want you to return to Pelagos and give this into the hands of King Stephan when he arrives for the wedding."

"What could happen? You are only going to the village to meet Christoff's sister," said Elieana.

"In the dead of night and through the bushes rather than the roadway. If anyone in the village sees us they may stop us from leaving. This is more important and must be given to the King."

Elieana took the packet and tucked it inside her fleece jacket.

"I will take it for now, but you will have it back when you return. It is a heavier weight than I can bear."

"You will not have to carry it for long. We will be back as soon as we have spoken to Magra," said Darec and he gave Elieana's hand a squeeze to reassure her. Before she had a chance to say anything more he stood and walked over to the cauldron sitting beside the fire, its contents cool with a congealing slick of grease on top. He filled a wooden bowl and wolfed the stew down as fast as he could, announcing to his men, as he ate, "It is almost nightfall. We will enter the village and go directly to the house of Christoff's sister. William, you come with me. Philen and Elieana stay here. Markus, you will take over guard duty when we leave. If we do not return before the moon is fully at its zenith you must break camp and ride for Pelagos. Do not wait until morning."

Shortly after nightfall Darec, Marcus and William left the camp. Elieana watched as they walked down the trail through the bushes, her feeling of trepidation even stronger than before. She crossed her arms tightly and squeezed to try and make the feeling go away then walked closer to the fire, hoping to dispel her fear with the comforting heat of the flames.

The men quickly covered the distance to the road and left Markus on guard at the entrance to the trail. Darec and William checked the road for any sign of late travelers. Upon seeing no one they jogged down the road until they found the trail to the village. They quickly found Magra's cottage, the only one on the outskirts of the village. Darec peered through the window and confirmed Magra had no one with her then gave the double knock Christoff used when he came to visit. When Magra opened the door, a large hand clamped over her mouth before she had a chance to scream. The men hastily entered the cottage, shutting the door. William drew the curtains across the window.

"Christoff has sent us," said Darec quietly into her ear. Pulling out the note Christoff had written, Darec held it up in front of her face.

"Do you recognize his writing?" asked Darec.

She nodded her head vigorously.

"You will not scream?"

She nodded her head that she would not scream and Darec removed his hand. She turned to look at him, wiping her mouth with her sleeve.

"Is he, all right?" she said.

"Yes," said Darec.

"Where is he? Where did you see him?"

"We met last night. He has told us about your problem. Where are your children?"

"They have been taken to the castle. That is why I have been unable to leave."

"Can you tell us more about this castle?"

"I believe Vasilis, Ambassador of Belenos, restored it for his own use before the war. Some of our villagers sought work there before the war broke out. As well, some of the young women went there to work and did not return. As they have not returned to the village there is not much known of the activities taking place in the castle, rumors, only evil rumors."

"Why have you stayed here?"

"I have only stayed because my sons have gone to the castle as stable boys. While they work at the castle, I must stay here in my village. If I do not, then their lives or mine could be in great danger. When Vasilis first started to rebuild the castle, the villagers welcomed his kindness. He gave them work and protection.

"Everything changed after the war broke out. We heard rumors of a woman at the castle. Some said he married and she came from Belenos, but it was just gossip, no one discovered anything about her. The women working in the castle could not speak with her."

"Can you tell me what she looked like? Have you ever seen her?"

"I have seen her only the once. She is very beautiful. Her skin is very fair, and her hair is long and reddish brown. It curled and hung almost to the floor. When I saw her, she looked at me, then ran like a frightened deer. She had such tragic eyes. I believe she stays in a room high in the castle tower."

"How is it that the people in the village hold you ransom?"

"The head man is the Ambassador's dead wife's kinsman and reports directly to him. If anyone who has been in the castle tries to leave he will have their families killed. He has warned me, if I leave, my sons will be in danger."

Magra wrung her hands together, her eyes brimming with tears.

"My sons are all I have left. Please, if you can, help us."

Darec looked at Magra, her face etched with lines of worry for her sons.

"As I have told Christoff, we will do what we can, but I cannot promise you anything. Can you describe to me the approach to the castle? Where are the guard towers and any defenses you can recall? You must tell me all you can remember."

Magra proceeded to describe the castle; she told him the best route to take to get as close to the castle as possible without being seen. She described the defenses as thoroughly as she could. She drew a small map to the tower room and where the sentries were posted. Darec spent a good portion of the evening with Magra until the sickle moon made its appearance.

"Thank you Magra, you have been a great help. I will try to let Christoff know you are safe and we will do what we can to free your sons. Unfortunately, I cannot promise this will be done but we will try. What are their names?"

"Arlen is the elder. He has thick brown hair and is big for his age. He walks with a limp. Gaere is the younger. He is wiry and quick. When last I spoke with them they were stable boys.

"I will be forever indebted to you, sir, if you can do this for me but I understand if you cannot. Before you leave, let me go out first to ensure you will not meet anyone. Watch for my signal."

Magra left her cottage and walked out to her animal pens. She hailed loudly at one of the village men passing by.

"Good evening, good sir, it is a pleasant night to be out."

"Yes, Magra, a good evening to you. I am out checking the pens. The animals are restless this night."

"I have not noticed anything with mine," replied Magra. "Perhaps it is the heat making them restless."

"You may be right Magra. If you hear anything, sound the alarm and we will come to your aid."

"Yes, I will. Good night then."

She leaned over the fence resting her arms on the top rung and watched the village man walk towards his cottage a short distance away. When he walked behind some thick shrubbery she waved for the men to leave.

She heard the latch of her door click, then the creak of the gate hinges. After the two men left, Magra remained by the fence for a considerable time, pondering their arrival. What of her sons? Would they find them? Would Christoff come back to the village to help her escape? She gazed up at the moon, a silently shining sliver in the deep darkness of the sky and said a prayer to her God for their safety and for the rescue of her sons.

She thought of her kindly husband, a good husband. He left their cottage on just such a night as this, to go off to the war, and never to return. She hoped this was not a sign the two men would die before they could help her as they had vowed. Magra's face flamed red and tears threatened. Her heart ached as she stood there watching as dark clouds partially covered the moon.

A gust of cool wind blew dead leaves across the roadway in front of her causing her to pull her shawl tightly around her shoulders not from cold but from the foreboding feeling of doom. Shivering she made the sign against evil spirits with her free hand, cursing her ability to recognize impending events before they took place.

The villagers of Delan feared her, including her husband's family, the reason she lived in this cottage at the outskirts. They wanted nothing to do with her. Her heart ached as she thought of her lost loved ones and with her head hanging low she returned to the loneliness of her cottage with only a small glimmer of hope in her heart that she might see her sons again.

Darec and William quietly left the cottage, carefully noting the direction the village man had gone. They did not want to cause more trouble for Magra, if they were seen leaving her cottage. As Magra said, if she raised anyone's suspicions, her sons could be in danger. Darec wondered about Vasilis' concern with anyone having knowledge of his castle. The more Darec learned of this Ambassador, Vasilis, the warier he became. He seemed a dangerous man. His threats against common people, to hide his dealings, revealed his nature.

Darec and William cautiously headed back to the camp but when they reached the trail Marcus did not come out to meet them. A flattened area in the tall grass remained, the only evidence someone had been there. Darec reached back, grasping William's arm for him to stop then put his finger to his lips for silence.

Quietly they proceeded along the trail but before reaching the campsite they turned off to circle behind the camp to the base of the rock cliff. Darec previously noticed a narrow path at the base of the cliff so they quietly crept along the base until they came to the spot where a path wound up between the rocks. They ascended silently, watching for loose stones which could fall and alert someone below.

At the final looping turn, before arriving at the top of the cliff, they spied a sentry standing silently in the dark. He didn't hear them coming up the path because he focused his attention on the camp below. The man, almost invisible, was dressed in black with a mask covering his face. Darec crept up behind the man and knocked him on the head with a rock. Before he fell, Darec looped his arm around the man's chest to pull him backward as he slumped, unconscious. The impact of the rock on the man's head was sickeningly loud in the dark silence of the night but not loud enough to be heard from the camp below.

They dragged the sentry out of sight behind a large boulder and bound and gagged him. Then they both crawled to the edge of the cliff and peered down into the camp.

A small fire lit up the camp and they could see Elieana and the rest of Darec's men bound and gagged except for one, Marcus, laying very still at the edge of the clearing. Other men stood around, their disguises still covering their features. One man had removed his mask and hood revealing thick, white hair although he was not old. He spoke to the men around the campfire but the distance being too great, Darec and William could not make out what he said.

Darec moved his body slightly causing a few small pebbles to slide over the edge of the cliff, rattling on the rocks below. He cursed himself for being so careless. The man with the white hair looked up, the sight of his face startled Darec. The man's eyes glowed luminously and although the darkness hid Darec from the man's view, it seemed as if his sight pierced the darkness and looked right through him to his very soul.

A shudder ran through Darec's body. He sensed pure evil emanating from the man below whose expression showed he saw Darec staring down at him. He waved a hand at one of his men who detached himself from the group around the campfire. It would take just a few moments for the guard to climb to the top of the cliff. Darec moved towards the unconscious man.

"William," Darec whispered, "Do you have the flask you bring on all our marches, to warm your soul?"

"Yes, but..." with a knowing look, he pulled it from his coat, opened it and poured some of the aromatic glava on the unconscious sentry's mouth while Darec released the bonds that held him. With a moment to spare they ducked out of sight before the second man arrived from below. He checked the sentry lying on the ground, sniffing his body. Darec and William heard the man growl low in his chest. He picked up the unconscious sentry and threw him down over the edge of the cliff to land with a sickening thud at the feet of the white-haired man.

What kind of men were these who traveled through the night and captured the rest of their party? The man's actions shocked them both and they realized their men, and Elieana, were in terrible danger.

Awhile later, another man climbed to the top of the ridge. The odds of overcoming the raiders were poor, even with one of them dead. They had no chance of success in overcoming these two men without endangering their own men and Elieana. The two men quietly talked together while they stood guard over the camp. Snippets of conversation gave away their plan.

"We travel just before sunrise," said one, "and then north to Delvar."

"We should make the castle by noontide," replied the other. "It will be good to rest before our next foray."

"Yes, and once we leave the prisoners to be questioned; we will give some proper discipline to that woman down there."

"I am done with these forays and I want no part in 'disciplining' the woman," said the other man.

"I am going to take some time to see my wife and child." Anger and disgust filled the man's voice.

"Stop your grumbling. If you do not like what we are doing there is a good sleeping place down amongst the rocks where our friend lies," said the other man.

Silence settled over the cliff top, broken only by the muffled mumbling of voices from below.

Darec and William stayed behind the boulder until the two sentries descended from the cliff top a little while later. When it was safe to come out of their hiding place they quietly crawled on their bellies to the edge of the cliff, making sure the overhanging shrubbery screened them from view.

They watched helplessly as the raiding party with the rest of their men and Elieana rode away. The man with the luminescent green eyes and white hair glanced up to where they hid before he pulled his mask back over his face. A chill ran up Darec's spine, certain the man knew they hid on the cliff above.

* * *

The bandits left the dead man behind, laying amongst the scattered remnants of the campsite. Anything of value they took with them. Darec wondered what Elieana had done with the packet, if she managed to hide it or if it they took it from her. He smiled grimly. "They took Marcus with them," he whispered. "At least we know he lives. They have no use for a dead man," and he pointed with his chin at the dead bandit laying below.

William nodded, running his hand over his forehead as if to wipe away the worry he felt for his comrades. They remained on the cliff top until the bandits left, their path revealed by the sway of trees and shrubbery as they passed. After waiting, for what seemed like hours, they climbed down to the campsite. The still burning fire shed some light so they could salvage anything they could use on their journey.

"These men, whoever they are, have no loyalty to their fellows, even in death," said Darec angrily. "They left their man to rot, as food for scavengers."

"Well," replied William, "At least we know Marcus still lives. He must have put up a fight and they clubbed him for it."

"Yes," replied Darec, breathing easier. "He is a good man and a friend. I don't want to lose any more men to this dire business."

Darec searched throughout the entire camp and eventually found the packet. Elieana hid it nearby where she had been sitting, in a crack in the cliff wall.

"Good girl, Elieana," said Darec quietly.

"I think our only hope is to go back to Magra's village. Perhaps they will loan or sell us some mounts, so we can follow the bandits," said Darec.

"They won't believe we were attacked if we go there looking as we do now," replied William.

"Right. Rough up your clothes so it looks like we fought them off," said Darec, who began to rub dirt on his clothes, face and hands.

William tied a dirty rag around his head, first dipping it in some of the congealed blood of the dead man on the ground.

Revolting as it seemed he believed he had best play the part of an injured man well.

"I hope there is no healer in the village who will insist on stitching me up. It would be quite a surprise to find I have bled from the outside in."

Darec grinned sardonically at him, "If you are concerned about your disguise not being realistic I can crack you on the head for good measure."

William grimaced in mock fear of Darec then he slapped his hand on Darec's back. "Come, my friend, we have work to do and our friends to rescue."

They left the clearing and its grisly contents behind, with a plan to use the dead man to their advantage. By telling the villagers of an attack, with one dead man in the clearing, Darec hoped the story would ring true. He had no doubt the villagers would check their story. From what Magra told him they did not sound like a trusting lot. If the villagers would not help, then they would return by night and take what they needed. Darec hoped his men would delay the bandits so that he and William could ambush them before they reached the safety of the castle walls.

When the sun rose the next morning Darec and William set out again for Magra's village. Dust rose in dry puffs, thoroughly coating their boots as they walked. When they reached the main road Darec saw the telltale path he and William left the evening before. He pulled up a handful of long grass and used it to obscure their footprints. In their haste to visit Magra, they had endangered her life. Angry with himself for not thinking of this he stormed down the road towards the village. Any villager seeing his agitation as they approached would not be surprised upon hearing their story of attack by bandits.

The light of day revealed Delan as old and run down, something they had not noticed the night before. Moldy thatch covered the roofs of the cottages, fences needed mending and most of the inhabitants were long past their prime.

Sullen old women, sat on a rickety bench and watched the two men as they plodded into the village. William nudged Darec's arm as they passed by a pen of shaggy ponies, their heads hanging low, their coats dull, and most likely insect ridden.

"If we do have luck buying a mount from these people I think we will end up carrying it," whispered William.

"From the looks of this village it is not money they will request from us in exchange for their animals. Have you noticed there are few men here," said Darec.

"I have. There seems to be only old men, young boys and cripples. What do you suppose has happened to them?"

"Magra did not mention this oddity to us last night. The village men can't all be casualties of war."

"We may get our answer now; the head man is coming to meet us."

The head man approached them, followed by a group of dirty faced children, old women and Magra, anger apparent in hard lines on her face. Darec believed, if they were alone, he would receive a tongue lashing to make him cringe, but he knew Magra would say nothing, so he directed his attention toward the head man.

The villagers surrounded the two men. Questions flew at them from every direction, who were they; where they came from; why they were here; what they wanted, the villager's intense animosity toward them was palpable.

The head man pounded his staff hard on the ground, jangling the numerous bells hanging from it. The jangling drowned out the babbling and eventually quieted the crowd.

"I am in control here," he bellowed, "Go about your business."

He waved his staff back and forth in a sweeping arc, clearing a path through the crowd and beckoned for the two men to follow. Forewarned of his kinship to the Ambassador they would guard their words well.

CHAPTER 3

Darec and William followed Delan's head man to a large house on the outskirts of the village. Stairs led up to a wide porch, facing the Barbicon Mountains to the north. Two spires of rock rising higher than all the other peaks marked the blocked pass to Sangan.

Darec stood gazing out at the distant mountains until the jangling of bells disrupted his thoughts. The head man had an annoying habit of pounding his staff on the ground to get people's attention. He introduced himself as Yannis, not a name from the surrounding villages. From his sing-song accent he obviously came from somewhere else. Odd, Darec thought, that the villagers chose Yannis as head man. Yannis motioned for them to enter the house. They climbed the wide front stairs and crossed the open porch.

Rich furnishings graced the first room they entered, surprising William and Darec who quickly exchanged glances at such lavishness not normally found in poor villages.

Darec reached out and touched the smooth, dark wood of the pillars supporting the upper floor.

"Denati wood, from the foothills of the Barbicon Mountains," Yannis said cheerfully.

“I have heard the wood of the Denati tree is resistant to fire,” said Darec.

“It is most amazing, yes,” Yannis said, puffing up with pride. “Come, I will show you.”

Yannis motioned towards a second room, its entrance graced with a huge, beautifully carved, wooden door. Darec gazed at the door, thinking he recognized it, but he could not remember where he had seen it before.

Yannis gestured for them to enter the room then he closed and bolted the doors. “I do not let my servants see my demonstration. It is better that way,” and he smiled wickedly. He raised his eyebrows up and down a few times, as if he were sharing a secret with them. Yannis led them to the center of the room where a huge copper fire bowl, the width of a man’s outspread arms, stood on carved wooden legs. "Come, be seated," Yannis gestured towards huge cushions surrounding the bowl.

"This is a very comfortable room," commented Darec as he took a seat on one of the cushions, hoping to draw Yannis into conversation, still trying work out where he had seen the door before.

"Yes, it is," replied Yannis but he didn't speak further. Busying himself with a large ring of keys he walked to one side of the room where he unlocked a wooden box sitting on a shelf. He removed a few pieces of dark wood and a small bottle of liquid. “You see, gentlemen, there is a magic about this wood that most do not know,” he lowered his eyebrows and glanced around as if someone might hear him.

Yannis put the pieces of wood into the fire bowl with some kindling and dried moss from a nearby basket. He took a flint from a pouch on his belt and struck it against the edge of his knife. A spark flew instantly onto the moss and soon a merry flame burned. The kindling soon blackened and smoked then caught fire but the Denati wood did not change. It did not even smoke.

Looking closely Darec saw the ash on the bottom of the fire bowl. He reached out and picked up a piece of the Denati wood. It felt warm to the touch but remained unmarked. Darec looked over at Yannis who smiled in return, his eyes twinkling.

"Put it back and I will show you another trick," said Yannis.

Darec did so. Yannis opened the bottle and sprinkled some of the liquid onto the Denati wood. The liquid on the Denati wood burned with an aqua flame. He picked up the Denati wood which continued to burn in his palm. He did not even flinch. The wood burned until only a small, dark, lump remained which he dropped into Darec's hand.

"Does this not surprise and delight you?" said Yannis happily, as if he had just discovered it himself.

"What liquid did you use?" said William.

"Ahh, that is my secret," said Yannis. He put his hands on his knees, pushing himself off the cushion he sat upon. "Now I must have my servants bring you some refreshments," he said and walked towards a door on the opposite side of the room.

Darec protested but Yannis raised his hands as if to say their discussion was at an end.

"I will be but a moment. If you wish to refresh yourselves there is water, soap and towels in the next room."

Yannis left Darec and William alone in the room to discuss quietly what they had just witnessed.

"What do you think caused the Denati wood to burn like that, with no heat?" whispered William.

"I don't know," said Darec, "but whatever it is I think we should find out. It seems magical and what fear and awe it would strike into simple villagers' hearts if they saw such a thing."

Darec got up and crossed the room to examine the strange wooden box. He had seen it before, in the great Hall of the Healers in the walled city of Belisle. He ran his hands over the top of the box then reached down on the backside to find a small indent in the carving. He moved his hand sideways until he found a bump and pressed. He heard a ticking sound and then a small drawer on the back of the box sprung open, revealing a small silver dagger, its handle encrusted with jewels. He pressed the drawer shut, leaving the dagger in its place.

Darec realized then that the doors to this room were also from the great hall. The carved scene on the door depicted the great battle at the pass through the Barbicon Mountains. At that time, the Balticans and Pelagonians fought together against the Sangan hordes, many hundreds of years before.

He pondered on what happened in Belisle after he left. How could this man in the middle of a decrepit village have come into possession of the wooden box that belonged to the greatest healer of all time, let alone the doors to the great hall? However, the head man came into possession of these things was anything but honest.

Darec had not returned to Belisle after the war but learned looters ransacked the hall then razed it to the ground. The looters killed healers or drove them out of the city. The people of Belisle, a superstitious lot, believed the healers used devilish ways to heal their patients. It distressed him to think that seat of learning had turned so backward.

The battle depicted on the two doors had been fought very close to this village. Yannis must have a very important patron to have received it as a gift or perhaps Yannis took it for himself when the destruction began. He walked back and sat next to William.

“Did not the Sangan warlords enlist men by force to fight their battles? Do you recall from your lessons of old what they did to those men and how many they took?" Darec whispered.

William didn't answer right away so Darec continued. "In the battle against Sangan, were not the armies of Pelagonia and Baltica almost decimated?”

William paused a moment then responded. "The Sangans used a very strong drug to control the soldiers. If they survived the slaughter, and after the drug wore off, they went insane when they realized what they had done.”

“Yes, I suspect this is what has been done to the men of this village and the others Christoff told us of. It all fits. I see treasures from the Hall of Healing in Belisle, in this very house. How else might they get here if not by subterfuge? I think maybe this head man sees us as potential recruits for the army they may be building."

"Darec, how can you suggest that with no proof?"

"I do not have proof, but I believe Yannis will offer refreshments with something extra added. If that is the case, then we must avoid eating or drinking what he gives us."

"Yes, but both of us cannot avoid it. One of us must partake and distract him so the other can avoid eating or drinking. You, Darec, are the one who must not eat or drink. I will partake sparingly to keep the effects of the drug as light as possible. And, if there is no drug, I will probably have had a good meal." William smiled at his jest.

"As you say," said Darec. "This will also give me an opportunity to watch how the drug affects you and plan our escape, so we can find our friends."

"It is agreed then. I am depending on you to make sure I do not become a member of the supposed army," said William.

A short time later two servants entered, bearing trays heaped with fruits, meat and cheese as well as an assortment of drinks. The servants passed the platters to Darec and William along with cups brimming with a purple liquid. The drink's fruity flavor would mask the taste of any type of poison or drug that may have been added.

While the servants remained in the room Darec wandered around looking at various objects. He carried the plate of food the servants had offered but did not eat and only pretended to nibble. His stomach rumbled softly in protest as everything smelled delicious. He took only a few small pieces, hoping the servants did not notice and tried to keep his back to them while they were in the room.

William downed some of the fruity punch and Darec watched for symptoms. Sure enough, William's speech became slurred but before he completely passed out William diverted the servant's attention giving Darec a chance to dump the contents of his goblet into a tall urn standing nearby. Darec then mimicked William's behavior, stumbling to a cushion and collapsing in a heap.

After Darec collapsed the servants cleared away the food and drink, leaving the two men sprawled out on the cushions, snoring loudly. Darec remained still and limp, feeling certain Yannis lurked somewhere nearby, waiting for the drug to do its work. As if on cue Yannis returned to the room, muttering to himself. He went over to Darec and kicked his foot. With difficulty, Darec remained sprawled on the cushion, not responding to the assault.

"You are a strange and dangerous man, my friend," said Yannis, no longer sounding cheerful but mean and vicious. "How is it you knew of a secret door in the box and why is it I have not yet found it?" Yannis kicked Darec again. "You will make a fine addition to our army and when you awake perhaps I will discover from you the secret of that box.

"Remove them to the cart," Yannis commanded his servants. Darec tensed slightly when they removed his weapons, worried the men would find the packet. They only searched for weapons, however, and paid no attention to the bulky pocket in his jerkin.

The servants carried the two men down a flight of stairs and dumped them unceremoniously into a large cart, covering them with straw. Darec lay still, waiting impatiently for the cart to start moving. He heard the servants talking and slowly their voices faded as they walked way.

When he could hear them no longer, Darec pinched William to awaken him, but to no avail. William lay still as if dead from the potent effects of the drug. His breathing slow and shallow, but evident, gave Darec some comfort.

Darec thought about this drug as he lay in the cart. He had not used anything like this when he apprenticed as a healer in Belisle. He could see the benefits for a drug this potent, perhaps for a surgery. The guild believed a man should be awake, so the surgeon could speak to the patient while operating. They believed a mere man played God, to make a man sleep and not feel any pain. Darec and many others had always felt this was barbaric. It was likely one of the reasons why the guild was practically torn apart by the people of Belisle. No one should subject people to such excruciating pain. The people of the city grumbled that the guild had turned into a place of torture rather than a place of learning. Had the surgeons used this drug perhaps they could have prevented the revolt and the outbreak of war.

Sometime later Darec heard voices approaching the cart. The men climbed aboard, the seat creaked as they sat down. A crack of a whip and the cart, pulled by a pair of bedraggled little ponies, jerked out onto the dusty road away from the village.

William still did not respond to repeated pinching and Darec soon dozed off, waking only once when they hit a large bump. At last the cart stopped and Darec awoke fully alert but stiff from lying in one position. The driver shouted at someone to open a gate. The gate rasped, metal on metal, as it opened and then the clopping of hooves on cobblestone echoed against stone walls.

Another shout, a second gate rasped and screeched then Darec could feel the cart moving down a slight grade. Carefully, so as not to attract the attention of the men in the cart, Darec moved the straw from his face. A tiny lantern swung from a pole at the front of the cart, lighting up the ceiling of a tunnel. He could only assume they were being taken directly to the dungeon below the castle.

Certain this was his only chance to get away he pushed the straw aside and moved up behind the cart driver and his partner. One of the men looked back but before he had time to react Darec grabbed both men's heads and banged them together as hard as he could. Stunned, both men slumped down on the seat. Darec jumped down and stopped the ponies, patting and soothing them.

Small alcoves built at regular intervals along the tunnel held lit torches. He snuffed one out against the stone wall leaving the alcove dark enough to hide William in until he awoke. He pulled William down from the cart, tucked him into the alcove and covered him up with a blanket he found under the cart seat.

Darec removed the cart driver's weapons, strapping on the sword belt and tucking a dagger in his boot. The rest of the weapons he pushed into the alcove under the blanket with William. He pulled the unconscious men into the back of the cart, tied them with a length of rope he found under the seat and covered them with straw then he climbed back aboard the wagon and drove it to the end of the tunnel where he stopped at a locked gate.

A wizened looking man sat at a small desk placed against the rock wall in a large circular chamber on the other side of the gate. Several barred doors blocked off other darkened passages, lit only by the dim light of flickering torches. From that location, the man had a good view down each passage. On the far side of the circular room a smaller gate led to a set of stairs winding up out of sight.

“Well, it took you long enough. What happened, lost your way?” The man cackled and grinned, revealing toothless gums and walked over to unlock the gate.

“The drug was starting to wear off, I had to put them back to sleep,” replied Darec as he got down from the wagon seat. Odd, he thought, the man knew they were coming, but at that moment he did not have time to be concerned as to how they did it.

“That accounts for the goose eggs on their heads,” cackled the man again after he pushed away the straw. Darec stepped back slightly in case the jailer recognized the men but also from the smell of stale sweat and urine hovering about him like a cloud.

“Well, times a wasting," said the little jailer; rubbing his hands together in anticipation. "Let’s get them out of here.

We'll put them in with the last group of new comers. Grimm is going to start on them in the morning."

Grunting in reply Darec pulled one of the unconscious men from the cart. The jailer removed a set of keys from his belt and unlocked one of the barred doors. Darec followed him into the tunnel, dragging the unconscious man. They passed a set of stairs descending to a lower level. Flickering torchlight lit up the stairwell below which, Darec guessed, led to where Grimm worked. He shook his head and hoped he had arrived in time.

They walked to the last cell, large enough to hold many inmates. Inside, Darec's men, bedraggled and bleary eyed, sat with their backs against the wall. Philen looked up when the two men approached, recognition flickering across his face. Darec winked at him and Philen hung his head so the jailer could not see his smile of relief.

The jailer picked up an iron bar leaning against the wall then unlocked the door. He entered the room swinging the bar back and forth to keep the men back while Darec set down his burden. The jailer backed out of the cell and locked the door.

"These ones are wild," said the jailer, "Every time I open the door they swarm it. I'll wait here while you get the other one."

Darec jogged back down the tunnel. He hefted the second unconscious man over his shoulder and took him to the cell. Again, the jailer repeated swinging the bar back and forth. As they backed out of the cell Darec grabbed the bar from the man's hands in mid swing and thumped him on the head. The jailer sank to his knees then fell face first on the floor, letting out a loud grunt as he landed.

"It's good to see you Darec," exclaimed Philen as he jumped up. "You have come with only a moment to spare."

"And you, Philen. Have you discovered what these people are up to?"

"We have seen groups of men taken from the cells kicking and fighting. They never return. The jailer said that once they have met Grimm they are ready to die for him."

"I did come with not a moment to spare. You were next on the list to visit Grimm. We must leave before someone discovers what has happened here."

Darec looked around the cell, examining every face and then more gruffly than he intended, asked where Elieana was.

The men all hung their heads as if guilty of a crime.

"They took her the first night," someone said quietly.

Darec's throat constricted.

"Did they say where they were taking her?"

"No," said Philen. "Elieana told them she was a healer. Someone came a short time later and took her away."

Darec clenched his teeth and his hands tightened into fists.

"I think, to see a woman," said Philen, almost apologetically.

Darec gave Philen an odd look then he turned away, waving for the men to follow him.

"You men leave this place and quickly. I will search until I find her. Bind and gag those three, Philen, we don't want them calling out before you have gotten clear of the castle."

Philen, assisted by Marcus, dragged the three men to the furthest corner of the cell. They stripped off the men's outer tunics and shirts. Tearing the shirts into strips they bound and gagged them then partially covered them with straw. If anyone looked inside the cell it would appear they were sleeping. They locked the cell door then ran down the tunnel to join the rest of the men.

Darec turned the cart around and drove it to where William still snored soundly. Marcus and Darec lifted William into the back of the cart. Philen climbed in beside him. Darec placed the weapons into the cart and then covered them all with straw. Marcus and Feder donned the tunics taken from the two cart drivers and climbed into the cart. They would drive what they hoped looked like an empty cart back to the gate and safety.

"Marcus, you are in charge. If anyone stops you, you are returning to Delan. Say no more. The cart is from Delan village; with luck, there will be no questions. When you are outside of the gates continue until you can leave the roadway without being seen. Leave a guard near the road to keep watch for me when I return. Wait until noon of this day. If I do not return, go back to Pelagos and tell Jorian what has happened here, so he can warn the King. Good luck to you." He slapped the rump of the nearest pony, then jogged back down into the dungeon.

When he reached the circular room, Darec took the ring of keys from the desk where Philen left them. He let himself through the gate that blocked off the stairwell and ran up, two at a time, hoping to find an entrance into the castle. At the top of the stairway he found an unlocked door. Pushing it open just a crack Darec peered out into a wide, well-lit corridor, running to the left and right of the door. He slipped silently into the hallway and crept down the corridor until he came to a large archway. Heavy draperies pulled back on each side of the archway revealed the wide-open doors to a large chamber. The walls of the chamber were hewn out of the rock of the mountain.

Further down, the corridor ended at a large gilded door but before Darec could continue the sound of voices alerted him. He ran back to the archway and slipped behind the drapery on the far side. As he waited for the people to pass by he recognized one of the voices. He peered between the stone wall and the edge of the drapery just as Yannis, from Delan village, walked past. Darec moved his head back, to ensure they did not see him as he listened to their discussion.

"The flyers, are they yet ready or do they require further time to prepare?" said one man.

"They will be ready in a fortnight, once the final training is complete," said the other man.

As they passed by, the white-haired man with Yannis glanced at the archway where Darec hid. Sensing someone or something hid behind the drapery he reached out to pull it aside but was distracted when another man approached them. The man was tall. His long, dark hair was pulled back in a queue and tied with the same fabric as his deep-blue, knee-length robe. His silver sash matched his shimmering shirt. Underneath, black leggings were tucked into fine leather boots. He clapped both men on the shoulder and motioned with a nod of his head towards the end of the hallway.

"Vasilis," said Yannis as he gave him a hug and a kiss on both cheeks. "It is good to see you again."

"And you, Yannis, welcome. Come Egesa, Yannis, we have much to discuss."

The white-haired man glanced back over his shoulder towards Darec's hiding place as Vasilis guided him towards the gilded door. Vasilis opened the door, motioned for the men to enter and the door shut behind them with a thud. Darec waited for a few moments, to ensure no one else remained in the corridor then he jogged away in the direction the men came from, resuming his search for Elieana.

Darec turned a corner, nearly bumping into a guard standing at the bottom of a wide stairway. Recalling what Magra said about a tower built facing the mountains he felt certain this stairway led to the tower. Taking a gamble, he blurted out, gruffly, “I have come for the woman, to return her to the dungeons.”

The bored looking guard moved the long pike he held, blocking Darec's passage. He pondered Darec’s request then nodded his head without saying a word and lifted the pike so Darec could pass. Surprised the guard didn't question him Darec nodded back and proceeded up the stairway. He had prepared himself for a fight and it took great effort to turn his back on the guard.

Darec climbed steadily; passing rooms and other short passageways and saw no one. The castle was virtually empty. The stairway ended at a smaller archway beyond which a set of narrow, winding steps continued upwards. When he reached the top, as he guessed, another guard stood on the landing beside a closed door. "I've come for the woman," he said, trying to make himself sound bored and annoyed with this task.

"On whose orders? Vasilis meant for her to stay until the end of the day."

"Yannis is here, he wants to meet her," said Darec firmly.

The guard shrugged, pulled a ring of keys from his belt and turned to open the door. Darec wrapped his arm around the man's throat as hard as he could, choking him. The guard struggled, trying to free himself, but Darec had the advantage of surprise. The man lost consciousness and Darec slowly lowered his body to the floor. Darec pulled off the man's belt and used it to secure his hands. He removed the man's weapons, taking them for himself, then dragged the guard's inert body to one side of the landing, propping him up against the wall away from the door.

Darec unlocked the door. When he pushed it open he saw a beautiful woman sitting on a bench staring back at him. She glanced to the side of the door nervously and as he turned his head to see what she looked at a heavy object struck him on the head. Just before he hit the floor he thought how like Nada the woman was, then he passed out.

When Darec finally opened his eyes, he saw two of Elieana staring down at him, a look of concern on her face. "Oh, Darec, I'm so sorry. I thought you were the guard coming to take me away. I'm so sorry. What are you doing here? How did you know where to find me?"

Darec sat up and cautiously rubbed the lump on his head. "It's a long story but one that must wait." He shook his head, attempting to clear his double vision. "What did you hit me with?" he said as he shook his head again, wincing from the pain the shaking produced.

"Well, we only had one chair, so we took one of the legs off. It made a serviceable club," said Elieana with a tone of satisfaction in her voice.

Darec glanced at the woman who sat very still on the bench. "Who is this lady?" he said.

"Darec, I'd like you to meet the Lady Antonia, from Belisle, King Stephan's wife."

The woman was undoubtedly Nada's mother. They had the same shape of face and color of eyes. Her wavy hair resembled Nada's with the exception that it hung almost to the floor. He saw a deep sadness on her face, not at all like Nada. In the few times Darec had spoken to Nada, even in her pain, he saw she had a fire this woman did not possess.

Darec rose from the floor, keeping his hand firmly on the door frame for support. "It is an honor to meet you my lady," he said as he bowed deeply.

"I am happy to meet you, Darec, Elieana has told me much about you," said Antonia as she nodded her head in acknowledgement.

The niceties completed and believing they had no time to delay, Darec immediately started to question her. "Lady Antonia, can you tell me, is there another way out of this tower?"

Antonia glanced nervously at Elieana and clutched her hands tightly together.

"There is," said Antonia, "But you may not choose to go that way, it goes even further into the mountain. The tunnel leads to the aviary. I am sure the birds would welcome us, as a meal. That is the reason I seldom leave here." She paused and then morbidly continued, "Although I have thought many times to go to the aviary and just feed myself to the birds. Alas, I have not the courage to do that. I have been naive and am destined to live with guilt for the rest of my life," her voice became high-pitched and she closed her eyes as she spoke. "That is my punishment," she whined.

Alarmed, Darec glanced at Elieana. She lowered her eyebrows, as a warning for him to say nothing. Antonia stared intently at Darec, not noticing Elieana very subtly shaking her head. Warned, Darec did not speak of Nada although it was almost out of his mouth before he even thought about it.

"Have you ever been to these aviaries, My Lady?" said Darec, trying to keep his voice soft and calming.

"Yes, many times. The birds are wonderful creatures. They imprint on their masters when the eggs hatch, but they are not a creature to get close to if you do not belong there."

"Do you have one such bird?" he asked, attempting to gain her trust.

"Alas, no, my brother will not allow it." She shook her head as if her desire to own a bird were thwarted. "He tells me the birds only imprint with males, but I do suspect they will imprint to man or woman if they were there at the right time."

“Why are they kept in a cavern?” said Darec, curiosity getting the best of him.

“They are young yet. The cavern is warm and fed by an underground spring. It is somewhat safe although there are other dangers there.” Antonia leaned closer to him and whispered, “Vasilis also is keeping their presence a secret until the time is right.” She became silent then, gazed down at her lap and fiddled with the trim on her gown.

Darec was taken aback by her behaviour and wanted to ask her more but first they must escape. There would be time enough to ask further questions when they were far away from the castle. “Well, I think we must go the way through the aviary. Perhaps you could show us the way to get out of the castle?” he said.

A quizzical expression crossed Antonia’s face as she looked up at him.

“Why do you want to leave?” she said. Her eyes grew wide and her brow wrinkled with concern.

“We must get back to our city. Our child, Nada, is waiting for our return.”

Elieana glanced at Darec, her brows knit together in a frown, surprised by the word "our" but more concerned with Antonia's response.

“I had a child once. Her name was Silanne. She was killed in a carriage accident many years ago.”

“What of your husband, surely you will want to return to him?” said Darec.

With that question, a shadow crossed over Antonia's face. She stopped talking and slid sideways on the bench, so she faced the wall, lost in memories of the distant past. She tilted her head back and forth, as if someone spoke to her, a voice only she could hear. She bent her head forward and silently wept. Tears splashed on her hands and soaked into her gown. She did nothing to wipe them away.

“My Lady," said Elieana. She crouched down beside the bench and gently took Antonia’s hands in hers. “My Lady, how may I comfort you?”

“There is no comfort," she moaned. "I am destined to spend the rest of my days, alone, here in this tower, for what I have done. I have broken a trust I held dear. My youth and ignorance led me to believe others and not my husband on matters I knew nothing about. I left him and took our child away from him because I believed what my brother, Vasilis, told me. He said my husband was evil. I was terribly wrong, so wrong.

"Vasilis is the evil one. He will destroy this land for his own ends. He will kill all who stand in his way.”

Her sobbing became uncontrollable, her body tensing with each great sob. Her hands clenched painfully onto Elieana's. When she completely exhausted herself, she lay down on the narrow bed and pressed her face firmly against the wall. Her breathing slowly became regular with the occasional breathy sob until she fell into an exhausted sleep.

“I have never met a woman like her. She is very puzzling. “What more can you tell me about her?" whispered Darec.

“Only that she changes from being happy and carefree one moment to sobbing uncontrollably the next. She has been like this since they brought me to this room. They did not tell me what I should do, only that I would remain until she asked the guard to take me away."

"Has she told you anything else, what Vasilis is planning or better yet, how to get out of here?"

"She has free rein in the castle. Wherever she wants to go they allow it. She told me she goes often to the aviary and watches, but she never goes further. It is the one place Vasilis told her not to go. When she goes there she uses a secret path. I think she can get there from this tower without descending the stairs. There has to be a door or some entryway that will take her to other parts of the castle as well, she told me she has even spied on Vasilis when he brings his counsel together."

"Did not Christoff say this castle was once a bandit lair?" said Darec. "It makes sense that secret passageways were built throughout the castle in the event they had need of an escape route. I think you may be right, Elieana, there must be a way to get out of the tower. If there is then perhaps Vasilis does not know about it.

"Let us search while she is asleep, if she has been here as long as she says, then she may have discovered the passage by accident."

Elieana nodded and rose from the bench. "I'll search this room; you take the other."

Darec walked into the adjoining room which held a large tub and a mirror on the opposite wall. He carefully ran his hands over the walls, searching for an indent or something that would trigger a door to open. Finding nothing and about to give up Darec sat down on the edge of the tub and stared at his reflection in the large, ornate mirror. As he pondered where a secret door could be hidden a small ball of fluff caught his attention as it rolled slowly across the floor and came to rest at his feet, as if the slightest of breezes touched it.

He walked over and examined the mirror, overly decorated with carved flowers, small birds and animals in a woodland setting. A carved ribbon wound this way and that throughout the scene until it reached the top, crowning the mirror with a large, slightly crooked bow.

The bow must be the key, he thought. Being careful not to touch the glass and leave smudges he twisted it. He heard a small click and the mirror popped straight out from the wall. He ran his fingers behind the mirror until he found a latch and when he lifted it the mirror silently opened, revealing a narrow passageway.

An unlit torch hung in a bracket on the wall in the passageway. Darec took out his flint and scraped it with his knife until a spark caught and the torch flared to life. He lifted it from the bracket and held it out so that it lit the stairway below. The light revealed a steeply winding staircase, choked with spider webs. He hung the torch back in the bracket and went to get Elieana.

"I have found the way out. We must hurry now. I told the guard at the bottom of the stairway I had come to take you to Vasilis to meet one of his guests. He will be wondering why we have not returned. We should also bring the other guard into the room. We can leave him gagged and tied up, that way he will not raise an alarm."

"Yes. I must wake Antonia," said Elieana. "We have to take her with us."

"Wake her when we are ready to leave," said Darec, glancing at the sleeping woman. "I am afraid she may fight us and not want to leave. She is so ridden with guilt I believe she will want to stay here in this tower until her dying day, just to punish herself."

"You're probably right. I'll help you drag the guard into the room."

They went out into the corridor and dragged the now semi-conscious guard inside. Darec thumped him on the side of the head and the guard slumped into unconsciousness again.

"Darec, let's leave the door ajar so the guards think we are somewhere in the castle," said Elieana.

"Good idea. When we have Antonia in the passageway I will go back and open it."

Elieana gently shook Antonia to awaken her. "My lady," she whispered. "We are going to leave the tower now. You must come with us."

"No, I cannot," she whimpered. "I have no life anywhere but in this tower. I will die here."

"No, you will not die here. There are others on the outside who wish to see you again."

Antonia's face pinched with emotion. Expecting that Antonia would cry out Darec picked her up off the bed and hugged her tightly to his chest.

"You must come with us," he whispered in her ear. "I believe what you say, that Vasilis is evil. I believe he is planning something that will hurt a great many people. You can help save them. That will be your way of making up for what you did in the past. If you do not want anyone to see you I will take you wherever you want to go once we have stopped Vasilis from carrying out his plan." He relaxed his hold on her but still held her firmly so that she could not run away from him.

Antonia nodded in agreement but the desolation on her face made him wonder if they were doing the right thing. He wondered if she had the will to stop Vasilis. He led her into the bathing chamber where Elieana waited for them. Darec placed Antonia's hand into Elieana's to ensure she did not follow him back into the bed chamber. Antonia stood there, trembling so Elieana wrapped one arm around Antonia's shoulders. They sat down on the edge of the tub, before Antonia's legs gave out, while they waited for Darec to rejoin them.

Darec opened the door of the tower room, leaving it slightly ajar, hoping any guards making a search for them would look in other parts of the castle first. He ripped up a blanket and used it to blindfold and gag the unconscious guard then dragged him behind the bed. Perhaps this might save the man from death for allowing the prisoner and Antonia to escape. He recalled, with revulsion, how the white-haired man, Egesa, as he now knew him, dealt with his own men in the clearing outside of Yannis' village.

The rest of the strips he tucked in his jerkin and then he returned to the bathing chamber. The fear on Antonia's face was palpable. Darec helped her to her feet and led her to the passageway. When they were inside he used the remaining strips of the blanket to tie the hidden door shut. Slowly they descended the spiral stairway, their way lit by the flickering light of the single torch.

The stairway spiraled around upon itself leaving it impossible to judge how far down it went. It had not been used for some time judging by the thick spider webs choking the stairway.

Antonia let out small squeaks of displeasure when the webs caught on her face and arms. She continually wiped them away and waved her arms frantically to keep them from sticking to her. Her strange behavior made Darec wonder how often she had come this way to get out of her tower room.

Vasilis had left Antonia alone to wander at will believing she would remain in the castle. There was nothing for her to do and nowhere for her to go. She had fallen into deep despair over leaving her husband and losing her child. He knew she did not pose a threat to any of his plans.

Darec tried to calm her by whispering encouragement to distract her from her preoccupation with the spider webs and the darkness of the stairwell, fearing any outburst from her would alert someone on the other side of the wall.

As they descended, Antonia told them Vasilis had convinced her that her husband was bent on wicked purpose and she had left Belisle only to protect her daughter. She had not realized Vasilis was using her to get to the king, so he could further his own ends. She believed her beloved brother, who then betrayed her, and with that betrayal she lost both husband and daughter.

Darec realized now why Elieana had not told Antonia of Nada. At times Antonia seemed completely normal and at others she seemed somewhat deranged from the grief and guilt she carried.

As they descended the stairway they passed many other passageways branching off into the dark bowels of the castle. Curious, Darec asked, "Antonia, there is a large hall, at the bottom of the stairway leading to your tower room. Not far down the hallway is a large chamber. I saw several men enter it. Do you know of any passageways behind the room?"

"Yes, there is one. I can take you to it," she replied eagerly, almost too eager for Darec's liking.

"Is it safe? Will the men in the room...Vasilis, will he know we are there?"

"Vasilis will not know but if one of the Sangan Chieftains is there, he will know. They have pure white hair and strange, frightening eyes that seem to look right through you. I was listening once, and he looked directly at me as if no wall stood between us. I could feel a presence about him so overwhelming I had to leave. I feared to go back there again."

"I saw a man that looks like the one you describe. He is in the castle now. He led the band of men who captured Elieana and my men. I felt the same thing, a repellent impression in my mind. Do you know what he is here for?"

"No, only that he frightens me," said Antonia, her voice now only a trembling whisper.

"Can you take me to the passageway, so I may hear what is being said?"

“I will take you to the passageway, but I will go no further. You must go to the spy hole on your own,” she said, now sounding petulant and disagreeable. Antonia became silent then, refusing to answer further questions. It suited Darec that she refused to go with him to this spyhole; she could put their lives in jeopardy if she started to talk or became agitated.

They descended the twisting stairway until they reached a much narrower passageway forking to the right and gradually ascending. Antonia stopped and pointed down the passageway. "You have to go that way," she whispered, and her voice quivered. "Just before the passageway ends you will find a recess in the wall to your right. The spy hole is there. Do not put the torch near it as the light may reflect into the room. It is part of a mural constructed of tiny mirrors. There is a circular center in the mural and an image of the room reflects onto another mirror in the passageway. You will be able to observe who is in the room and hear what they are saying. The mural is of such intricate design no one will know you are there." She stopped speaking as abruptly as she had started. She didn't look at Darec and didn't lower her arm as she pointed the way.

A quizzical expression crossed Darec’s face, he opened his mouth as if to say something then shook his head, as if thinking it better not to ask her any further questions. His shoulders brushed against each side of the passageway. In places he had to walk sideways to get through. When the tunnel abruptly ended, it didn’t take long for Darec to locate the recess behind the mural. He looked through the tiny portal and saw the men seated around a large table. Yannis sat on the right side, with the white-haired man sitting to his left. Three other men, Darec didn't recognize, sat on the opposite side. Darec assumed the dark haired, richly dressed, man sitting at the head was Vasilis. A servant poured wine while another served their meal on golden platters then both servants left the room. Vasilis raised his glass in a toast. "To the successful conclusion of our plan, gentlemen."

The others raised their glasses then they ate, discussing no more than pleasantries. Darec was about to leave when another servant entered and spoke softly with Vasilis. He nodded to someone out of range of the mirror then a man stepped into view. The man wore the livery of one of the houses of Pelagos. Darec had seen it before but did not know which house claimed those colors. The man saluted and stood waiting to speak.

"Yes, Arturo?" said Vasilis, slightly inclining his head in acknowledgement.

"I have a message for you from Girard."

Surprised at hearing the name, Girard, Darec listened intently, guessing it might be Girard, the assassin he had hunted for so long and who seemed always one step ahead of him.

"Go ahead, you may convey the message, we are all partners in this scheme."

"Girard sends his good will and to inform you that a young maiden belonging to the house of King Stephan stays in his house. He asks about arrangements for her travel to Delvar or if she should remain until you arrive for the wedding."

Darec could not see Vasilis' face but could see something was amiss by the way he tightly gripped his goblet. Vasilis' guests looked inquiringly at him, but he recovered quickly.

"Ah, gentlemen, my young niece who went to visit the City of Pelagos; to learn something of the city's history. She is not of King Stephan's house but is related to my dear departed wife." His voice oozed with falsehood, but the men seemed not to take notice except the white-haired man whose gaze lingered on Vasilis.

"Excuse me for a moment while I draft a reply. We don't want her to be in any danger. I must arrange for her removal immediatcly."

A surprised expression passed across Arturo's face which he masked immediately. He had not become Girard's right-hand man by being slow to understand hidden meanings in conversations, but the confusion was on his face long enough for Darec to be suspicious about who they referred to and the danger Vasilis wanted to keep her from.

Vasilis exited the room, followed by Arturo, the other men remaining in quiet conversation. Suddenly it dawned on Darec that the girl Arturo spoke of could only be Nada. As far as he knew Vasilis' wife was an only child and Antonia's family consisted of Vasilis and a younger brother cloistered in a monastery high in the Razor Mountains. Somehow the Girard they spoke of had found out about Nada and taken her. Jorian should have spoken with the king about Nada and had her moved to the royal chambers but it was possible someone else discovered her before they could do so.

While Darec stood thinking about all he had heard he did not notice Egesa rise and walk to the mural. Darec again looked inside the room and saw the man's unusual pale eye, with a slit for a pupil, staring back at him. Egesa whispered just loud enough for Darec to hear. "I have sensed your presence three times now, once on the outskirts of the village of Delan; once in the hallway outside this very room and now. We will meet soon, you and me. You have much to lose, I fear. Be on your guard, I will find you."

Startled Darec jumped back, bumping his head painfully on the wall behind him. He retreated, as quickly as the width of the tunnel allowed, to where he left Elieana and Antonia. When he reached them, he did not stop to tell them what he heard. He helped Antonia up from where she sat and rushed them along the passageway. "Elieana, Antonia, we must get out of here, now.

Antonia, tell me, is there a quick exit out of the castle?" said Darec, trying to keep his voice calm so as not to startle her.

"There is not," she said in a flat, emotionless voice. "There are three ways out, back the way we came and through the castle; through the cavern and up to the aviary on the plateau where the newly hatched birds are taken; or, across the deep lake. On the far side of the lake I have heard there is a passageway leading to the forest beyond, but I have never been there, I have only heard about it."

"What have you heard?" said Darec, "You must tell me everything if we are to get away safely."

“The stories frighten me," she whined. "Vasilis has told me of large creatures in the water of the lake. I have heard the soldiers have thrown men in and the creature swallows them in one huge gulp.” She started to tremble, causing the torch she carried to wave dangerously close to Darec's face.

Darec grabbed Antonia's hand to steady it. “It would not surprise me, Lady Antonia, if large creatures did inhabit the water. There are many such creatures in the sea. Do you know if the creature takes men from a boat? If that is so, then it would not be safe to cross. If the creature does not, then we should be safe to take a boat, if there are any. What I am most concerned about are the birds you speak of. How large are these birds?”

Antonia seemed to take courage from Darec's hand holding hers and spoke without trembling. “They are large enough for a man to ride upon. Vasilis brought the Sangan men here along with the eggs many months ago, once they have hatched and imprinted on the men who will ride them they are taken to the aviary until they are fully grown and trained to carry soldiers. Vasilis is planning on using them for war. They are carrion birds. It is so frightening.” She hid her face in her hand and when she again looked up at him her face looked like a death mask.

Darec patiently listened to Antonia describe the immense birds, large enough to carry a man; brilliant blue feathers on their heads; the head more like a lizard with a large mouth and large teeth; a long paddle like tail with blue and white feathers and huge wings. Once imprinted they became linked until either one or the other died. An army of them could travel great distances and from the sight of them, strike fear in the hearts of men. What amazing creatures they must be, he thought and the more she told him the more wondrous they became. Antonia seemed to enjoy describing these fearsome birds, becoming more relaxed as she talked.

They arrived at the end of the passageway, seemingly blocked by a large boulder but on closer inspection a crack at one side gave enough room for them squeeze around it. When they emerged on the other side a huge cavern spread out before them. Stalactites hung from the ceiling and at some places they joined the stalagmites reaching upwards, like giant pillars holding up the towering ceiling. Some formations seemed so delicate that with the slightest touch the whole formation would shatter. On one side of the cavern a stone waterfall flowed from centuries of moisture running down the walls. Flickering torchlight in the cavern added to the illusion of it slowly flowing downwards.

On two sides of the cavern, large fires burned, burnishing the walls in a shimmer of gold. Spreading out from where they stood lay a level area covered with mounds of sand. On top of each mound sat a large creamy colored egg the size of a very large barrel. The warm sand beneath their feet and the slightly humid air in the cavern was obviously the reason the eggs would hatch in the cavern without a bird nesting on top of them. Some of the eggs were so translucent in color the shadow of the growing embryo showed through. Antonia stepped up behind Darec and held onto his waist as she peered around him to gaze at the scene in front of them.

"There will be watchers about," she whispered, "We must be very careful. They watch for cracks in the eggs and then they bring a soldier to wait by it, so he will be imprinted to the bird when it hatches." She pointed to an egg towards the middle of the group, already showing signs of small fractures in the shell.

Silently they crept along the outer edge of the cavern, staying as far away as they could from the egg mounds. When they could no longer walk near the cavern wall they moved furtively between the eggs, always on the lookout for the watchers. As they came around the last mound the dark expanse of the lake spread out in front of them, its distant shore invisible in the gloom. On their left a narrow roadway led up out of the cavern. Nearby large wheeled cages stood beside a corral of dilhaas who observed them curiously as they munched on their fodder.

As she walked, Elieana gazed out towards the lake and the wondrous ceiling above, glimmering in the darkness like thousands of stars in the night sky. She tripped and fell against an egg. Her arms wrapped around the egg in a hug as she tried to regain her balance, there was a loud cracking noise and a piece of the shell fell at her feet. She looked up and a huge, savage eye stared back at her through the hole in the shell. She could not look away. She felt compelled to stare back into the eye. She couldn't detach her hands, they seemed glued to the shell. The top of the shell broke away and out popped a very ugly head covered with fine, damp, yellow feathers. The bird looked directly at her, continuing to stare. It started to make cooing noises. A link to this man-sized bird grew in her mind and she felt fulfilled somehow, as if she found something she had long sought for.

Strong hands pulled at her. She tried to fight the grip of the hands, she didn't want to let go. Her hold on the shell broke and immediately she felt a loss so painful she started to cry. "No, no," Elieana whispered as tears streamed down her face. Darec held her tightly as she struggled to get away from his grasp.

"Elieana. Elieana," he called out to her, "We must leave now."

Elieana blinked back her tears. She held her hand over her mouth, attempting to stifle the sobs threatening to escape. She allowed Darec to take her arm and he gently helped her move away from the egg. The bird frantically pecked at the imprisoning shell, screeching, and calling. Elieana's heart broke as she leaned on Darec and stumbled the rest of the way to the edge of the lake where some small boats lay on the shore. Darec had pulled one out into the water, where Antonia sat placidly, as if she were waiting to go on an excursion. Behind them angry voices joined with the squawking of the bird as Darec helped Elieana into the boat.

"Paddle into the middle of the lake as fast as you can," said Darec not once letting go of her arm.

Before Elieana had time to sit down, Darec shoved the boat as hard as he could, she lost her balance and sat down hard onto the seat. He ran back to the other boats and rammed his sword down through their bottoms. At the same time, the watchers Antonia warned them about ran out from between the eggs.

Darec ran out into the lake and some of the men followed but went no deeper than their knees. One man, braver than the rest, ran forward and tackled Darec, toppling him over into the water. The sounds of their struggles echoed off the cavern walls.

In the distance Elieana could see the bird trying to get the rest of the way out of its shell. An overwhelming need flooded into her mind. She should be there to help Euphemious, its name, the name she sensed when their eyes met.

One of the men remained by the shell, trying to help the bird. He pulled the shell away and tried to sooth and pat the bird, but it snapped at him and squawked loudly. At last, free of its shell, the bird struggled on its spindly legs to the edge of the lake. It wanted only Elieana. The man tried to coax Euphemious back towards the egg mound, but his attempts only infuriated the bird making it snap and screech.

As she watched this interaction Elieana realized the man should have imprinted with Euphemious. She could feel the anguish the man felt as he tried to get Euphemious to stay with him. She sensed he had visited the egg and touched it and had experienced the same feeling of attachment that Elieana herself felt when she fell on the shell. Elieana realized the man, Euphemious and herself were now linked together.

She sensed Euphemious, torn between the man who touched and caressed him and Elieana who had left him. Euphemious let out one final screeching cry, then gave up its search for her and flopped down in the sand. The man stayed with Euphemious, gently caressing the creature's head.

Elieana turned her face away from the scene, her grief for the loss of Euphemious too much to bear.

CHAPTER 4

The man tackled Darec and attempted to pull him out of the water. His comrades urged him on but none of them moved into the water to help.
Antonia's piercing scream cut the humid air in the cavern. Elieana turned towards Antonia, intending on berating her, then she looked in the direction Antonia pointed. A massive, slightly submerged log, passed by the boat. A flick of its tail revealed it was not a log at all. A scaly tail slowly propelled the creature towards the shallow water where Darec and his attacker struggled. The creature slowly opened its mouth, revealing its huge yellow fangs.

"Darec, the creature," Elieana's voice echoed eerily off the cavern walls.

Darec turned, distracted by her scream and at the same time the other man threw a well-aimed punch at Darec's jaw, throwing him off balance. Darec fell backwards towards the creature which was preparing to grab him by the legs. The creature's mouth was not fully open and as Darec fell he landed on top of its head then rolled off into the water.

Stunned from the punch Darec floated on his back not moving.

Darec's attacker furiously ran towards the shore but the creature lunged forward and grabbed the man's leg with its huge jaws. With one gigantic thrust the creature threw the man over its back into the water. The man shrieked in pain and fear as he struggled to regain his footing.

Antonia fainted, slumping down in the bottom of the boat. The oar she held slipped into the water and floated away. The cacophony in the cavern was deafening. The bird's screeches mingled with the screams of the injured man, again in the grip of the monster. The man shrieked in agony as the huge fangs pierced his body. Elieana felt her head would burst and in all the commotion she lost sight of Darec.

Lunging and splashing the creature attempted to get a better hold on its prey. Elieana couldn't tell if it was Darec or the man he had fought with that was hanging from the creature's mouth as it crushed him to death.

The thrashing from the creature's tail caused swells making the boat very unstable. Elieana paddled furiously with her oar so she could retrieve the one Antonia dropped. When she had the second oar she maneuvered the boat closer to the shore to search for Darec. When she couldn't locate him, she glanced out to the deeper water, hoping by chance the lunging and thrashing of the creature pushed him there.

She finally spotted him floating on his back and rowed the boat as fast as she could towards him. At the same time, she heard another loud shriek echoing on the walls and then everything went deathly quiet. Elieana stared at the shore and saw the creature sink down into the water, the man held firmly in its mouth.

The breaking of the waves on the shore and the oars hitting the water as she rowed towards Darec broke the deathly silence in the cavern. She maneuvered the boat alongside him then reached down and grabbed him by the shoulder pulling and shaking him.

“Darec! Darec!” Elieana called out as she shook him again and again until his arms flailed for her to stop. He rolled over onto his stomach, spluttering and splashing, trying to orient himself but he kept sinking down under the water. Suddenly Darec's head and shoulders popped up. Gasping for air he grabbed onto the side of the boat and heaved himself up out of the water, almost tipping the boat over. Elieana leaned back as far as she could, putting all her weight onto the opposite side of the boat as Darec pulled himself in. He slithered, boneless, into the bottom of the boat and lay with his arm over his face.

"That beast's hide is as tough as boiled leather," he said then smiled at Elieana as he sat up, using the sides of the boat for support.

They stared at each other for one poignant moment then fell laughing manically into each other’s arms.

"I thought the beast had you in its jaws," said Elieana, shaking with emotion.

"It almost did. If that fellow hadn't punched me I wouldn't have lost my balance and fallen clear of its bite."

Darec moved back so he could look at Elieana. Tears streamed down her face and he reached up to wipe them away. "I'm all right," said Darec. "What happened? I hit my head on the beast and it stunned me but what happened after that?"

Elieana wrapped her arms around Darec's shoulders, smiled and kissed him fully on the mouth then moved back to her seat. Her heart pounded, and she shook as she grasped the oars and pulled as hard as she could to get further away from the shore. "I will tell you more once we are well away from that horrid place."

Surprised by the kiss, Darec gazed intently at her, not saying a word.

As Elieana rowed away she watched the men on the shore. "They have retrieved their weapons, Darec," said Elieana as the first arrows flew over their heads.

"Surely, they are better shots, perhaps their aim is off due to the creature and the death of their comrade," said Darec. "A few more strokes and we will be out of range."

Elieana rowed as hard as she could until the arrows fell harmlessly short of their target, making plunking sounds as they sank out of sight in the murky water.

The further they rowed from the shore the dimmer the light became but it didn't entirely disappear. Elieana could still see the men milling around and then a group of soldiers joined them. The soldier's arrival bolstered the men's courage and they pushed the remaining boats into the water to begin their pursuit. A chorus of shouting signaled the discovery of the damaged boats.

Elieana smiled in relief as she pulled on the oars. The exertion felt good and as they glided across the water she felt the stress of the days slipping from her shoulders. She didn't know what they would find on the other side of this hideous lake; she just wanted to get as far away from that beach as she could.

The further they moved from the torch lit egg cavern the more noticeable became the dim light from the cavern walls and ceiling high overhead. It was a curious light, pale and ghostly. Whatever caused it she did not know but was thankful they were not left in total darkness. As she rowed further out on the glassy blackness of the lake the light from the egg hatchery slowly faded away until it finally disappeared completely.

Darec moved forward to take over the rowing from Elieana and as he did so he reached out and cupped her cheek. "The second time I have caused you to cry. I am sorry."

Elieana smiled back at him and shook her head as if to say, no matter, then thankfully passed the oars to him. They sat in silence as Darec rowed the boat through the cavern.

When Antonia finally began to stir she sat up, her hair matted about her ghostly pale face.

"Antonia," said Darec, "What have you heard of this end of the lake?"

She twiddled her hair about her fingers and stared at him, a vacant expression on her face. "Nothing, I do not know where it leads to."

Astounded by this revelation Darec's mouth gaped, as if he meant to say something then he clamped it shut, clenching his teeth. He felt, at that moment, like a blind man being led by a blind woman. It made no matter, however, they had to search for another way out. They could not return to the egg hatchery, where others either waited for them or at this moment pursued them in newly repaired boats.

Darec maneuvered the boat towards the left wall of the cavern and rowed alongside it, hoping to see an opening and a way out. "Elieana, look out for a landing or something that might be a way to get out," he said.

Elieana moved to the front of the boat, rocking it gently as she tried to move past Antonia. Antonia squeaked like a mouse, holding onto the sides of the boat firmly, making this maneuver very difficult.

"Antonia, let go of the side of the boat so I can get around you."

"Noooooo," Antonia wailed. "You will tip us over. Stop. Stop rocking the boat."

Elieana grasped Antonia's shoulders and climbed over her outstretched arms, the muscles completely rigid, as if they were carved from wood. After much boat rocking and squealing from Antonia, Elieana settled herself at the front of the boat so she could peer out into eerie semi-darkness. They rowed for what seemed like hours but finally, out of the gloom, they could see a landing in the distance.

"Darec, there, over there," Elieana whispered, as if afraid to be overheard. As they rowed closer they saw a narrow stairway, hewn out of the rock, leading up out of the water. A rope railing knotted on rings ran up the cavern wall and in front of the stairway a huge creature lay with its head on the bottom step, blocking their access to the stairway and their way out of the cavern.

Darec looked to where Elieana pointed, shuddering involuntarily. He immediately realized they could not get out of the boat unless they could distract the creature's attention. He rowed the boat past the stairway and saw another way to climb up along the wall on the opposite side.

"Elieana," he whispered, pointing to the far side of the landing. "I'm going to row past the stairway and get out of the boat over there by that ledge. I'll climb along the wall and come at the creature from above." Hopefully, he thought, I will kill it before it kills me.

"When I get out you bring the boat around behind the creature. You must get up the stairs as fast as you can when the beast is distracted."

Elieana stared at Darec in horror, fearing the outcome if he again ended up in the water. The beast was enormous. Its slightly opened mouth revealed huge teeth, that they now knew could rip a man in half. She took the oars from Darec and rowed the boat past the stairs and steadied it while Darec climbed onto the rock ledge. He clung to the wall like a limpet then pushed the boat with his foot as hard as he could. One of the oars splashed into the water as the boat slid backwards. The beast moved its head and watched the boat, with one of its malevolent looking yellow eyes, as it floated past. It hissed menacingly, and its mouth gaped wider as it moved backwards into the water.

Fearing the beast would follow her, Elieana rowed far out into the center of the lake and then turned the boat around, maneuvering it along the cavern wall behind the creature. The beast slowly moved its body as Darec climbed sideways on the rocks. Its body still blocked the stair and it cocked its head sideways, so it could still see the boat behind it. The further Darec climbed the more agitated the beast became, raising its huge tail and arching its head back. It slid sideways as it watched both Elieana and Darec. Growling noises coming from the creature rippled the water and a shiver of dread ran tingling up Elieana's spine. Elieana stayed where she was, trying to steady the boat with the oars so the beast focused its attention on Darec.

As she watched the beast, it seemed to grow larger, sort of puffing up. Its huge tail with spiny ridges all along the top and its scaly hide, mottled yellow and green, gave it an appalling look. It opened its mouth and growled, a sound that seemed to come from the subterranean depths of the world. Its monstrous teeth glistened in the dim light of the cavern. Elieana's stomach lurched with a visceral fear; her heart pounded so hard it felt as if it would jump out of her chest. She glanced at Antonia, sitting rigidly on the bottom of the boat. She held her eyes tightly shut, her back to the creature and Elieana was thankful that Antonia could not see it.

Suddenly the beast began flicking its tail back and forth, it snapped and bit at the water and groaned loudly, a warning that could not be ignored. Elieana gripped the oars tightly, turning her hands white and skeletal looking. She had to force herself to breathe slowly; to concentrate on loosening her grip. She tried to focus on Darec, now half way to the top of the stairway. Suddenly the creature shuffled its body, so it faced directly towards him as he moved along the rocks. Groaning and snapping the creature lunged upwards with a speed none of them could have anticipated. Darec was too far away for it to reach him but Elieana's fear burst out in a terror filled scream that reverberated on the cavern walls, over and over and over.

The creature's lunge proved to Darec that it moved too quickly for him to plunge his sword into its head as he planned. He also realized if the beast faced him it blocked Elieana and Antonia from reaching the stairs. The only comfort he had; the boat's distance from the beast's whipping tail. He needed something to distract the creature's attention, if only for a moment. He considered his options then decided he could use his belt to tie around a large rock. A weapon, of some sort, to hit the creature with from a distance. Using his knife, he pried at the rock wall until he broke off a sizeable chunk. He buckled his belt securely around the rock and crept slowly forward to the topmost stair. He pulled at the rope railing then sawed through it until the knot holding it in place fell to the ground. The beast kept its gaze riveted on him but did not lunge again.

Darec picked up the knot of rope and threw it out into deeper water. The beast slid backwards, moving its head in the direction of the splash but then immediately turned its gaze back to Darec. It raised itself up on its front legs hissing and threatening another lunge.

"Elieana," Darec whispered loudly, "Row to the far side and splash with your oars to attract the beast's attention.

"No," screamed Antonia.

Elieana started to move the boat as Darec instructed but then Antonia reached out and grabbed one of the oars. The boat tipped and bobbed and was in imminent danger of capsizing. The commotion, however, had the desired effect and the beast turned its malevolent stare towards the boat. As it watched the struggle it moved backwards until its body floated completely in the water. Elieana managed to grab the oar out of Antonia's grasp and shoved her roughly backwards, causing her to fall hard onto the bottom of the boat. "You crazy woman!" shrieked Elieana. "What do you think you are doing? You could have tipped us. The beast would be devouring us at this very moment."

Antonia curled into a ball, pulled her skirt up over her head and started moaning; the intensity increasing and decreasing repeatedly. Elieana worriedly watched Antonia. What am I doing, she thought, bringing this woman back to Nada. What kind of a mother can she possibly be? Elieana's fear for their safety as well as Nada's intensified in her heart.

Horrified, Darec watched the altercation between the two women, diverting his attention from the beast for a moment. As the beast watched the crazily rocking boat it sank down into the water, its cruel yellow eyes and the top of its long snout remained above the surface as it slowly swam towards the boat.

"Elieana," called out Darec, "You must row the boat to me."

Elieana saw the beast no longer blocked their way. She immediately rowed the boat to the stairway. As soon as the boat bumped up against the bottom step, Antonia leapt out. Her sudden movement pushed the boat away from the landing. At the same time, the beast burst forward hitting the boat with its snout, tipping it over. Elieana did not have time to hold on and slid into water between the boat and the rock wall.

Darec drew his knife, jumped onto the beast's back and stabbed it in the head. He wrapped his legs around the beast's body and held on as it started to roll over and over, trying to dislodge Darec from its back. Darec slammed the knife into the beast again and again. As the beast rolled it sank deeper into the water dragging Darec down with it. The spiny ridge on the creature's back and the boney scales on the sides of its body shredded Darec's clothing and abraded the skin of his chest, stomach and arms.

Elieana pulled herself out of the water onto the landing. Her back ached from hitting the edge of the boat as she fell. She crawled on hands and knees up the stairway. When she reached the top, she lay watching the horrific sight of the beast rolling and Darec clinging to its back.

Darec's lungs burned painfully from lack of oxygen. It took great effort not to breathe in deeply, filling his lungs with water. Whenever the beast resurfaced, and he could gasp in a breath he heard screaming but didn't know if it was himself, Elieana or Antonia. He had no time to wait for the beast to succumb to the wounds he already inflicted. He needed to end this now before he drowned. Darec pulled himself forward onto the beast's head inch by painful inch until he could wrap his arms around its neck. With one final burst of energy he reached down and slashed the beast's throat. A gush of warm blood pulsed from the wound and the beast's lifeblood created an ever-widening circle around its body. The rolling slowed.

It gave one last heave and lay still, exposing its pale, scaly, vulnerable belly.

Darec burst out of the water gasping for breath and dizzy from lack of oxygen. Treading water, he nervously eyed the beast, expecting it to lunge at him again but the huge jaws lay slack.

The beast's thick blood surrounded Darec. Repulsed he rolled onto his back and paddled slowly back to the landing. He used his remaining strength to pull his body out of the water where he succumbed to exhaustion. Darec awoke to throbbing pain in his hands, slashed from the beast's scales. He pulled himself upright, his legs as weak as a newborn babe, climbed the stairs and lay down beside Elieana. Just as he started sinking into oblivion Elieana tugged at his arm.

"Darec, we have to get out of here. They are coming, I can hear them coming."

Darec shook his head; he just wanted to rest. His whole body hurt as if someone had slammed him repeatedly with a stick. He couldn't hear anything; the screaming had ceased; only Elieana's insistence stopped him from passing out again. He wanted her to go away and waved his hand at her to stop talking.

"Darec, get up. Those men are coming." She pulled at him and then the screaming started again. Elieana flashed an angry look at Antonia, "Woman, will you stop your screaming," she snarled.

All Antonia could do was point out into the water. Elieana turned her gaze to where Antonia pointed and saw a creature, even larger than the ones they already encountered, swimming towards the dead creature in the water. Its huge jaws clamped down on the carcass and with a slow roll it pulled it down under the water.

Darec looked up in time to see the creature staring back at him before it sank down out of sight. Fear of the beast shook him from his stupor. "Help me, Elieana," he said as he grasped her shoulder and leaned against the stone wall to push himself upright. "We must get out of this accursed place."

Elieana put her arm around his waist and together they staggered towards the passageway leading out of the cavern. Antonia stood at the entrance, pure terror etched on her face. She pushed herself tight against the wall as Darec and Elieana passed, then followed closely on their heels, into the darkened passage.

CHAPTER 5

Elieana entered the pitch-dark tunnel blindly searching the walls for a torch or something to light their way. She found nothing. "There has to be something," she spoke aloud. "They could not possibly come across the lake with lit torches, there must be something here."

She left Darec sitting just inside the entrance of the tunnel, urging him to rest, then went back to the landing where they left the boat. Amazed at the faint light emanating from the cavern ceiling a thought suddenly struck her. Never had she seen anything as wondrous as those glowing rocks, perhaps they could give enough light in the tunnel to see a few feet in front of them. She drew out her knife and chipped at the rock wall by the landing. When she had a handful of pieces she re-entered the tunnel and held them in her outstretched palm. The rocks gave off a soft, greenish-glow, lighting the tunnel walls where she stood.

Elieana moved her hand from side to side so the glow lit the walls as she passed by. Eventually she found a small alcove hewn out of the rock wall and a pile of old torches, slightly burned but dry. She slipped the rock chips into her pocket then lit the torches, giving one each to Darec and Antonia. Elieana stuffed the remaining torches into her belt, seeing no point in leaving them for their pursuers. She went back out and retrieved the rope left from the railing on the stairway and tied it around her waist. Before she re-entered the tunnel, she peered out into the gloom to see if any boat approached. The lake lay like black glass, smooth and without a ripple.

She could no longer hear the angry voices she heard before and considering this she thought it was probably an echo coming from the egg hatchery. Elieana took one last look, thankful they would not have to cross that horrible lake again, then re-entered the tunnel.

By the time Elieana returned, Darec had rested enough from his ordeal to move on. Before they started out Elieana tied the rope around Darec and Antonia's waists then reached out to take the torch from Antonia, but her face pinched into a frown. Elieana raised her hands in surrender, not wanting Antonia to start screaming again. "Keep the torch Antonia," she said then stepped back a pace.

Antonia looked back at Elieana and smiled with all her teeth. It was not really a smile just a lifting of her lips to display all her teeth. She took her place behind Darec, carrying her torch gripped tightly in her outstretched arms. Elieana shook her head and took a deep breath to calm herself, silently asking the Goddess to provide her with patience to deal with this strange woman.

They had no idea in what direction they walked; they just knew they wanted to be far away from that deadly lake. They walked for a long time until the tunnel suddenly branched in opposite directions. Elieana felt sick with the prospect of them having to split up.

Darec untied the rope from his waist. "I will go. Hopefully there will be an exit. This tunnel goes up, so I suspect it will come out somewhere above the castle," said Darec.

"We will wait for you here," called out Elieana lamely as she sat down alongside Antonia and watched Darec as he walked down the passage until only the light of his torch bobbing up and down showed his presence. Eventually it became just a pin prick of light then winked out altogether.

Darec jogged as quickly as he could along the cramped tunnel. It proceeded straight and at a slight incline and took no more than five or ten minutes to reach the end. Light filtering through vines and shrubs covering the exit was a welcome sight. He doused his torch and pushed aside the shrubbery just enough to see outside and was astonished by what he saw.

A flat, open field, surrounded by a heavily treed forest spread out before him. Small sheds occupied a spot close to the trees. Nearby his hiding place he saw a corral full of dilhaa and horses, a large building and another corral full of nervous, bawling cattle. In the center, a large, domed building dominated the field.

A group of men moved back and forth from the building near the cattle corral to the domed building, pushing wheelbarrows of what looked like fresh meat. Darec could hear the squawking of many birds emanating from the dome. When the men entered with the wheelbarrows the squawking reached crescendo.

"It's a rookery for the infant birds," he whispered out loud. "This is where they bring the hatchlings."

Just as he wondered how they could get the birds up from the cavern he observed a large group of men, laughing and joking with each other, approaching the dome from the opposite side of the clearing. One man walking by himself seemed the butt of their jokes. Behind the group of men, a dilhaa pulled a cart with a large cage mounted on it. Inside the cage sat a newly hatched bird. The man fell further behind the group, waving his arms in an agitated manner. He waited for the cart to reach him then walked alongside it. From the set of his shoulders, his agitation with the other men and the way he walked and waved his arms Darec speculated this man should have imprinted with the bird when it hatched. Had Elieana not bumped the egg and sped up the hatching the man probably would have succeeded with the imprinting. The unhappy bird snapped and screeched at the driver of the cart and the man walking alongside it. The man’s distress increased with the taunting of the other men and the more he tried to coax the bird to notice him the more aggressive and agitated it became.

The roadway passed very close to where Darec hid in the tunnel. He let the vines slip back into place and stepped back, away from the opening. As the cart passed by his hiding place he could hear the man speaking endearments to the bird, struggling to calm it, but to no avail.

Elieana's fall against the egg seriously affected the bird, so much so that the man could no longer imprint with it. Darec wondered then if Elieana still had a tie to the bird and wondered what the bird would do if it ever saw her again.

He saw enough to realize access back into the egg hatchery and the castle was much too risky. Vasilis would have posted additional guards in the event they found this escape route. He wondered then why no one pursued them through this tunnel. It would have been simple to catch them. An ominous feeling settled upon him, as if someone walked over his grave. He shook the feeling off, not wanting to succumb to fear of the unknown.

Darec picked up the torch from where he left it and walked back down the tunnel. When he could no longer see the vine-covered entrance, he stopped to re-light his torch, then he jogged back to where Elieana and Antonia waited at the other fork in the tunnel, their only way out.

Darec hoped his men were well on their way back to Pelagos. In hindsight, he should have entrusted the packet to one of his men rather than carrying it with him. It did no good to them now, trapped in the mountains with very slim prospects of returning to Pelagos before King Stephan's declaration of Michael as his heir.

Elieana welcomed Darec back with a huge sigh of relief. It seemed they waited hours for him to return. He told them all he had seen and his thoughts on the unlikely possibility of returning to the egg hatchery and then escaping through the castle. He looked down at Antonia, still sitting in the same spot on the floor of the tunnel. "Antonia, do you know if the clearing where they keep the hatched birds has a road leading into the forest below?"

She looked at him but did not answer. Darec glanced over at Elieana and she shrugged her shoulders. "She has been like this since you left, Darec." Then she stood up and motioned with her head down the tunnel. Elieana whispered, "She will not answer me and when I speak she turns away. I regret now bringing her with us; I think she will endanger us further, if we ever get away from here."

"Well, we cannot stay here, and we cannot leave her," he replied. "If she will not talk, perhaps she will follow. The only way out I can see is for us to go down the other passageway. Do you want to wait here while I go and check it?"

"I will come with you. Perhaps she is angry because you left us. If we go together maybe she will stop this childish behavior. I want nothing more at this moment than to get out of this darkness and into the light," replied Elieana.

"All right, I feel as you do. It will be better to get out of these tunnels and be able to see what is coming from the front or rear."

They walked back down the tunnel to find Antonia standing up, staring at them. "Why did you leave me? I do not want to stay here in this place alone. Do not leave me again." She stamped her foot down hard, ordering them both as if she stood again in her court and addressed her servants.

Elieana wondered if she truly was crazy from all the long years she lived in isolation or if she was as sane as them but spoiled and unruly and just punishing them with her behaviour.

"My lady," replied Darec diplomatically. "We only left you for some moments to determine which tunnel to take. I felt it better to explore first before asking you to follow. Will you not come with us now? I believe there must be a way out if we follow this other tunnel." His courteous appeal had the desired effect. She graciously nodded, putting out her hand for him to take as if being escorted into a grand ball.

"I will lead again, my lady, in the event something ahead may endanger you."

"Thank you, sir, you are most brave," replied Antonia who looked at Elieana with disdain and then purposely bumped into her as she followed Darec down the passageway.

Elieana shook her head in bewilderment as she watched Antonia. She was undoubtedly the strangest woman she had ever met. In her travels throughout the land she worked with some not right in their minds but never one so obviously peculiar. She did not want to say Antonia was crazy, she did not think so, she believed Antonia was lost somewhere in her mind and didn't really know anymore how she should conduct herself. This seemed very odd and very dangerous.

Absentmindedly Elieana touched the sheath where her knife hung from her belt. The last thing she wanted was to have to protect herself from attack by Antonia, but she also did not want to be caught off guard. Realizing she stood alone in the tunnel, and the light from her torch was the only thing keeping the dark at bay, Elieana set out at a jog to catch up to Darec and Antonia. The tunnel seemed to go on and on until they hungered for sight of sunlight as well as food and water.

At last they came to a sharp turn and saw a tiny rectangle of light in the distance.

"Wait here, My Lady; Elieana. I will look first to ensure it is safe to go through the opening," said Darec as he passed his torch to Elieana.

Darec proceeded to the exit, his silhouette as he went through the opening, a dark shape against the light. They waited for just a few moments and he reappeared in the doorway. He sounded pleased when he rejoined them. “It opens onto a little meadow and a small stream, flows there, at least we will have water. Come now, let us leave this place,” said Darcc.

He took his torch from Elieana and they proceeded at a quick pace toward the mouth of the tunnel. The excitement of getting out into daylight engulfed Elieana so much that she felt a bubble of laughter well up inside her.

When they reached the opening, blinding bright sunshine welcomed them, the babble of a small stream nearby like music to the ear. Thankfully, Elieana breathed deeply of the fresh sweet air, wonderful after the dank, musty smelling tunnel. She allowed herself to smile and laugh with relief as she leaned her head back and took the bright sun full on her face.

Darec observed Elieana and then laughed with her, he felt the same way. They walked to the stream, each slaking their thirst, splashing water on their faces and enjoying the coolness of the water.

After Elieana scrubbed the grime off her face she surveyed the meadow. The stream fell from a ledge high above them. It landed in a small pool nearby and then flowed away downhill. She followed the stream and looked for anything edible. Eventually she found a pathway, overgrown with tall grass. Before long she found herself standing at the top of a cliff where the pathway wound down to a large, flat plain spreading towards the horizon. She could see clumps of vegetation and enormous trees. Huge herds of animals, clustered closely together as they grazed. Much larger animals grazed in smaller groups and still larger ones picked leaves off the trees while they balanced on their hind legs.

Never in all her travels throughout Baltica or Pelagonia had she seen plains such as these and animals as large. Her mouth opened in an exclamation of, "Oh," and an icy trickle of fear slid down her spine when she realized they had traveled through the mountain. She stood in Sangan.

CHAPTER 6

Elieana ignored the stinging slap of branches against her legs as she ran back to where Darec and Antonia waited in the meadow. Her face, white with shock, announced something was terribly wrong.

"What is it?" said Darec as he grasped her shoulders and searched her face for answers.

"Darec, we have emerged on the wrong side. We are on the Sangan side of the mountain." She pointed towards the overgrown path. "The path leads to a wide open plain. There are herds of huge animals I have never seen before."

"Show me," he grabbed her hand and they ran back down the path, leaving Antonia staring after them. Darec and Elieana reached the cliff edge and gazed out over the wide expanse of land before them. Darec held onto Elieana's hand so tightly she had to pry his fingers away to loosen his grip.

"We could never have known, in that labyrinth of tunnels, which direction we walked. It is not surprising we are here. What we need to do now is find a way back." Darec ran his fingers through his hair, leaving it standing on end as he looked out at the vista in front of him. He felt a tug at his shirt and looked around to see Antonia behind him, crouched down and looking up at him, much like a beaten mongrel sidling up to its cruel master.

"Please, can we go away from this place? I am terribly afraid. What if someone sees us?"

"Who would see us?" he said, sounding impatient and angry.

Antonia cringed even more.

"The Sangan Chieftain brings the eggs through the tunnel to the nesting ground," she said. "He has a pact with Vasilis to provide them to him," then she flinched as if expecting to be struck.

"Antonia, you are a most vexing woman," he replied gruffly. She shrunk away from him again and without a second look at her Darec walked briskly away.

"Come, Elieana, Antonia," he called over his shoulder, "There is nothing we can do now. We will build a shelter and try to rest, night is almost upon us."

Elieana took Antonia's hand in hers but Antonia shook her hand away and trotted ahead so she could keep Darec in her sight, leaving Elieana staring after her in surprise.

Darec walked until he reached the wall of the mountain towering above. He searched and found a cleft in the rock wide enough for them to sit and keep them safe, at least on three sides, in the event anyone or anything approached during the night. He cut boughs for bedding off nearby fir trees with his sword and straight branches off a leaf tree for the remaining open side and top. Wedging the branches between the rocks he then piled more fir boughs on top, making a snug and cozy shelter large enough to have a small fire inside to keep them warm. The activity served to release some of the pent-up anger he felt towards Antonia for constantly giving information far too late to assist them in any way.

As soon as Darec finished the shelter Antonia crawled inside and sat with her back against the wall and stared out at them. Darec suddenly felt very guilty for being so abrupt with her. "Stay here, Antonia, we will be back soon, hopefully with something for you to eat." She didn't acknowledge what he said with either a nod or a reply. She just sat and stared and smoothed the fabric of her gown repeatedly.

Darec looked at her for a few moments then strode away from the shelter, his boot heels leaving deep marks in the soft soil. Elieana followed him and when she caught up with him she reached out and touched his arm. He slowed, then stopped. When he turned to face her, she saw the fury he held in check. He ground his teeth in frustration, the muscles of his jaw bulging.

"Darec, she has done nothing to help us, but it is not her fault we have ended up here."

"I know, I needed to get away from the woman. She has much knowledge but doesn't share it until it is too late," said Darec, the tone of his voice showing his impatience.

Elieana let go of Darec's arm and shrugged her shoulders in exasperation. "She has lived in intentional isolation in that tower for many years. She betrayed her husband. She believes her child is dead and that she is responsible and loathes herself for it. It has eaten away at her. She is confused and doesn't know what to do to help herself or anyone else. We have knowledge that will relieve some of her self-loathing. We need to tell her about Nada."

"You have come a long way in accepting this since we first spoke in your chamber. You are right, but I wonder what that knowledge will do to her. Will she regain the courage to live, to again see her daughter or will she descend even deeper into a pit of insanity she will never climb out of?"

Elieana shook her head sadly. "Whatever happens we have to tell her. If we never make it back to Pelagos she needs to know she did not kill her child."

"We will tell her tonight," he said with a tone of finality then he walked away to search for something to relieve the hunger cramping his stomach.

Elieana watched him walk away, realizing that he wanted to be alone so that he could control the anger he felt towards Antonia. She went to the stream and took a long drink of the crisp, cold water. After satisfying her thirst she searched the banks of the stream, looking for something edible and found some small tubers. She recalled eating tubers in the forest after her escape from Belisle, they were tasty and would relieve the empty pain in their stomachs. She stuffed them in her pockets and her upturned shirt and returned to the shelter.

As Elieana walked towards the shelter she found a small nest filled with oval-shaped eggs about the size of her palm. She took three from the nest then returned to the shelter and found Antonia lying curled up in a tiny ball, soundly asleep. A pang of grief pricked Elieana's heart as she looked down at the face of the sleeping woman, seeing the uncanny resemblance of mother and daughter. With her face relaxed in sleep she looked like a slightly older version of Nada. Elieana missed Nada terribly.

The noise of kindling and sticks falling to the ground heralded Darec's return and startled Antonia awake, her face again fixed in the frown usually present on her face. Darec's expression revealed how much he disliked Antonia. He paid no attention to her and barely acknowledged her presence. Antonia watched Darec build the fire but did not speak to him, recognizing his hostility, she kept her distance.

When the fire burned merrily with comforting snaps and pops Elieana pushed the eggs in close to cook but not burn. She didn't care what kind of bird or reptile laid them, deciding it didn't matter because she was so hungry even insects seemed appealing. She stuck the tubers on the ends of some sharp sticks and gave one to Antonia. They sat silently roasting them over the fire until the skins crisped and peeled away from the soft yellow meat inside. Antonia pulled the eggs out of the fire with a stick and in a surprising act of selflessness distributed the food, making sure Darec had an ample amount. A look of surprise flashed across Darec's face and he looked at Elieana, one eyebrow raised in question, but she shook her head, not knowing what to think. Antonia changed from a whining bitch to a docile lamb in seconds.

When Elieana finished eating she crawled out of their shelter and walked into the meadow to watch the last light of day fade from the sky. In a spectacular exit, the sun changed the fluffy clouds overhead from white to pink and yellow, then deep purple as it slowly slid below the horizon. Darec came and stood beside Elieana and they watched as the first stars flickered in greeting. Antonia whimpered and stood as close to Darec as she could without touching him. Afraid of the dark, Elieana thought in annoyance, huffing loudly. Darec reached over and gave Elieana's shoulder a little squeeze to let her know he understood.

The sounds of night insects filled their ears along with the occasional huge bellow or shriek from the plain below them. The first loud animal noises they heard startled them, the sounds of predators, animals not found in their land. Both Elieana and Darec knew the snarl and growl of the huge cats in the forests of Pelagonia and Baltica but never these fearsome sounds.

"I'll take the first watch," stated Darec as he nodded his head towards the shelter.

They walked back and crawled inside. The shelter kept off the night breeze but even so, Antonia snuggled close to Elieana, again surprising her. Antonia curled up and laid her head on Elieana's lap, falling instantly into a deep sleep and making small puffing noises as she snored lightly.

Darec pulled extra boughs across the opening to keep in the warmth. If anyone came into the clearing they could smell the smoke from their fire but not see it because the breeze blowing from the plain dissipated the smoke against the rocks. At the least the shelter hid them from sight if anyone approached. Darec knew they could not protect themselves from an armed attack but at least he would not be killed in his sleep. He could still give some resistance if someone discovered them. He leaned against the stone wall and watched Antonia as she slept, raising his eyebrows in question to see her lying with her head on Elieana's lap.

"She just curled up into a ball and fell asleep in my lap," whispered Elieana. "I can't tell from one moment to the next what she will do or say."

"Well, as you said earlier," he whispered back, "We must speak to her about the world outside her tower."

Antonia's eyes popped open, unnerving Darec, having thought her soundly asleep. She pushed herself up to a sitting position and smoothed her hair back from her face, as if she had been sitting there awake the whole time.

"Yes, please tell me what has taken place while I have been in my tower. What news do you have from Baltica?

They sat and talked for some time about small things that had taken place in the world while she shut herself away, exiled from the outside world. Antonia listened, occasionally making a comment or asking a question. Elieana wanted to tell her that her daughter lived but every time she started to speak Darec nudged her foot with the toe of his boot, greatly annoying Elieana. As the glow from the fire faded and Antonia drowsed off again Elieana blurted it out. "Antonia, we must talk about your daughter. She lives."

A frown of wary concern crossed Darec's face, concerned that the news could send Antonia spiraling down into the depths of despair. He readied himself for her to begin screaming.

"We agreed, Darec, she must know," said Elieana sharply.

"Yes, but I did not want to upset her." He did not want to give the real reason, that he did not trust Antonia and did not want to give her any information to cause them regret later.

They watched Antonia, waiting for some response, but she just stared at them. She seemed to glow with this news of her lost daughter, then in a quiet and very calm voice she spoke. "Why did you not tell me this before?" She raised her hand to stop them from responding. "No, do not answer, I know the reason. You do not trust me. You believe I have lost my mind from grief and guilt. In many ways, you are right. I had nothing to live for. I betrayed my husband and because of my betrayal I lost both my daughter and my King. I cannot now go back to Belisle; my life is forfeit. Now I cannot go back to my tower. My brother could not kill me but his Sangan chieftain could, without compunction. Now, I would very much like to hear news of my daughter. Please, tell me all you know."

A sudden transformation took place before their eyes. This woman who seemed completely lost in her mind reemerged with hope, a reason to go on. Elieana told Antonia about Nada from the day she found her to the day she left her in search of proof she was the daughter of King Stephan. Antonia exclaimed with pride for her daughter and tears of joy and wonder rolled down her cheeks as Elieana described Nada, a daughter to them both. Sometime during all this Antonia grasped Elieana's hands in hers and stared raptly into her face as she listened. They talked like this for what seemed like hours until they both fell asleep in each other's embrace.

Darec fell asleep while they talked and in the early morning hours woke abruptly. He rubbed his face vigorously, silently berating himself for not taking care to stay awake. The fire had burned to hot ash. He stirred it to life feeding in small sticks until eventually it flickered and burned, warming the shelter. Quietly he moved the boughs from the entrance. He took one look at Elieana and Antonia sleeping soundly, curled together for warmth, then crawled outside, replacing the boughs to keep the warmth inside.

He shivered in the chilly dampness of the air as he walked a short distance away to relieve himself. He stretched his cramped muscles and then walked to the cliff side to look down upon the Sangan plain. As he watched, the sun rose in brilliant hues of pink and orange but clouds in the distance gave the promise of rain. Hearing a screeching cry overhead Darec looked up and saw ten or so large birds swooping from high above towards a herd of large animals grazing below.

The herd, sensing danger, started to run, raising a huge cloud of dust. They ran for their lives and as he watched one of the birds swooped down and hit one of the animals with its talons. The bird's immense size dwarfed the huge animal running below it.

Darec slowly backed away into the trees, so as not to attract the attention of the bird riders, then rushed back to the shelter. He crawled inside and gently shook Elieana awake. She smiled up at him and stretched leisurely. Her tousled hair fluffed up around her face like a cloud. He smiled back at her, put his finger to his lips for her to be quiet then motioned for her to follow him outside. Darec replaced the boughs back on the entrance to the shelter then motioned for Elieana to follow him, leading her away from the shelter and making sure they remained under cover of the trees.

"The bird soldiers are out hunting on the plains," said Darec. "I am going to scout around to find a trail to take us up and out of here. Be wary they do not see you. Don't add more wood to the fire. We don't want the smoke attracting their attention."

Elieana's eyes widened slightly at the news, then she smiled and lightly touched his cheek. "I will have something for you to eat when you return, even if it is only cold tubers and eggs.

Her touch warmed him, and he smiled, very much wanting to take her into his arms and hold her but instead nodded and left to search for a trail to take them over the mountain and back to Pelagonia.

Elieana found large leaves to wrap up the tubers and eggs. She wrapped the food in the leaves and pushed it into the embers at the edge of the fire then she patted Antonia on the arm until she awoke.

"I slept well, Elieana, did you?" Antonia asked.

"Yes, Antonia, I did. Darec built a very cozy shelter for us and now he is searching for a trail to take us up over the mountain."

Antonia nodded then looked at the dying fire and reached for some sticks to add to it.

"No," exclaimed Elieana who then berated herself for sounding alarmed. "We must let it smolder only because Darec saw some of the bird soldiers hunting on the plain."

Antonia's hand stopped, hovering in mid-reach over the sticks as she looked wide-eyed back at Elieana. She didn't say a word and slowly withdrew her hand setting it in her lap. She gazed down at her hands, as if she held something very precious, then began to twist the fabric of her gown. Elieana watched her, waiting for Antonia's screaming to begin but this time she sat quietly, twisting and twisting the fabric.

After what seemed like a very long time Darec removed the boughs from the entrance to their shelter and stuck his head in. It had started to rain, and his wet hair stuck to his face and dripped onto the embers of the fire making it sizzle and steam. He found no more food but the look on his face showed pleasure in the news he brought. "I have found a trail. I hope it will take us up to the other side of the mountain. I recall the ancients blocked off a mountain pass for the safety of the people of Baltica and Pelagonia, to keep the Sangans out but also to keep the large animals at bay as well. I believe this is where we are now. The trail is hidden amongst the trees opposite the exit from the tunnels. It leads upwards but seems to curve around to the north. Once we have eaten we should set out. I fear Vasilis may still be searching for us, we must cover as much distance as we can."

Elieana nodded then passed him a large leaf filled with chunks of warmed tuber and egg which he ate with enthusiasm. When he had eaten his fill Elieana wrapped the rest of the food in leaves and stuffed them in her pockets. Darec scattered the ashes of the fire and covered them with dirt and then they walked to the stream to wash and drink before setting out towards the trail.

The rough state of the trail gave them confidence they would not meet anyone as they climbed but it also made the climb difficult and treacherous. Their clothing became thoroughly wet from the sodden shrubbery as they passed. Although they cursed the thick shrubbery when they started their climb it became a godsend. They eventually climbed higher than the plateau where the young birds squawked loudly in their huge rookery. The shrubbery screened them from anyone on the plateau who might casually glance in their direction.

The rocks on the trail were slick with the steady, misty rain. Elieana and Darec were better equipped with heavy shoes and clothes for the cold but Antonia was not, because of her light shoes she continually lost her footing. When they finally stopped to eat a cold meal, her knees and legs were covered with scrapes and bruises. Both Darec and Elieana waited throughout the morning for her to voice complaints or refuse to go on, she did neither. Her spirit, renewed with the news her daughter still lived, could not be thwarted. She determined to go on until at last she could hold her daughter, Silanne, in her arms.

As they sat eating their meager meal Antonia built up the courage to ask why they came to the castle. "You can't have known I was there, why did you come?" she asked timidly.

Darec told of the capture of his men; of Magra and her sons and the packet of papers Elieana found in the wrecked carriage.

Antonia gasped when Darec finished speaking. "After the accident, Vasilis questioned me for days. He wanted the packet and the wealth for himself. That is why he kept me in the tower room. He thought if he isolated and deprived me I would reveal its hiding place. I finally did tell him where he could find the packet but by the time his men went back to the carriage Silanne...Nada and the packet had vanished."

"I am so sorry for being the cause of your grief for so many years, Antonia," said Elieana. "When I saw the dead horses, partially devoured, and no one around.... when I heard her cry out..." Elieana's voice choked with emotion, she tried to finish but couldn't.

"Do not feel so, Elieana. I am glad you took her. Although my heart ached with grief for her loss, living in the castle with Vasilis and that Sangan," she said venomously, "It would not have been a good life for her. You have been a mother to her. I thank you for loving her as your own." She bowed her head and clenched the fabric of her dress tightly then she lifted her face and it shone with tears and happiness. "You cannot know how happy I am to learn she is safe. Now can we please be off and make haste to Pelagos? I have such a need to see my daughter again." Antonia hurriedly got up and tried to pass Darec on the path, but he held her back.

"Wait, Antonia, let us wrap your feet so you will not injure yourself further. We can use strips off the bottom of your gown, which will make it easier to walk as well. It won't be catching under your feet and tripping you."

Smiling for the small kindness Darec exhibited Antonia sat down beside him, allowing him to rip strips off the bottom of her gown and bind them around her feet.

"I thank you, Darec," she said shyly, "I do not deserve your kindness after the way I have been behaving."

Embarrassed by her statement he replied somewhat gruffly, "Well, it will give padding to your feet somewhat but will get very dirty. I hope it will keep you from slipping. We cannot have the Queen of Belisle arriving in Pelagos with bruised knees."

Antonia's face blanched at the comment, she did not expect anyone to call her queen. She looked at him and pleaded, "Please, Darec, I am queen no longer, just call me by my name and no other. I will not use that title again in my lifetime, I am certain."

"I apologize for embarrassing you, my lady...Antonia," replied Darec.

An uncomfortable silence hovered about them, so Antonia got up and led the way at a surprisingly quick pace, the strips of cloth tied around her feet giving her better traction on the slippery rocks of the trail. With renewed energy Antonia managed to climb quite far in front of them. She passed around a clump of stunted trees then they heard her gasp. As they approached they saw her squatting on the ground and anxiously motioning for them to get down. Darec squatted down beside Elieana, a look of bewilderment on his face.

"What is it?" he whispered.

"We have climbed level with the plateau where they keep the large birds," Antonia whispered. "Look through the shrubbery; you will see the army they have amassed. It is frightening to behold." Her hands shook uncontrollably as she pointed back over her shoulder.

Staying at a crouch Darec climbed up the path to where Antonia knelt on the ground. He pulled aside some of the shrubbery and looked across at the plateau opposite to where they hid. Hundreds of huge birds were each secured to a stake in the ground, far enough apart so they could not peck or harm each other. An extremely agitated dilhaa, its bleats loud and fearful, pulled a cart loaded with a mound of fresh meat between the lines of the birds. As they passed each bird a man walking behind the cart casually threw the meat, the birds catching it in their beaks before it hit the ground.

On the opposite side of the plateau tents pitched for an army of men spread out across the plateau. Shaken by the sight, no one spoke. Darec had not heard anything about such a large army amassing on their borders. He looked grim and his mouth clamped tightly in a thin line as he estimated the encampment held at least a thousand warrior birds and at least three times as many men.

He slowly let the bushes slip back into place and took a moment to think what they could do to get word back to the King but the only way to get word to the King was to ensure they were not captured. He attempted to reassure Antonia, seeing hysteria building by the look on her face, her body shaking, and her eyes opened much too wide.

Elieana, sensing something very seriously wrong, duck-walked to where they waited for her.

“I have never seen anything like this," whispered Darec, nodding with his chin for Elieana to look and when she did her face drained of all color.

"Antonia, have you heard Vasilis speak of who he plans to attack?" whispered Darec. This time Antonia met his gaze straight on.

"He said many things about his plans when he met with his Sangan Chieftain. There were times," she whispered, her forehead creasing as she thought of the past. "There were times when Vasilis made me dine with them. They ignored me. He did not care what he said in front of me. I was his captive but his blood, so he did not kill me," she said bitterly. "They talked of attack on Baltica and Pelagonia. I believe they plan to attack the cities, perhaps with the birds." Her body shook, and her voice became flat and defeated, "Yes, I believe it will be with the birds. They will attack from the air. They will surprise the people and take the cities. I do not know why they will do this." Tears streamed down her face. "Why are they planning this terrible thing?" she asked them, her voice quivering. "Why did Vasilis make me a part of this terrible plan?"

"I do not know, Antonia," said Darec. "We must not wait to find out why. We must get back to Pelagos as soon as possible. They must be warned. A surprise attack from the sky will have devastating effect. I fear though, we cannot go on further until nightfall, they will see us from the encampment because the bushes along the path here are too sparse to give us cover."

Darec didn't share his thought that if the soldiers saw them they could probably use arrows and hit them easily. The bird soldiers might also just fly the birds across and pluck them off the trail with ease as they did to the creatures on the plain below. They must not be captured. They must return to Pelagos and bring warning of this growing peril.

"I agree, Darec, this is a good place to stop, we can observe them until night falls and perhaps have more knowledge of them before we leave," said Elieana who then shuffled closer to Antonia and put her arm around her shoulders. Darec moved to Antonia's other side and they sat huddled together for warmth for they dared not light a fire and reveal their presence. The rain pelted down throughout the afternoon. Cold and uncomfortable they ate the last of the tubers and eggs. While they waited in their hiding place for night's concealment they sat quietly and observed the soldiers and their birds.

Groups of mounted birds continually flew over the huge herds of animals on the plain below. Each bird carried a leather sack strapped onto its breast. When they flew over their target the rider pulled a strap which opened the bottom of the sack and large rocks tumbled out. They seemed to be practicing but also hunting as they dropped the rocks onto the beasts. The volley of rocks from above scattered the herd but for every drop at least four or five beasts lay stunned or dying.

After the herd had moved the birds swooped down and plucked up a dead or dying beast in its huge talons and carried it back to the plateau. They dropped the beast on the plateau where men waited to butcher the animal. The sight was horrifying but the birds were fascinating to watch and as they hunted, their screeches were echoed by the ones tethered on the plateau.

Although the sight of the hunt was horrifying, Darec, Elieana and Antonia, at times couldn't help but laugh at the riders desperately working to keep from falling from the tiny saddles strapped between the bird's wings. They saw that although a bond existed between man and beast some of the men remained fearful and with good reason. They witnessed one man harnessing his bird when it reached out with its opened beak. The man lashed back with his hand, hitting the bird's beak and it immediately bit off the man's arm. Antonia let out an involuntary shriek and for the rest of the day they sat in fear of discovery.

Teams of birds and their riders took to the skies in search of the woman whose scream they heard. The failing light was on the fugitives' side, the shadows created by the bushes they sheltered under hid them until night fall. At dusk, the birds flew back to the plateau where the soldiers staked them out until morning. A point, Darec would remember, this enormous bird army did not fly or attack by night.

When night enveloped them with its silent cover they resumed their climb. Their limbs were stiff after sitting in the cold, but they needed to move on, stealthily taking advantage of the night. The trail now more treacherous because heavy clouds blocked any moonlight they thanked the goddess for the additional concealment.

After a few frightening experiences on the slippery trail they finally reached level ground. They continued to stumble along blindly, tripping on rocks and low shrubs growing beside the path. Finally, the sickle moon peeked through the clouds and enabled them to move at a faster pace and they reached the highest point of the trail by the time the moon reached its zenith.

As they climbed up onto the summit a cold wind blasted them, chilling them to the bone through their wet clothes. It was there that the trail disappeared completely. Weary and very hungry but being too dark to forage they unanimously agreed to stop until daylight, hopefully to find the trail before any birds took to the air in search of them.

A mound of rocks offered some protection from the wind where they shivered uncontrollably for what seemed like only a few minutes when the sun peeked over the horizon. The rain clouds had dissipated overnight and at the very least even if their bellies were empty their clothes would start to dry out. Antonia, now courageous compared to the woman they met just a few days before, did not complain. She stirred for a moment as Darec arose then curled up closer to Elieana and fell back asleep.

Darec went in search of food and the trail. He walked through the scrub brush until he found a narrow rocky path, concealed by brush and grass. He hoped to find a crunchy tuber in a small spring fed pool but found only a broad-leafed plant that he did not recognize, growing in the water. At least they could slake their thirst before their long climb down off the mountain. The pool drained into a nearby cave which offered a place of shelter if they needed to conceal themselves.

He retraced his steps to the rocks where they spent the night and saw Elieana and Antonia crouched beside a large boulder. Elieana waved her arms like a bird flying. Darec glanced towards the plateau and saw a flock of five large birds flying towards them. Even from far away the birds seemed to fill the sky. The bird riders were again searching for them and if they did not hide or get away they would be forced to fight these armed and mounted soldiers. The night before they saw how easily the huge birds plucked their enormous prey from the plain below, how much easier for them to pluck up a slower moving human. He doubted capture was a high priority for the soldiers; their only hope, to take shelter in the cave he found.

"Elieana, Antonia, slowly move around the rocks to me. I have found the path and a small cave we can run to it and take shelter there."

"Darec, I don't think we will be fast enough. They have already seen us," replied Elieana in a loud whisper. "I think we should try to find what cover we can here in the rocks."

They watched with dread as the birds flew towards them, flying so close together they resembled one large creature. The wings flapping up and down, a sinister movement, a promise of death, unlike any attack by mounted soldiers on horses. Darec had to admit to an overwhelming sense that these huge creatures may be invincible. Archers might defeat them in a battle, if they had enough archers to fight the huge army encamped on the plateau. Except for the wings, the birds were also very well armored. How could he now fight these swiftly moving birds with only his sword?

A ripping sound coming from the boulders where Elieana and Antonia hid, drew his attention. Elieana was busily ripping strips from one of Antonia's underskirts. "What are you doing Elieana?"

“I have an idea. I remember a toy we used as children in my home town. Not really a toy, my cousins used it to capture birds that ate the fruit in our orchard. They tied rocks to each end of a long thin rope and then threw it. The rope tangled around the bird’s body and the rocks injured it when they hit. The weapon may not injure these birds, but it may disable them when they become entangled. I hope it will give us a better chance of surviving this attack.”

Darec nodded, grateful for any assistance in this fight. By the time Elieana had two of her weapons ready Darec could make out the faces of the soldiers flying towards them. He directed Antonia to crouch down behind the rocks, hoping they offered protection enough for her. He then shifted his attention to Elieana, but she had already climbed to the topmost rocks, a better vantage to use her sling weapon. The soldiers split into two groups. Darec could do nothing to help her, someone needed to stay and protect defenseless Antonia.

He briefly watched Elieana before three bird soldiers swooped down towards him causing him to focus all his concentration on surviving the onslaught. The birds swooped and flew up and away continually, before he could swing his sword. As he wielded his sword in huge arcs he watched the birds, trying to determine what their strategy might be. They seemed to do the same maneuver repeatedly and, Darec realized, the soldiers’ inexperience in handling the birds caused the repetitive attacks.

These soldiers only practiced their attacks on passive prey. This new prey fought back. Their inexperience showed, and they did not work well in unity. As he watched, their tactics became obvious, and if he swung after one bird swooped away he could hit the one that swooped in to take its place. He waited for his opportunity, swung his sword in a wide, gleaming arc and it cut deep into the soldier's leg. Blood sprayed profusely, a death blow.

The blade also hit the front of the bird's wing, crippling it. The bird floundered, as it tried to fly, but its damaged wing caused it to collide into the next bird as it swooped down. They both fell to the ground in a tangled heap. The uninjured bird flopped about, trying to regain its feet, at the same time it ripped at the injured bird beside it. The uninjured bird's rider jumped free but could not prevent the birds from attacking each other.

As Darec directed his attention to the third bird swooping up and down but not coming close to him another one joined in and the swooping maneuver began again. Seeing the fourth bird come to the attack Darec's heart clenched, thinking the soldiers defeated Elieana. A shiver rattled through his body then he straightened up and stood at the ready as the attack started again. He screamed in a loud voice, "Come, you bastards. Join your brother on his way to the underworld." He swung his sword then crouched ready for the onslaught watching for one of the soldiers to make a mistake.

Neither of the two bird soldiers came close to engaging in battle. They flew above Darec, swooping down but never coming near enough for Darec to attack. He jumped down to where the other two birds on the ground struggled, helplessly entangled in each other's harness. They pecked and ripped at each other ruthlessly while the uninjured rider watched in horror.

Darec ran towards the uninjured bird and with a quick, stabbing stroke drove his sword through the bird's heart. He then dispatched the injured bird with a slashing stroke to its throat. For a single moment, deathly quiet settled over them and then a blood curdling scream shattered the silence. The uninjured soldier ran at Darec, his face fixed in a mask of anger and grief at the loss of his bird and the powerful bond between them.

Both accomplished swordsman, they thrust and parried and circled around each other, at times gaining ground, and at times losing ground, like a macabre dance, the partners each determined not to guide the other but to step in for a kill.

A scream from above startled Darec and he glanced up at the rocks where Elieana stood. His pause gave the other man an opening to thrust. Darec deflected the blade in time but received a nasty slash on his arm. They moved about each other as if in slow motion until the soldier tripped over his fallen bird. Darec moved forward and dispatched him with one quick thrust then he turned his back on the bloody mess and sought out Elieana. He didn't know who screamed but thought it must have been Antonia, seeing that she had joined Elieana on the rocks. While hiding safely below, her hands had not been idle, her dress more tattered than before, she had busied herself making more weapons. As fast as Elieana threw them Antonia passed her more, screaming at the top of her lungs, urging Elieana on.

Elieana flung her weapons, some flying wide and landing harmlessly on the rocks below. The ones that hit the birds and their riders took their toll; one of the rider's arms hung limply at his side, having received a direct blow. Still a formidable opponent, he guided his huge avian to swoop down upon the women, but the bird fought his control. It flew back and forth, swooping down but not close enough for its talons to grab its quarry. Elieana hit it once making it wary of her. It occurred to Elieana as well as it had to Darec that the birds trained only with slow moving animals which did not fight back.

Darec climbed up the rocks as swiftly as he could; he needed to get Elieana and Antonia away before reinforcements arrived. "When the next avian swoops in, Elieana, crouch down," said Darec, his chest heaving from the climb. The bird swooped down and Elieana dropped to her knees giving Darec a chance to make his attack. He slashed the bird across its chest with his sword, the point slashing through the armor on its chest. It screeched in pain and flew up, spraying crimson droplets down upon them. The blow was not life threatening but enough to stop the attack for the moment. Perhaps a moment long enough for them find shelter in the cave.

They watched from their perch on the rocks while the injured bird flew back towards the plateau. One of the remaining riders pulled a horn from his belt and commenced sounding the alarm. The soldiers circled their birds above them as they waited for reinforcements to arrive. Moments later a large flock of birds, perhaps thirty or more, took flight.

They darkened the sky like a large undulating cloud moving towards them.

"Run, as fast as you can," hollered Darec. Our weapons will be as toys to them." He helped Antonia down from the rocks and then he and Elieana, one on either side, pulled Antonia along as fast as they could go. Elieana stumbled once and when she stood again her leggings were ripped, revealing a bloody cut on her knee. She wavered for just a moment then ran on down the trail. The bushes slapped at their faces and arms. Brambles clung and tugged at their legs. Their breath came in ragged gasps as they ran from their attackers as the two remaining bird soldiers from the first attack flew above them, marking their progress down the trail.

"There," Darec pointed, "Do you see the bush with the red leaves? There is a small pool of water and a cave in the rocks behind it. Run, get inside."

He let go of Antonia's arm shoving her forward then looked back and saw the birds closing on them. Armed with bows, strung and ready, the riders pressed their birds forward. Darec pushed Elieana in front of him to protect her with his body and then he stumbled. His shoulder suddenly felt numb. He regained his footing then glanced at his shoulder and saw the shaft of an arrow protruding. He focused his attention on the cave, no longer seeing Elieana satisfied him she reached safety. He dove through the brush in front of the cave opening with one last leap but before he reached the cave mouth another arrow hit his leg. He scrambled through the opening, dragging himself forward with his uninjured arm and leg.

Elieana helped Darec farther into the cave as arrows clattered harmlessly on the rocks, spraying branches and leaves inside. They rested for a moment where it was wide enough for them to sit without getting wet. Elieana called out to Antonia for help and the two women pulled Darec's arms over their shoulders and dragged him further back into the cave.

When they were far enough back to be safe from the attack Elieana took from her pocket, the rocks she found in the cavern. They immediately gave a comforting glow and enough light to see. She went to the cave opening and took a branch which had fallen inside the cave. She used this to make a torch from a sleeve ripped off her shirt. She struck her flint and lit the torch, hoping it would burn long enough for her to bind Darec's wounds. Elieana cut off Darec's shirt with her dagger and inspected his shoulder, gently touching where the arrow penetrated the skin. The arrow shaft stuck out of his flesh and the wound bled but not so bad to be concerned for blood loss. She touched the other side of his shoulder and felt the tip of the arrow head just under the skin.

“Antonia,” said Elieana, “Can you rip some more strips of cloth for a bandage?”

"I soon will be naked," remarked Antonia and then she immediately started ripping strips from her petticoat.

Elieana looked over her shoulder at Antonia for a moment, they had used her clothing to wrap her feet and make the weapons they used on the birds. "You are right, Antonia. Perhaps we should make you a skirt of grass."

Antonia didn't comment, bending her head to her task, ripping narrow strips for bandages, but Elieana felt certain she heard her chuckle. "Darec, I am going to push the arrow head through. It is going to hurt."

"No more than it does now, Elieana," he whispered in a weak voice which startled her.

"Help me pull off my belt," he said as he tried to move and undo the buckle.

"Let me do it, Darec, lay back, let me help you." She gently pushed his hands down and pulled off his belt. Darec took it from her, doubled the leather and stuck it between his teeth then clenched down as hard as he could. Elieana hoped he could not see the concern on her face in the dim light. He seemed very weak. His wounds were not life threatening, convincing her that poison on the arrowhead caused his increasing weakness.

Elieana shoved the arrow forward. Darec grunted with the pain. The arrowhead broke the surface of his skin and Elieana pulled it through as gently as she could. When it pulled free Darec took a deep shuddering breath and slumped against the cave wall.

"Antonia, help me with Darec so I can wrap the bandages around his shoulder," said Elieana as she took the belt from Darec's mouth. Antonia did not respond. While Elieana ministered to Darec she had not noticed Antonia prop the torch against the wall and move out of the light.

"Antonia," she said loudly. Antonia did not answer. A scrabbling noise of someone moving from the direction of the cave mouth put her on guard.

"Antonia, is that you?" whispered Elieana as she picked up the torch, ready to use it as a weapon if it turned out that a soldier approached.

"Yes, I'm coming," said Antonia breathlessly as she crab-walked towards them out of the darkness. She grabbed Elieana by the arm, her fear cracking her voice as she whispered, "They are sealing us in."

The hair on Elieana's body stood up and her blood suddenly felt like ice in her veins. Antonia shook, and her teeth rattled together, her grip on Elieana's arm digging into the flesh. Shock, Elieana thought as she gently peeled Antonia's fingers off her arm, noticing how cool her skin felt to her touch. In a few seconds, thought Elieana, she is going to scream. How am I going to deal with Darec's wounds when I have a hysterical woman clutching at me?

Elieana grabbed Antonia's face with both hands and squeezed it tight, bringing Antonia's face an inch from hers. She saw the flickering torchlight reflected in her eyes like an omen of destruction. If she could run away from the woman, she would. She steeled herself against the fear threatening to overcome her and whispered, "Antonia, Darec is seriously injured. You must sit calmly and wait while I bind his wounds then I will come with you to the entrance of the tunnel. We will see if we can move some of the rocks, if only just to let some light in. Please, you must wait until I am finished, for Nada... for Silanne's sake."

Elieana held Antonia's face close to hers for a few seconds more as Antonia slowly calmed down, the shaking decreased, and her breathing became more controlled. She helped

Antonia move to the side of the tunnel and noticed that the stream was shrinking and realized that the rocks closing off the entrance to the cave were diverting the stream.

Briefly, Elieana let herself imagine the stream drying up altogether and dying of thirst. She shook the feeling off, silently berating herself for becoming more like Antonia, fearing every challenge and every change. She scrambled back to Darec, her feet slipped, and her injured knee came up hard against the rocks, causing her to gasp in pain, but the pain made her think of what was taking place right then rather than imagining what could happen. When she looked at Darec's face it startled her, his eyes looked like holes in his ghastly pale face. He looked cadaverous in the wavering light, so she unkindly pinched him, fearing he died. He batted her offending fingers away and moaned.

Elieana wished she still had the flowers Olaf pointed out to her the first night on the trail, she could use them now. She finished binding his shoulder wound then rolled him onto his stomach, so she could deal with the arrow in his leg.

CHAPTER 7

Startled from sleep Jacq found himself staring into the face of a strange looking creature. He scrambled like a crab, scuttling across the sand, trying to get away. Frightened and confused because he didn't know where he was he called out frantically for Carlotte.

The last thing he remembered before he fell asleep was Carlotte beside him and the pungent smell of the tree they lay under. Never having slept under a tree before he wondered if the pungent scent caused this nightmare. The creature slowly followed him, its hands out-stretched towards Jacq and then he noticed other creatures standing nearby silently watching them.

"What do you want? Where am I?" Jacq shouted. He rapidly surveyed his surroundings, looking for an escape route as the creature herded him into a small enclosure, with one side open to a lake. Benches lined the side near the water along with small buckets and brushes. One of the creatures sat down on a bench and started to scrub its body.

"What kind of insane dream am I having. I'm in a bathhouse," Jacq spoke out loudly. "No, I'm dreaming about a bathhouse, I'm asleep under the tree." He pinched himself, trying to wake up. "The smell of the tree sap must be giving me bewildering dreams. Carlotte will soon wake me. Carlotte," he yelled, his voice edging on hysterical. One of the creatures raised its finger in front of its mouth and gurgled. Jacq thought it was telling him to be quiet.

He shushed me, he thought, this is a crazy dream. "Carlotte," he yelled again.

The creature gurgled again at Jacq and then another creature came from behind and put its hand on Jacq's shoulder. He struggled to get away from the creature.

"Carlotte," he yelled.

The creature squeezed Jacq's neck and he fell limp beside the bench. One of the creatures handed Jacq a bucket and a scrub brush and pointed towards the bench. Looking up from where he lay on the ground he watched the creature point at him then squeeze its nose or what resembled a nose. It again gestured in the direction of the bench. Realization struck him, it was telling him he stunk and that he should bathe. Jacq rose and stumbled to the bench. He pulled off the vile smelling clothes he wore and dropped them in a heap on the ground then took up the brush and began to vigorously scrub his body until it tingled. He poured the contents of the bucket over himself. It was soapy water, so he scrubbed his hair as well. Feeling clean all over he looked back at the creature who nodded its head in approval.

The other creature finished scrubbing its skin then waded into the water and ducked below the surface. Jacq watched it swim under the water, back and forth, without coming up for air. Suddenly it leapt out of the water in a beautiful arc then dove back in, leaving hardly a ripple.

Tentatively, Jacq stuck his big toe into the water. He disliked the thought of going in after his encounter with the beast a few days earlier, but this pool seemed harmless. Nothing attacked the creature already in the water. Slowly he waded out, finding the water pleasantly warm. He felt embarrassed after watching the creature swim like a fish, lacking any swimming skills himself.

He held his breath and slowly crouched down under the water and opened his eyes. The swimming creature seemed to sense him watching and swam directly at him, stopping inches from his face. Surprised, Jacq stood up, gasping for air. The creature stood up beside him then let out a strange gurgling sound, its mouth wide, and its head thrown back. The noise sounded strangely like laughter.

Jacq didn't really have anything funny to laugh at but the joy emanating from the creature seemed to be catching, as it bubbled up inside him. Jacq laughed out loud with pleasure, his anxiety crumbling away in the soothing waters of the pool.

The creature touched Jacq's shoulder motioning for him to leave the water. He patted Jacq on the back then gurgled something to him as they both sat down on their separate benches. A pile of fresh clothing lay on the bench where he left his old clothes. He didn't miss them and hoped they would burn them. The new clothes were worn and old, but clean. It struck him as odd these creatures had clothes here, they did not wear them.

After Jacq dressed the creature took him out of the bathhouse. He saw Carlotte stretched out on a mat, sound asleep. The creature pointed to Carlotte then walked away toward a cluster of buildings, leaving Jacq to make his way to the mat where Carlotte slept. As the creature walked away Jacq noticed it had a long, ugly scar on the back of its head, one distinguishing feature setting this one apart from all the others.

CHAPTER 8

The bearers carried the palanquin, with Nada inside, right into the castle. She did not have to walk up a single flight of stairs. She felt very uncomfortable having these men carrying her. It seemed a little odd they did not allow her to walk inside the castle. When the palanquin stopped she peeked out of the curtained enclosure. It sat in the middle of a very large, beautifully decorated room. She climbed out before the bearers opened the curtains causing them to display their annoyance in exasperated puffs of displeasure.

"There is no need to help me," she said when she saw the men's reaction. They didn't speak to her in response and just gave her surly looks. Taken aback by their reaction she watched with relief as they backed out of the room, closing the huge, ornate door, leaving her alone in the room.

Nada wandered throughout the large, airy room towards the balcony on one side. Luxurious draperies, hung on both sides of the balcony, were pulled aside to reveal a spectacular view of the sea. The brilliant sunshine reflecting off the water bathed the room in warmth and light.

Nada drank in the view, enjoying the sun on her face. She gazed down upon the sea, never having seen it from this vantage point before. Pearly white froth trimmed each wave upon wave as they lapped on the shore. The rhythmic sound had a calming effect on her mood. A slightly salty breeze rippled the curtains and sent tendrils of her hair tickling her face. As she gazed out at the amazing view before her she almost forgot why she was there.

Fleetingly she remembered Carlotte and Jacq. Her youth and the events of the past few days overpowered her and although she knew she should send a message to Jorian, she could not bring herself to do so. "I will just rest here for a time and think about them later," she whispered aloud. "After that horrible experience, they can't find fault with that."

Bored, Nada wandered back into the room, touching a bowl, looking at herself in the mirror, picking up small objects and setting them down. The sound of water trickling diverted her attention. She looked behind a thin curtain and found a large bath. A woman kneeled nearby and when Nada walked in she arose, smiling. "I am here to take care of any needs you may have, Princess. Let me help you with your bath."

Nada looked at the large tub. Flower petals floated upon the water and steam rose in fragrant curls, scenting the air. Soft, fluffy towels nestled in a basket and combs and ribbons for her hair were laid out in a neat row upon a dressing table. Enticed, Nada nodded, never having experienced such extravagance before.

The woman helped Nada remove her soiled clothing then helped her into the bath, where she lay back, groaning with pleasure. "First, I will bath, then I will think about what I can do for Carlotte and Jacq," she whispered to herself. She lay there, letting the water soothe and comfort her. The woman brought scented soap and washed Nada's hair, leaving it clean and sparkling then she left Nada alone to soak. The warmth of the water and the luxurious scents relaxed her and for a moment she fell into a light sleep until the woman came over and gently touched her shoulder. She held up a large towel for Nada as she climbed out of the tub.

"What is your name?" asked Nada.

"Ammera, Princess."

"Do you..." Nada wanted to talk to someone, tell them what happened to her, but she sensed she should not confide in the woman. She clamped her mouth shut, stopping in mid-sentence before she asked any questions or said anything she might regret later.

"Yes, Princess?"

"Nothing, it is nothing."

A quick look of annoyance crossed Ammera's face, but she hid it just as quickly. Ammera led Nada to the dressing table and proceeded to comb the tangles out of her hair. She put Nada's hair up with pins and a ribbon. She brought her a tunic and loose pants to wear then suggested Nada lay down and take a nap. Nada thought this suggestion completely ridiculous but didn't say anything and went, as instructed, to lie down on the bed.

The soft pillow, lightly scented with fragrance, relaxed her and she felt as if she could sink down into the bed. Ammera pulled a soft coverlet over her. Nada lay there listening to Ammera move about the room as she tidied up. The sound of the door closing lifted her momentarily wakeful, then silence, and she fell into a deep, dreamless sleep.

When Nada awoke, she thought it must be early afternoon. Her stomach grumbled hungrily. She stretched her arms, yawned and sat up to see Ammera sitting quietly in a corner, awaiting her command. The fact Ammera sat there while she slept unnerved her. She was a stranger; it was not the same as when Aldred came to stay with her after Elieana left. Her heart clenched at the memory of Aldred and Elieana. It seemed so long ago she had seen either of them. Had it only been a few days?

Her eyes welled up and she took a deep breath, blinked and fought back the tears. She rose from the bed and walked to the balcony where she sat in a chair with her knees tucked up under her chin. She wrapped her arms around her knees and stared out at the sea.

The day wore on and on. Completely bored, with nothing to do she thought of all her friends and how much Elieana meant to her. She got up and wandered through the room, stopping to look at her reflection in a huge, polished-bronze mirror. The image reflected at her, not Nada but someone who looked selfish and self-centered. Why she turned her back on Jacq and Carlotte, she couldn't explain, even though Jacq was responsible for her being there in the first place. She felt guilty for not immediately helping them both.

In all her young life never had she regarded herself as she did now, dressed in fine clothes and her hair styled in the latest fashion. Ashamed she reached up and pulled out the ribbon and pins holding her hair in place. It fell around her shoulders and fluffed out like a cloud. At the same time, she heard a slight cough from Ammera, the maid, who stared at her, her brow wrinkled in annoyance that Nada had ruined her creation. Nada cocked her head to one side and shrugged her shoulders grinning impishly. “I guess I like it down. You can leave now.”

The woman bowed and backed up towards the door. She tapped lightly, the door opened then she exited the room. After the door closed Nada went to the door to leave but found it locked.

“I'm locked in,” she said, incredulously. “Why am I locked in?” she yelled and banged on the door but to no avail. Whoever stood on the other side made no response. The door remained closed.

"You out there, let me out. I don't belong here," she yelled as loud as she could, slamming the flat of her hand on the door. "There has to be a way out of here," she mumbled to herself. Being locked in, to Nada, was a challenge for her to find a way out. Slowly she observed her surroundings and the balcony drew her attention. The view should have again distracted her, but her attention was drawn to garden balcony thirty feet below. In the center of the garden gurgled a small fountain. The garden was surrounded by a low wall and then a straight drop to the sea.

Nada leaned as far out as she could, to see if a path led from the garden to the water below. She saw nothing but sheer cliff. As she peered out she caught a glimpse of sand far below her. She knew the beach well; she always sat there at low tide behind the log, hidden from passersby on the road to the castle and where she recently slashed her foot.

While she peered out over the railing a noise in the room caught her attention. "Ammera, is that you?" she said as she turned around, but instead of Ammera a young woman stood by the opened door. The woman looked back over her shoulder, spoke to someone behind her then entered the room. A guard reached in and pulled the door shut. When they were alone she walked towards Nada and as she did her pretty features transformed into a wicked sneer.

“So, you are Silanne, or should I call you Nada?” She said Nada's name in such a way it came out sounding common and distasteful. The girl walked slowly around Nada making her feel as if she was on display. She touched Nada’s clothes and flipped Nada's hair making it hang down over her face. "Those are my clothes, you know. You realize you being here has changed my future.” Her voice sounded hard and mean.

Nada guessed this was Princess Verenase. She didn’t think the girl wanted her to answer; rather, she was making a statement.

The princess snorted in disgust and gave Nada’s hair a sharp, painful tug. Nada wished she had left the pins and ribbon in her hair; at least it would have been somewhat organized rather than a wild mess around her face. She resisted the urge to push her hair back and shook her head slightly to move the hair out of her eyes. Nada stood up as straight as she could, thinking of Elieana who constantly told her to do so.

“So, I’m told they found you hiding in a cave. Hiding with criminals. I imagine you don’t know those criminals have escaped.” Princess Verenase looked directly into Nada’s eyes, her face inches from Nada’s.

“Did you help them?” she snapped.

Her face was so close, Nada could smell her breath, fresh and minty. She had eaten something, leaving a small green speck on one of her teeth. She had pale, icy-blue eyes. Nada knew immediately this girl would never be her friend and her intimidation of Nada would continue if she didn’t respond.

“Did you know," asked Nada, ignoring her questions and in the sweetest voice she could, "You have a speck of food on your teeth?”

The princess didn’t move or respond except to inhale deeply; her nostrils flared, her eyes narrowed to slits and her mouth pursed and wrinkled. She slapped Nada across the face and in a flurry and rustle of silk stomped towards the door. “Guard,” she shouted. The door opened, Nada, heard the guard say, "Princess," before the door slammed shut behind her.

Nada walked to the door and pulled on the handle, but it was already locked. She could hear the princess’ angry voice but couldn’t make out what she was saying. Having a guard posted at the door and after the interview with the princess, Nada realized her safety in the castle was limited. The princess hated her. Her only option now, to escape as soon as she could find a way out. Being mid-afternoon, she had time before they brought a meal, if they intended on feeding her at all.

She searched the room and found a small pair of scissors in the bathing room then she ran to the balcony and looked down at the garden below, her only avenue of escape. Nada yanked down the curtains surrounding the balcony and shred them into strips. She knotted the strips end to end, making one long rope, then tied one end to the huge bed, the other end she threw over the balcony railing.

Nada took a firm hold on the railing, carefully climbed over and then slowly lowered herself down, hand over hand, clinging tightly to the curtain rope. She focused on the wall in front of her as she descended, afraid to look down at the very long drop to the rocks below. Twice she slid a short distance before regaining a firm hold. She had never climbed like this before. Her vicelike grip on the strip of curtain the only assurance she would not plummet to her death.

When she reached the top of the doorway to the lower balcony she wedged her feet against the wall and listened to hear if anyone occupied the room beyond the balcony. Hearing nothing, she let herself down the rest of the way. When she felt solid stone under her feet she felt as if she could finally breath. Her arms shook from the exertion, her heart pounded in her chest and her hair was pasted to the back of her neck.

Nada splashed water from the fountain onto her face and took a long drink. The water came from a small spring bubbling up into the top of the fountain and then draining away through a hole in the bottom of the bowl. Curious, she wondered where the water drained to but then reminded herself she had no time to dawdle, someone would soon discover she was missing and start searching for her.

Nada dipped her feet into the fountain to cool them after standing on the hot stone floor of the balcony then she peeked into the tiny room beyond. It looked unused which struck her as odd considering the happy little fountain and the lovely view from the balcony. She walked across the room and tried the door. Finding the door locked she lay down on the floor to rest before she started her descent to the sea below. The cool stone floor felt good after the heat outside, she relaxed and let it sooth her then fell asleep.

Nada awoke a while later feeling slightly groggy and confused. She rolled onto her back and stared up at the murals covering the walls from floor to ceiling. The sun, just above the horizon, shone into the room, giving the walls a pleasant pinkish hue and making it easier to see the detail in the murals.

Agitated voices filtered down from outside and shattered the peacefulness of the room. Nada kept herself hidden in the shadow of the archway leading out to the balcony and listened. The voices came from the room above where someone had discovered the shredded draperies.

“Search the cliffs and the sea side below,” screamed a female voice, "She will pay for destroying this room."

Nada recognized the princess’ voice giving the order for the search and nervously moved back further into the room. “I don’t trust her one bit,” Nada whispered to herself. A movement just above her head caught her eye, she looked up and watched as the strip of cloth, her only avenue of escape, was slowly being pulled up to the balcony above. She wanted to reach for it and pull it back but couldn't give away her hiding place. It was only a matter of time before the soldiers came and found her.

The Princess' behaviour confused her and she wondered aloud. "If I am the daughter of the King of Baltica why does the princess hate me so much? Why lock me in a room? Why did King Stephan not come and see me?"

The more she thought, the more she began to wonder if something had happened to King Stephan or maybe he didn't yet know she was there. "I thought Jorian told him I was here," she spoke aloud and then walked back into the room and sat down on the floor beside the door to wait for someone to open it. She sat there waiting, resigned to the fact that she would be locked up again and let the warmth of the last rays of the sun comfort her as she watched it slowly sink into the sea.

It seemed as if the sun also set on the scenes in the paintings. The scenes told a story of Pelagonia, the castle and the sea. A battle scene spread out before her, men on horses fighting fierce flying creatures. It showed a mountain pass and a wall being built to block the pass. As she looked at the picture and the sunlight moved across the wall Nada noticed a small crack, invisible, had the light not shone directly on it.

Boot clomping on the flagstone floor outside the door to the room and the murmur of voices distracted her. Someone jiggled the latch but finding the door locked they shouted. "Find the chatelaine, he will have a key to this door."

She sat frozen to the spot, listening. The person seemed angry and determined to find her, making her feel very vulnerable as she listened to them talking in the hallway. Nervously she traced the crack on the wall with her finger.

If she was a princess, as they told her, then why lock her in? Why were they angry she escaped and why were they pursuing her like this, as if she were a criminal? The more she thought on this the more nervous she became. She wished Elieana or Aldred were there to help her. They would demand to see the king. She considered then that she should call out and demand to see him but remained silent, reminded of the night Girard kidnapped her and waking up in the dark, underground room. Nada reasoned out in her mind that being in the castle she should be safe, but she could not trust someone like the princess who behaved the way she did. Elieana always taught her to go with what felt right and this whole situation felt very wrong.

Nada ran her finger up and down the crack in the wall until it occurred to her that the crack seemed more like the edge of a door rather than a crack in aged plaster. Hoping this could be a secret door she put her full attention into tracing the crack and trying to find a way to open it. She could feel the anger emanating from the people who stood outside in the hallway and it made her feel weak with fear. She traced the line to the floor and found nothing, but she was sure it was a door. Slowly she slid her hands back and forth across the wall, feeling for a bump or latch or something to open it. After searching, nearly the entire wall she found it, a small raised portion disguised as the center decoration of a soldier's shield. She pushed it with her thumb and heard a tiny click and the door popped open just a crack. She pried at it with the tips of her fingers and it swung open just wide enough for her to squeeze through.

At the same time, she heard a commotion out in the hall, a key clicked in the lock and the soldiers burst into the room. The hidden door closed with the click of the latch falling home, the sound muffled by the noise of the soldiers as they pushed their way in. Expecting to find their quarry when they entered the soldiers saw only the splendid view of the setting sun reflecting off the dust motes they disturbed when they entered.

"She must have jumped," said a burly, mean looking soldier who sauntered over to the balcony edge and looked down, thoroughly expecting to see her broken body on the rocks below.

"Well, she's been here, look at the footprints on the floor." He pointed at Nada's wet footprints, still damp on the floor where the sun did not penetrate inside the room.

"Looks like she disappeared into thin air," he said. In response one of the soldiers furtively made the sign to ward off evil spirits.

Meanwhile, Nada sat shivering in the dark chill of the secret room, afraid to move a muscle. She felt overwhelmed with the enormity of everything that had occurred in the past few days. Confused and lonesome she felt the tingling of tears threatening to flow like a torrent down her face. She took a deep breath and in that quiet moment became stronger and more determined to fight back for her freedom and against the tyranny which seemed to be taking hold in the kingdom.

"Well the only thing that could have happened to her is she probably climbed down," said the man who spoke before.

"She didn't climb down," growled another man.

"Well then how did she get out of this room?" sneered a third man, "The door was locked."

"Someone has helped her. We will report back to the princess; she will want to know there is someone in the castle working against her.

"Bring the handmaid, Ammera, to the princess for questioning," said one of the soldiers as they exited the room.

The voices of the men faded as the door closed with a loud thump. Nada waited for a few minutes before she started to move, first stretching her cramped legs in the small space and then cautiously feeling around the tiny room, hoping to find an exit. She soon discovered the room was a passageway paralleling the main corridor on the other side of the wall. At times, she found small slits in the wall where she could peek out into the corridor. The flickering torch light shining in through the slits gave her enough light by which to see so she could continue walking in her search for a way out.

The passageway zigzagged and climbed up and down and seemed as if it circled around rooms in the castle. She climbed small stairs cut in the stone and crawled on her hands and knees. Her only hope was that she would find an exit near somewhere familiar, so she could escape the castle.

Eventually she came to a narrow stairway stretching down into inky blackness but part way down she could see a thin line of welcoming light. She descended towards the strip of light at a small landing.

Nada kneeled and put her ear near the crack to listen for voices or any movement on the other side of the wall. No sounds filtered through the opening. Determined to get out of the dark she felt along the wall and found a small latch sticking up from the floor. Nada pushed down on the latch and the door popped open a crack. She held her breath as she pushed the door open just a bit, so she could peek out. She saw a landing beyond the door and a flickering torch hung on the wall. The bright torchlight blinded her after being in the dark and she blinked like an owl to get her eyes accustomed to the light. She pushed the door open a bit further and saw a window then stood up to see what direction the window faced. She knew this place. She pushed the door fully open and saw the familiar stairs leading down to the chamber she shared with Elieana.

Before descending the stairs, Nada removed one of her shoes and wedged it into the door, the other she tucked into her pocket, then quietly slipped down the staircase in her bare feet. She went slowly, peering as far around the wall of the winding staircase as she could, then proceeded until she came to the door of her chamber.

A quiver of exultation went through her as she thought of her home. Her heart thudded in her chest as she listened at the door then quietly opened it and slipped inside. What met Nada's gaze as she entered tore at her heart. Elieana's treasured books strewn on the floor amidst broken mugs and crockery, every cupboard and drawer pulled open and the contents thrown on the floor.

She wanted to scream out in anger. Most of Elieana's herbs and medicines were ruined. Nada rooted around in the mess and found a sack to salvage what she could, wrapping them neatly with pieces of paper the way Elieana taught her. She loaded the sack with the medicines; a small loaf of stale bread from the food cupboard; some hard cheese; a stone bottle which survived the ransacking of the room and some warmer clothes. She looped the straps over her shoulders and with a heavy heart she turned towards the door to leave.

Nada reached for the door handle and in dismay watched as the latch slowly lifted. Panicked, she looked around for somewhere to hide and then frantically scanned the room for a weapon. She spied a piece of half burnt wood in the fireplace. In one fluid motion Nada picked it up and raised it above her head, all the while watching the door. As the person entered she brought it down as hard as she could on top of his head.

The man fell like a stone and as he fell Nada saw it was Jorian. She took a quick look outside, seeing he was alone she grasped Jorian's outspread arms and slowly dragged the rest of his body inside the room. He was a big man but her work in the kitchen, lifting the heavy pots, had strengthened her arms and her back. After she dragged him inside she barred the door and then tied his hands and feet with the braided rope from the curtains hung around her bed. She disarmed him of his sword and his knives from the sheaths at his waist and his boot, placing them on the far side of the room, then sat down to wait for him to regain consciousness.

Jorian's eyes fluttered and he groaned with the pain in his head as he tried to make sense of what had happened. He lay at an awkward angle amidst a pile of books strewn across the floor and a little dust ball slowly floated in front of his face. Confused, he couldn't remember why he came to this room. He tried to reach up to touch the tender spot on his forehead and felt sudden panic at not being able to move his arms and then he realized his hands were tied.

He lay on his side and could turn his head slightly. He saw a pair of dirty bare feet dangling above his face or was it four bare feet, he couldn't be sure. He knew the feet belonged to Nada from the large cut the length of her foot and saw through the dirt that it appeared to be healing nicely. He lifted his gaze higher and saw two of Nada sitting on the bed. The room spun wildly as he looked up. He closed his eyes, waiting for the spinning to subside. "Nada, did you hit me?" his voice came out in a croak.

"I didn't know it was you, Jorian, until after I hit you," replied Nada.

"Why did you leave your room?"

"Why did you have me locked in?" she said angrily.

"Nada, I'm sorry, the princess ordered it."

"It seems the princess would be happy if I no longer existed, did you know?"

"Yes," he replied. "Nada, I have loved you as a daughter. I cannot deceive you. She has threatened my family if I do not do as she says. The princess does not want you to reappear.

Your reappearance will stop her from becoming Queen of Baltica when your father dies. She ordered you locked up until she has time to dispose of you."

"So why are you here? Searching for me, to take me back to the princess?" she spat the words out with contempt.

"No, I came here to think. Michael, the princess' betrothed arrived just before my men found you on the beach. She is completely and utterly mesmerized by him and will do whatever he says. They are watching me to make sure I do not leave or warn the king. I believe it is only a matter of time until I also am killed, along with my family. I know too much about you; I am a liability to their cause. I came here to think of some way to get my family out of the castle."

"I can help you escape Jorian. We can also help your family to leave but I must have your allegiance. You must swear on your honor and your family's lives you will protect me and not fail me."

Jorian looked intensely at Nada. She seemed changed in the mere few days since her injury and even since seeing her that morning. She seemed more self-assured, more determined, a young woman.

"I swear my fealty to you, Nada, my Lady."

Nada started to cut the bonds on his hands but before she finished she reached over his shoulder and grasped his chin, turning his face painfully towards hers.

"If you betray me Jorian I will kill you," she said without any emotion.

Taken aback at her forceful speech he suddenly feared the change in her. "There is something more you must know before you set me free," said Jorian.

"Girard, the man who took you, is my wife's father. I did not know this until recently. Mia and I were out taking the evening air along the sea walk when he approached us. He acted as if he did not recognize Mia at first; he just started conversation as we looked out over the sea. Mia knew him immediately. I did not, at first, realize that he is the Girard we have been hunting for so long. He told me I must hand you over to him or he will harm my wife and son."

Nada stared at Jorian, not entirely sure she could trust him, but perhaps if her family were threatened she might do the same.

"Do you tell me this because I have told you I will kill you if you betray me? Two threats on your family, it seems farfetched."

"I tell you this when I am bound so you know I have placed my life in your hands. You have sworn to kill me if I betray you. I swear I will not. I swear, Nada, on my son's life I will not betray you. I am your man."

Nada nodded. Satisfied she could trust him, she cut the rope. Jorian sat up and rubbed the circulation back into his hands. He flexed his shoulders then stood up, suddenly grasping the bedstead as the dizziness caused him to lose his balance. He shook his head, attempting to clear it, wincing at the pain. "What did you hit me with?" he asked, through gritted teeth.

"Oh, I'm sorry; a chunk of wood from the fireplace. You have soot on your forehead from it," she said.

Jorian reached up and rubbed his forehead where a large bump grew above his eye.

Nada poured water on a cloth and passed it to him, so he could wipe his face. She rummaged amongst the debris on the floor and found a tin with a few peppermint leaves in it. "I can make you some tea with this peppermint, it should help your headache," said Nada as she held out the tin for him to see.

"We don't have time, Nada...my Lady. We must leave at once before anyone comes to search this part of the castle again."

Nada looked at him curiously. How strange, she thought, before he entered the room he looked for a child; now I am his Lady which he has sworn to protect. "You must call me Nada, as always, Jorian. The title is too large for me. I think it would be safer for me to be just Nada."

"As you wish," he replied.

"Well then," said Nada. "Let us leave. I have some food in my sack that will last us for at least one meal."

Jorian picked up his sword and knives and put them in the sheaths where they belonged. He shook his head in amazement, a slight smile on his face, at Nada's courage.

Nada tucked the tin of peppermint leaves into her sack then led Jorian out of the room and up the staircase to the hidden door, her shoe still wedged inside where she left it. She stopped long enough to pull the remaining shoe out of her pocket and put them on then she pulled the door open and slipped through the opening. They descended the narrow stairway, unbeknownst to them both, the same one Darec and Elieana descended just days before. Upon reaching the bottom, it seemed as if the exit had been sealed permanently but after much searching they found a small rusted latch. With a few tries, the door opened to reveal the sea lapping at the wall just below the doorsill, closing off any avenue of escape.

"Well, I think we will just have to sit and wait for the tide to turn unless swimming is something you might consider," said Nada.

Jorian looked down at his young charge. "An encounter with a large sea creature is one I do not welcome. There is one nearby, as you probably know," he said with a hint of a smile on his face, thinking about what his men reported to him before they brought Nada to the Hall of Justice.

"If we must wait for the tide we may as well have the food I took from my room," said Nada. "The bread is stale, and the cheese is hard, but it will fill our bellies. I only wish I had stopped to fill the bottle with water, it would have softened the bread to make it easier to swallow."

"No matter," replied Jorian as he squatted down in the doorway next to Nada. "This will do fine."

Nada pulled open the bag and brought out the bread and cheese which they shared in companionable silence as they waited for the tide to turn. They watched the water lap against the rocks and the sea creatures, not seen during the daylight hours, now visible. Schools of phosphorescent striped Tunga fish swam rapidly back and forth, giving the appearance of many greenish-blue ribbons blowing in the wind. A small dog-like creature pursuing the Tunga fish occasionally raised its head up out of the water, looked about, then sank back down leaving hardly a ripple to reveal where it had been.

As the night wore on Nada slowly slumped down until her head rested on her knees. She slept soundly, making little puffing noises as she breathed. Jorian reached over and pulled her close, wrapping his arm around her to keep her warm. He gazed out at the ocean and listened to the lapping of the surf. It mesmerized and calmed him, so he could think and plan what to do next. Worry for his child foremost in his mind it was crucial he get word to his family and get them out of the city as soon as possible. With the passage of each day since the discovery of the sword his feelings of foreboding grew stronger. Each day without word from Darec and the rest of his men the more worried he became.

Slowly the water receded until in the early morning hours a narrow strip of sand allowed them to leave the rocky ledge they perched on. During the night Jorian decided old Peter Bondar could help them and perhaps even send word to his wife.

He gently shook Nada awake and they climbed down over the rocks and set out towards the fishing village to Peter Bondar's shack. They saw no one about, being too early for the beach scavengers. Any guards patrolling the shoreline now returned to the castle at dusk after the murder of the young soldier on the beach some few days before. Confident they would follow orders and remain close to the castle gates until sunrise Jorian and Nada could get to the village without being seen.

They walked close to the receding water, which obscured their footprints as they passed, and as they walked the sky slowly brightened. They arrived at Peter's shack and Jorian rapped once, twice, then a voice from within called out.

"Who is there at this hour?"

"Friends, looking for a haven," replied Jorian.

Peter peeped out from behind the ragged curtain covering the window. Seeing Jorian and Nada he opened the door and ushered them in, with open arms. "It is a strange hour for you, Nada, to be gracing my doorstep, also you, Jorian," said Peter when they entered his little shack.

"What brings you to my humble home at this hour?"

"I have brought Nada to you for protection for a short time. Can I count on you to keep her safe?" asked Jorian.

"Upon my word. Nada is loved by all, no harm will come to her," replied Peter as he gave Nada a hug.

"Thank you, Peter. I have another favor to ask. My wife and child may be in danger. I must get them out of the castle. It may put you at risk, and you must say no if you do not want to take that risk."

"Jorian, you are an old friend and friends help friends. I will go to your wife about some fresh fish. She will come and then when the sea is safe I will take her and little Joel fishing to the islands."

"Thank you, Peter. I owe you much. I do not know when I will return but if you could go to her this morning you have my thanks."

"Once I have settled Nada in I will go and visit your wife. The earlier the better, if I may say so myself. Come Nada, you look hungry and tired." Peter motioned to a chair for Nada to sit.

Nada stared at Jorian and by the expression on her face he knew immediately what she was thinking and responded. "Nada, have no fear, no harm will come to you. I will return as soon as I am able."

She nodded once then sat down on the chair Peter offered. Jorian quietly left the shack taking a circuitous route through the village on his return to the castle.

"Nada," said Peter, after Jorian left, "I think perhaps I should find you something more suitable to wear. Please, rest awhile, you may lay down on my bed. I will be gone for a short time and when I return I will make you a nice breakfast before I go to fetch Jorian's wife and little Joel."

Peter left, to fetch Jorian's wife and son, leaving Nada in the cool, dimly lit shack. It had only two rooms, one with a small cook stove, a tiny fireplace and a table with two chairs. The next room was Peter's bedroom, but Nada could not see past the curtain drawn across the doorway. A large window faced the sea and a smaller one faced towards the castle. Nada moved from her chair to look out the window facing the castle She pulled back the curtain and she saw Jorian walking towards the gate. He stopped to talk to a soldier and as he did he pointed back towards the village, causing Nada's heart to skip a beat. Could she trust Jorian or did he just tell the guard where to find her? She desperately wanted to run away and hide, her new-found courage draining quickly away. As she watched, the soldier slapped Jorian on the back and they both entered the castle gate. Nada let the ragged curtain fall back into place and took a deep breath, she mistrusted everyone.

***

A little while later the door opened, and Nada jumped up from the chair where she had fallen asleep. She scanned the room, looking for a way to escape. Peter stood in the doorway, a worried look on his face.

"What has happened to you, Nada? What makes you so frightened?" he asked, his brow wrinkling with concern. It took some minutes for him to calm her and convince her she was safe. She started to tell him about the events of the past few days. He didn't say a word while she told her story, he just exclaimed with "Oh" and "Ah" nodding his head as he listened.

When Nada finished telling Peter of recent events in the castle he shook his head in concern. He set down his basket, full of fruit and a few small fish along with a paper wrapped package which he gave to Nada. She carefully opened the paper wrapper and found some well used boy's clothes. Peter gestured towards the curtained room.

“Go, put those on. No one is looking for a young boy who is working for me on my boat. While you change, I will cook you some food,” he said as he gently pushed her in the direction of the room.

It took a few seconds for Nada to move then she pushed the curtain aside and entered the room. A thick feather quilt covered the bed. Peter's clothes hung from pegs on the wall along with other things such as a scabbard with a small knife, a bow, some fishing gear and a net.

A collection of items cluttered the room, possessions Peter could not part with, pebbles, flowers long dead in their vase, various seashells, some very tiny and others quite large. One shell, sitting on a special stand, had strangely shaped pointy edges resembling tiny arms. A carving on one side depicted a scene of men in boats fighting a large serpent. A wooden mouthpiece had been attached at the narrow end and, Nada thought, the shell must be some type of horn.

After she changed her clothes they ate a breakfast of fried fish and fresh fruit, a feast to Nada, who had not eaten properly in a few days. Had it been only a few days since Elieana left? She shook her head in astonishment. A tightening in her throat reminded her how sad she had become since Elieana left and she wondered when she might return.

Once they finished their meal Peter braided Nada's hair in the way young men normally wore it. He tied it with a leather cord and tucked the ends inside the braid then he melted some wax around the cord to keep it from slipping. Satisfied Nada no longer looked like the young girl the soldiers searched for, they walked towards the dock and Peter's flat-bottomed boat. Peter leaned his head towards Nada and spoke quietly to her. "The boat," Peter told Nada, "has a flat bottom so I can keep it in the shallows where none of the large serpents can venture. The shallows are rich with huge schools of fish and crustaceans that take refuge amongst the rocks and coral on the sea bottom. As we travel we will fish and ah, the meals we will have." He patted his ample stomach. Peter went on to describe sauces and fish soup and even though Nada just ate, her mouth watered, and her stomach growled.

As they walked along Peter waved and nodded to friends he saw along the docks. "My new helper," he called out to anyone who noticed them.

Peter's boat gently rocked at its moorings, bumping up against the thick, skin covered bladders lining the dock. They crossed the gangplank and Nada's stomach did a little lurch as it bounced under their weight. Once aboard Peter gave Nada some odd jobs to do below deck so as not to attract attention to herself. After Nada was safely below deck he went off to fetch Jorian's wife and child.

Peter headed back in the direction of the castle and as he trudged up the hill from the village he saw a group of soldiers near the gate. One of the men broke away from the group and walked in Peter's direction. Peter didn't recognize Philen until he got closer to the boy. Although Philen hadn't changed physically since he borrowed Peter's dilhaa and cart, he displayed more confidence. Peter could see it in the way he walked.

Philen clapped the old man on the back, "Peter, how have you been? I have had many adventures since last seeing you."

"I'm sure you have Philen, if you have been spending time with the likes of your fellows at the gate."

Philen looked over his shoulder toward the group of men. He realized, looking back at them, they were rough and unkempt looking. "Ahh, they are not so bad. We just arrived home from our travels. They are rough company at times, but we have seen huge mountains, rivers and wild animals. It is a much more pleasant way to pass the time, traveling with their like than shelling beans for Aldred," referring to the last day he spent in the castle kitchen when Darec pulled him away to help them search for the missing soldier.

Peter nodded and moved to go around Philen and continue on his way. "I must go, Philen, I have a date with the tide, if I am to fish today."

Philen looked at him oddly and wanted to say he went in the wrong direction but held his tongue. "Well, I will escort you; there have been bandits in the castle, and killings."

Startled, Peter looked at Philen. "Killings, you say?"

"Yes, Mathilde, the owner of the bath house on Washerwoman's Alley, murdered and found by her maid. The guard at the gate told us when we arrived today. There are also escapees from the dungeon, two of them, a man and a woman. It is believed they killed Mathilde because the escaped woman worked for her and..." he paused, a confused look on his face, "Nada is missing."

"Nada, you say?" replied Peter, beginning to fidget.

"Peter, have you seen her?"

"No, no, I have not seen her for some time," Peter lied. He fidgeted more and pulled away from Philen to continue walking towards the gate.

"Peter," said Philen as he watched Peter walk away.

Peter waved his hand, without turning to look back, and walked quickly through the gate. As soon as he could he turned down a side lane to avoid any more questions if Philen should follow him. Peter broke out in a cold sweat. He didn't want to say anything to Philen, even though he knew Philen and Nada were friends. He wanted to get her and Jorian's wife and child away as soon as possible. When Peter set his mind on a task he could not allow himself to be diverted. He liked to talk, and he knew, had he stayed, would have divulged everything. He glanced over his shoulder once to ensure no one followed him and then continued, taking a roundabout route towards Jorian's house.

CHAPTER 9

The avian soldier blew on a large shell horn, calling for reinforcements. He watched for a moment to see if those on the plateau heard his call. When he saw men running towards their mounts he turned his attention back to the three escapees scrambling away from the security of the rocks. He saw a flight of birds take to the air and knew they could see him flying high above the rocks where the fight took place, so he maneuvered his bird around to follow his quarry.

The escapees ran towards a small hump of rocks in the distance. The soldier, thinking they sought refuge for another fight, urged his bird faster. Capture or kill was much easier if the quarry had no place to hide. A sneer of hatred spread across his face as he thought of the men and mounts of his squad they killed in the first attack. Determined to get first blood he kept his eyes on the man who ran towards the cave, his back a perfect target.

As the soldier closed the distance between his victims he saw the entrance to a cave in the rocks they were running towards. Urging his bird on, he felt its body shudder as it flapped its great wings faster. He loved the exhilaration as they flew, the wind streaming across his face. He lowered his woven visor to block the wind then calmly nocked an arrow; drew, aimed, released. Just as he released the arrow his bird screeched and began spiraling down, its energy spent from the gaping wound in its chest. The wound inflicted by the man running from him now. The arrow flew high and lodged itself in the top of the fleeing man's shoulder.

The bird soldier took satisfaction from the shot, injuring the man who dealt the deadly blow to his bird. As he rode his dying beast to the ground he saw the man stumble and fall face forward into a pool of water in front of the cave. The man gained his footing and waded towards the cave, his arm hanging limply by his side.

A shadow from above caught the soldier's attention. He glanced up and saw the new contingent of avian soldiers flying overhead. They let loose a volley of arrows which clattered against the mouth of the cave and splashed into the now muddied water of the pool. The injured man dove inside the cave but not before he let out a bellow, his comrades hit their target.

The wounded bird landed hard on the ground and the soldier jumped from the saddle to cradle its head in his arms. Gazing deeply into the bird's fierce eyes the soldier felt the glint of life slipping away, along with the mental and physical bond they shared. The bird tried to stand but collapsed and died in the soldier's arms. The soldier screamed out in agony as the bond they shared ripped from his being. He couldn't leave his bird and stayed for a long time, patting the silky feathers covering its head. They shared each other's strength when the two were together, a strong force. The loss of the bond left the soldier drained and exhausted.

When he could stand, he plucked the two large feathers sticking up in a tuft from the top of the bird's head. He tucked them inside his jerkin, taking care not to crush them. He unbuckled the leather straps of the riding harness and carried it a short distance away then gathered some dry brush and twigs. He gently tucked the kindling around the body of his bird and lit it. The flames quickly spread. For a moment, the man desired to go to the Gods with his bird, to ride forever in paradise, but when the flames became too hot to bear he stumbled back and watched the flames consume his bird's body, its feathers seeming to melt in the intense heat.

Overwhelmed by grief he turned his back on the pyre and staggered to where his comrades waited for him. It would take many days for the soldier to recover from his loss. He moved towards one of the gigantic war birds from behind, its rider grasped his hand and pulled him up onto the bird's back.

The grieving soldier rubbed his sleeve across his face, dashing away his tears as he looked back to the pyre, then he turned his eyes forward and readied himself as the war bird leapt into the air, its powerful wings flapping as they flew back to the plateau.

CHAPTER 10

Vasilis and Egesa, the Sangan Chieftain, watched as the soldiers returned to the plateau. They carried no captives. The fugitives either escaped again or were killed, their corpses left as carrion for the flesh eaters with only bones to mark their passing.

Egesa's pale, merciless eyes gleamed; the oblong pupils shrunken to tiny pinpricks. He remained motionless, watching as the men landed their mounts, removed the riding harness and secured the birds to their perches. Servants ran up to throw chunks of meat to the birds, ensuring they stayed a good distance away from the razor-sharp beaks.

Egesa and Vasilis waited for the soldiers to kneel in front of them, heads down and right fist pounded against their chests. Egesa spoke, his voice as cold and unyielding as the stones of the mountain. "What of your captives? Where are they?"

"We have sealed them in a cave on the upper plateau," replied one of the men.

One of Egesa's eyebrows rose, "Very resourceful of you. Were you intending to leave them there or go and retrieve them?"

"We intend to leave them there. The male is injured. The women together cannot lift the stones heaped in the opening of the cave. They will have water and not die of thirst, but he will die of his wounds and the women will die of fear and hunger."

Egesa's mouth transformed into a malevolent smile. He looked at Vasilis, questioning, a beating for the woman Antonia, perhaps, but not death? No argument came from Vasilis. He was Egesa's pawn. Vasilis did not know the soldiers would do Egesa's bidding regardless of whether they were Vasilis' kinsmen or countrymen. Egesa ruled by fear but he also knew the strength of the bond between the men and their birds. Once they imprinted with their birds they would follow without question. Their birds were more important than anything, more important than life itself. It had been this way from the beginning of recorded time. Soon, thought Egesa, we will regain our land. The land Vasilis called Baltica and Pelagonia.

"You have done well." Egesa clapped his hands and dismissed them. "Go find your reward, food, drink and women."

The men rose in unison and marched towards a large building on the opposite side of the plateau. Egesa and Vasilis provided food and drink in abundance and the men had their choice of the many whores Egesa brought from the mountain city of Ganita in Sangan. There were many Sangan men in Egesa's army. They must have their needs met by a woman who knew what a Sangan male wanted. Vasilis provided some from Baltica, but they were weak and soft and did not have the strength to stand in the embrace of a Sanganian male.

Egesa watched the men walk towards the building, his disdain for anyone not Sangan not lost on Vasilis. The Sangans, tall and well-muscled with white hair, the sign of a pure Sangan, all very similar. Some Sangans had yellow hair, they were not pure Sangan, but their size set them apart from the humans.

The Baltican men were not small men but all were different. Egesa trained the Balticans himself and they could compete in mock fighting with the Sangans but often they chose to watch the Sangans compete against each other. The Sangans were ruthless. When they killed, they showed no emotion, not even if they killed a fellow soldier in friendly competition.

CHAPTER 11

Jacq rejoined Carlotte as the Wirliang instructed him. He couldn't figure them out. They seemed to change appearance even as he looked at them and when their appearance changed, when they touched him, it frightened him so badly he ran away. He sat down beside Carlotte and looked up at the towering cavern ceiling; it seemed to shimmer with color and light. As he sat there watching, a movement caught his eye. "Carlotte, have you watched the ceiling of this cavern?"

"No, why?" she replied, turning her gaze upwards.

"Well, it's strange, but it seems as if there is something hanging up there. A lot of something hanging up there and every so often something moves but I can't quite make out what it is."

Carlotte lay back, taking pleasure in the soothing warmth of the sand soaking into her back and watched for a few moments. "I see it. It looks as if there are long sacs hanging up there and they move every so often. I have never seen anything so strange. Come to think of it this whole place is strange. Have you noticed there are only adult Wirliang? There are no young ones. Where are their young?"

Half joking Jacq pointed to the ceiling. "Up there, hanging in those sacs, a good place to keep children when their parents are not around, kind of like an aerial child minding service."

"Well, perhaps you are right, Jacq, look over there," said Carlotte.

Jacq gazed in the direction Carlotte pointed. Far up on an outcropping, nearby the waterfall, they saw a lone Wirliang lift a smallish sized sac and gently carry it across to where another Wirliang hung suspended from the ceiling. As they watched the second Wirliang reached out to take the sac and then slowly moved across the ceiling to the spot where other sacs hung, gently moving back and forth like sea grass in water.

"Can you see the sac is moving? I think it is a young Wirliang inside," whispered Carlotte. The hair on her arms stood up and she shivered. "That must be what they do with their babies. I have never seen any creature so interesting."

"And you may never again," replied a deep voice that sounded strangely familiar.

Carlotte sat up abruptly. Standing in front of them was the old farmer whose body they brought from Pelagos. Stunned by his presence Carlotte scuttled backwards. Jacq spluttered, unable to speak and stared at the man in disbelief. It could not be the farmer come back to life, his body stunk with rot when they camped out under the tree.

"I am sorry; I seem to have shocked you. You did not see me killed and you did not bring my body back to the Wirliang people, it was Maka, a Wirliang, who took my appearance. We all felt it wise that Maka go to the village in my place because he could change if it became too dangerous there."

"Why were you there? Why was he there? Why was it too dangerous?" asked Jacq anxiously.

"You have many questions, young man. The Wirliang people have scouts all over the land. They do not want to assimilate into the human culture. They want to be left alone but they believe, and rightly so, if they do not know what is taking place in the human world then what befell their people hundreds of years ago may occur again. Their culture is old, very old. Once they roamed freely throughout the land and the females laid their young in the open. In times past the Wirliangs hung their egg sacs from the branches of the Candela tree.

"You would know it, Carlotte, as the tree the children stand under during the Slump festival in Girona."

Carlotte nodded, remembering the harvest time festival, the feasting, the delicious treats. She could hardly contain her excitement during the festival, when the children stood below the huge, spreading branches of the tree waiting to be showered with leaves as they fell over a period of hours. After the last leaf fell the tree stood, just as beautiful, its huge spreading branches covered with soft, light brown bark to be shed before spring, revealing fresh green bark below, such a wondrous tree.

The farmer continued his story, "Many, many, many years ago, a people came to this world, I believe we are their descendants. How they got here, I do not understand, but the

Wirliang stories tell of large ships floating in the air. When the people arrived, they hunted the Wirliang. I believe they were fearful because of the Wirliang ability to change shape. They also desired the beautiful skin of the female which changes to gold with rainbow hues when she lays her eggs."

He pointed to the ledge where the Wirliang worked. They could see Wirliang moving back and forth and as they watched they saw the most beautiful creature stand, with the help of another Wirliang. Her skin, golden hued, shimmering with many colors, as if just under the surface.

"I have never seen anything so beautiful," whispered Carlotte.

"Yes, neither had those who arrived here on their ships. They decimated the Wirliang population. Some Wirliang escaped and hid in these caverns. This is only one of many caverns, where they have resided since that time. Some humans felt a great affinity to the Wirliang and became their friends, vowing to protect the Wirliang population from extinction. This cavern is where many of the Wirliang stay when they go top side. They bring their mates here to be close when the laying and incubation time begins. The male will help his mate throughout the laying and it is his job to hang the eggs, so they can mature.

"In times past, when they hung the eggs in the Candela tree, they matured quickly. The survived and matured well when hung in the open. Now many eggs do not mature at all. The Wirliang population is still very small. In the Candela tree, the sun warmed the eggs and hardened the shells. When the leaves fell, as in the Slump Festival, the Wirliang eggs hatched. The Wirliangs also celebrated with a kind of festival of their own to greet their children into the world. They gathered around their family Candela tree to watch as their children emerged from their shells.

"While you are here you most likely will see some of the children emerge. I suggest you stay long enough to observe this event; it is most exciting. When you see how closely the family unit relates to each other then you will understand and may even pledge yourselves as protectors of the Wirliang."

"Well, I don't know," replied Carlotte, "I don't think I could live underground."

"The Wirliang feel the same way," said Rodolph, somewhat abruptly. "Their lands stretched from the delta of the Kofathi River to the Barbicon Mountains. Their largest settlement was near Girona where the largest forest of Candela trees grew. Most of those trees are gone, cut down for farmland. At one time, each family unit cultivated its own Candela tree, used by each succeeding generation. You can see there is much they have lost."

Carlotte wrung her hands together. Her family lived in Girona for many generations and she feared that possibly some of her ancestors were responsible for the Wirliang living as they lived now. "Can you show me more before I decide what I will do?" she asked.

Nodding at Carlotte the man turned towards Jacq, "And what of you, young man, will you take up the cause of the Wirliang?"

Jacq looked perplexed. "Still you have not answered my question. Why was it so dangerous for you in Pelagos?"

"There is a great army amassing in the south, amid the Barbicon Mountains. Many soldiers are training huge birds. They will use them to attack the cities. The man who killed my friend, Maka..."

A warbling call interrupted Rodolph. The Wirliang on the hatchery ledge anxiously called out for assistance. They ran back and forth, with as many egg sacs as they could carry. The somber formality they previously displayed when hanging the sacs now replaced with a frantic urgency to complete the task as quickly as possible.

The female Wirlean, in her weakened state, leaned against the wall of the cavern making low moaning sounds. Her color, vividly bright before, now changed to a dull, burnished gold. Rodolph led Carlotte towards the ramp leading up to where the Wirlean leaned against the wall, gesturing for Jacq to follow.

"Something grave has happened at the pool. You can help now. Carlotte attend the female, calm her. Jacq, you and I will help remove the sacs from the pool."

The Wirliang and humans worked together, removing the remaining sacs from the laying pool and hanging them safely out of harm's way along the cavern wall. Jacq touched the cavern wall and found it warm to touch. He realized what little knowledge he had of these matters. The warmth assisted in incubating the eggs, hardening the shells and eventually, hopefully, hatching all the younglings, as Rodolph called them.

"Well done, my friend," said Rodolph when they completed their work. He patted his large, work roughened hand on Jacq's back. Jacq's face split into a huge grin, his first experience of camaraderie from anyone. He felt genuine pride in this small accomplishment.

"Now let us go and find out what has caused the turbidity in the laying pool. Carlotte you stay with the female; she needs comfort. Once she is settled and resting, her mate will take you to see the last group of younglings to have hatched. They will be in the nursery, so to speak."

Jacq and Rodolph, torches in hand, walked around the laying pool and through a cleft in the rock not visible from the cavern floor. It led to a tunnel through which the underground stream ran from the surface. A narrow walkway built on one side kept them out of the water, to prevent muddying the laying pool.

As they walked, Rodolph explained to Jacq that the water became purified once the stream traveled over rocks and sand such a long way underground. Once purified, the water was suitable for the laying pool in the cavern below. They slowly proceeded upwards, pausing at times to clamber around large boulders, under which the stream ran. At times, they crawled on hands and knees to get through, but Jacq, used to being in the city's underground sewer system, felt entirely at home. He felt good, as if he was being cleansed in some way, just like the stream. A sharp, spicy smell, Jacq noticed earlier, seemed much stronger inside the tunnel. "Rodolph, what is that smell?" said Jacq.

"Ah, you noticed," said Rodolph, sounding pleased with Jacq's discovery. "A pool on the surface is fed by a warm spring, the scent is from an herb growing in the pool. Heated water rises to the surface from deep below the earth; the plant grows abundantly in the heated water; as the water flows over the plant it picks up the plant's medicinal qualities. Once the water flows back down through the rock, and is cooled, the temperature is perfect for the laying pool and the medicinal qualities of the plant help to keep the eggs healthy, so they will mature properly. It is a wondrous system; don't you think?"

"I... yes, I do." Jacq stumbled over his words, taken by surprise that Rodolph asked his opinion.

"When the Wirliang lived on the surface they diverted heated spring waters to a laying pool nearby the family Candela tree," explained Rodolph. "After the female laid her eggs the males immediately hung them in the Candela tree. You see, the Wirliang survival is dependent on the water, and the herbs growing in it, to purify the water. If the water is not purified the female will die when laying her clutch. It is a miracle they found caverns like the one below."

As they climbed higher the temperature of the tunnel became humid and warm. Sweat ran down Jacq's face, stinging his eyes. He stopped to wipe his face and rest for a moment. Rodolph, noticing Jacq had stopped, waited for him to catch up. As he waited he heard the murmur of women's voices. The voices sounded frantic, urgent. When Jacq reached him, Rodolph motioned for him to stay where he was. "I will go and find out who these people are. If I do not return you must go back and warn the Wirliang," Rodolph whispered.

"Yes," Jacq whispered.

Rodolph took the torch and moved further up the tunnel, leaving Jacq standing in the dark. Silent on his feet, as silent as any of the Wirliang, having lived with them for so long, Rodolph approached the people in the tunnel, taking them completely by surprise. Antonia let out a shriek when she saw the torch approaching out of the darkness. Elieana, so busy tending to Darec, did not see Rodolph until he stood behind her. Darec tried to rise when he heard Antonia's shriek but unable to gain a foothold he slipped in the gravel of the streambed falling hard on his injured leg.

Rodolph spoke sternly, his tone permitting no argument, "You must come with me to the cavern below. You are causing great distress to the settlement by stirring up the water here."

Rodolph handed the torch to Elieana then bent down to hoist Darec up and assist him as they walked through the tunnel. Darec grunted in pain and fell back against the cavern wall, bumping his head. He slid his body up the wall, by digging his feet into the gravel to gain his footing, and then leaned heavily on Rodolph's shoulder. Elieana led the way, carrying the torch, with Antonia following closely behind, anxiously twisting the hem of her skirt. None of them asked any questions, they proceeded obediently, resigned to the fact that with Darec's injury they could not escape on their own in either direction.

"Hold the torch high, my dear; we are looking for an opening in the wall to your right," said Rodolph. They proceeded about fifty feet when Rodolph called out, "Jacq, I have found our friends, come to my voice."

They waited a few moments, listening to rocks scrabbling in the darkness, then a thin, young man with shaggy hair emerged before them. He looked familiar to Elieana. She cocked her head to one side trying to think where she had seen him before. She started to ask if she might know him. “You seem to be familiar, do I…?” Darec let out a low, pain-filled moan.

“Yes, yes,” said Rodolph. “We must get this man below; he has grievous wounds. Nothing that we can take care of here, I am afraid. Proceed ladies.” Rodolph nodded his head towards Elieana, for her to proceed down the tunnel. "It is well marked; you should have no trouble. Walk on the side of the tunnel, out of the water. There will be an opening on the right side," he said.

Elieana paused for a moment, uncertain, as she did not want to leave Darec.

"Do not trouble yourself,” said Rodolph who waved his hand for her to continue walking. “Jacq and I will help your friend." Rodolph nodded again for her to proceed.

They descended further and squeezed through the opening Rodolph indicated. Jacq and Rodolph helped Darec who was becoming increasingly weak from his wounds but also, Rodolph thought, from poison. No one spoke as they proceeded through the narrow tunnel. Finally, the tunnel widened, seeming to get brighter as a glimmer of light grew in front of them. They went around a slight bend in the tunnel and a large opening revealed a huge cavern before them. They stepped out onto a ledge over which the stream flowed into a lake below.

"Rodolph, I know where we are," said Jacq excitedly as he realized they had circled around the cavern and overlooked the lake where he and Carlotte bathed.

"Yes, Jacq, now the only difficulty I see for some of us is there is no way to get down to the lake except jump."

Antonia looked at the man as if he had lost his mind. After their experience with the huge reptiles in the underground lake she had decided never to step in water over her knees again and only inside a bathing chamber. Agitated, she backed up against the rock wall. Her whole body became rigid like the wall she leaned against. Elieana realized she had to do something before Antonia became unhinged again with her unbearable screaming. She grabbed Antonia's hand tightly, pulled her forward in one fluid motion and jumped from the ledge. Antonia's arms and legs wind-milled followed by a piercing scream, which stopped the instant both women hit the water.

Darec watched them go over the edge, then his eyes rolled back, and he slumped down in Rodolph's arms in a dead faint.

"Come, Jacq, take an arm and over we go," said Rodolph.

Jacq did as Rodolph instructed and grasped Darec's arm tightly. They dragged him to the edge and jumped together. As he fell towards the water Jacq remembered he didn't know how to swim.

Wirliang from all over the settlement looked up when they heard Antonia scream and ran quickly to the water's edge. Wirliang males dove into the water and pulled the two women to the shore. Others swam to help Rodolph with Darec.

Jacq gasped for air, splashing wildly to keep his head out of the water when a large Wirliang came from behind, grasped him under the arms and pulled him towards shore. When he felt the creature's arms around him, Jacq lay back and relaxed into its arms. These creatures calmed him. He felt less anxious in their presence with each interaction. He trusted them, a new feeling for him, having never trusted anyone in his life, except for Carlotte.

When Antonia's head went under, water rushed into her mouth, almost choking her, cutting off her scream instantly. Strong arms grasped her from behind and dragged her towards the shore. She struggled for a moment then let her savior drag her through the water. As she floated along she admired the glittering ceiling overhead and then she saw Darec being dragged between the two men as they jumped off the ledge above. When they reached the shore, Antonia turned to thank the man who rescued her but was shocked to see a strange looking creature holding onto her. Her mouth opened wide, her shrieking started all over again, out of her mind with fear. She rolled over and scrambled on her hands and knees, crawling as fast as she could to get away from the creature. As soon as she gained her balance she ran across the beach surrounding the little lake, screaming and waving her arms in the air. No one paid any attention to her, being more concerned with getting Darec out of the water and attending to his wounds.

The creatures cautiously surrounded Antonia, as she ran in one direction, turned around and ran in the opposite direction. They didn't get too close, preferring to watch her from a distance, chattering to each other and pointing at her. Carlotte, saw that Antonia's screams and the blood from Darec's wounds agitated the Wirliang. Wanting to help she ran over and flopped down on the sand beside Darec, tore off a portion of her skirt and wrapped it about the wound on his leg, holding on tightly to staunch the bleeding. One of the two women who jumped off the ledge moved over to help her.

"You have done the right thing to hold tight. Thank you. I can take this from here if you could be so kind as to deal with Antonia. She is a bit excitable and needs calming. My name is Elieana if you need me."

"Carlotte. My name is Carlotte," said Carlotte, realizing instantly that this woman was Nada's mother, a capable healer. "Might we speak later when I have settled Antonia?"

"Surely," replied Elieana without looking back as she tended to Darec's wounds. Now she had light and a place where she could lay him out in comfort she saw he had fainted from loss of blood. One of the strange creatures came forward, offering bandages. Elieana took them, taking a moment to look directly at the creature. He or she did not appear threatening and its featureless face calmed her, almost.

"Thank you," said Elieana. The creature gurgled in reply then walked a short distance away, squatted down and watched as Elieana tended to Darec's wounds. Elieana heard someone else approach and glanced up at the elderly man who helped them from the cave.

"I will help in any way I can, as will my friend, Jacq," said the older man motioning towards Jacq who stepped forward nervously. Elieana looked at Jacq, who appeared very nervous and agitated about something.

"Thank you, sir. What is your name?"

"Rodolph, from Girona."

"Could either of you bring me some water for cleansing Darec's wounds?"

"The water in the lake will suit the purpose," said Rodolph. "It is very clean.

"Jacq, go to the bathing compound and bring a small bucket. You know where to find it now, don't you, young man?"

"Yes," Jacq stuttered and abruptly ran towards the bathing compound at the edge of the lake, relieved to be given a task and almost tripping in his haste to get away.

CHAPTER 12

After Elieana cleansed and bandaged Darec's wounds, two Wirliang picked him up and escorted the newcomers to a large building containing numerous sleeping pallets. Elieana lay down on a pallet between Darec and Antonia, exhausted but between that time of falling asleep and wakefulness. A feeling of loathing for Antonia welled up inside her. The woman screamed continually when they first crawled up on the edge of the underground lake, until suddenly it stopped when one of the creatures placed its hand on Antonia's head, gently, as if in a loving caress, then Antonia stopped screaming.

Elieana had worked on Darec's wounds cleaning them thoroughly, especially the one in his shoulder. The angry, red skin around the wound caused her much concern, that it may putrefy. She lay there thinking of the events that took place that day as slowly the tension drained from her muscles. In her last waking moment, she wondered how she would know if it were day or night, being underground. This piqued her curiosity and lifted her to wakefulness for but a moment then she slept.

A grumbling snore from Darec jerked Elieana awake sometime later. Panic fluttered inside her chest, like a bird beating its wings against her ribcage. She looked around the room, confused, having no recollection of walking into it or of even laying down. As wakefulness slowly seeped into her brain she sat up and reached over to touch Darec. His skin felt cool to the touch and he slept soundly.

Elieana briskly rubbed her hands over her face then looked to her other side and saw Antonia, sleeping as peacefully as a babe. What a strange woman she thought, recalling Antonia's last outburst of screaming. Her long years of being locked up in her brother's castle has taken its toll on her sanity, thought Elieana.

Redirecting her attention back to Darec, she rose from the sleeping pallet and looked fondly down at him. Impulsively, she bent down and kissed him on the mouth. She immediately stood up and looked over her shoulder. "Odd," she whispered quietly, "I could have sworn someone stood there watching me." Out of the corner of her eye she caught a tiny movement. The hair rose on the back of her neck and her heart pounded. The room was empty save for the three of them. She tried to rationalize and convince herself it must have been an insect or a mouse. Again, the tiny movement occurred. Elieana very slowly directed her attention to where she caught the tiny movement and briefly saw the outline of one of the strange creatures standing motionless against the wall. She knew it had not been there before because she looked around the room when she first awoke. She faced directly towards where she thought she saw it and caught a shimmer as if the air moved and then the shimmer seemed to wink out.

Never had she seen a creature quite like this one. It had been standing up against the wall and looking directly at her. It must have moved its arm or leg for her to catch a glimpse of it. Now she could not see it at all. She immediately feared for her two friends laying completely vulnerable on their respective pallets but then, she rationalized, if they meant any harm why help her tend Darec's wounds and let us rest here in this room, wherever here is.

Softly and without emotion she spoke in the direction of where she last saw the creature, "Please, show yourself, we mean no harm. Perhaps you can help us." The creature didn't move or become visible. Hesitantly she walked over to the spot where she briefly saw the creature standing and reached out but felt nothing. She warily moved back to the pallet and sat down with her back against the wall, thinking if anything came close the shimmer of movement would alert her before it attacked. The fear she experienced now was far greater than the fear of the gigantic reptile, knowing someone watched her but unable to see who it may be, where it may be and when it might move.

Elieana sat on guard and fought the exhaustion threatening to overtake her. Darec and Antonia still slept, oblivious to their surroundings or any possible danger. She pinched herself to stay awake, watching for anything that might approach them. After what seemed like a very long time, Rodolph, Jacq and the girl who helped with Darec, entered the room. Rodolph spoke first, "Ah, you are awake.

My young friends told me you looked much refreshed. This is Carlotte," and he motioned in the girl's direction.

Startled Elieana responded "How did they know? I... I didn't sleep. Someone watched us."

The man ignored her comment. "I see your friends still sleep. Come, we will let them continue their slumber." Beckoning her to follow him, he reached out for her hand but Elieana stood on her own. He shrugged his shoulders then led the way out of the room, Carlotte and Jacq following a few steps behind. They walked down a short hallway, lit by tiny oil lamps set into the wall. Rodolph pushed open a door, holding it for Elieana, motioning for her to enter. The small room, richly appointed with thick carpets on the floor and hangings on the wall depicting familiar scenes from the world above felt warm and inviting.

A low table, spread with a bountiful feast, sat in the middle of the room; bowls of steaming vegetables, platters of meats, a large basket of bread and small cakes and a huge pitcher of red colored liquid. The savory aromas wafting up from the table caused Elieana's mouth to water and her empty stomach let out a very loud grumble. Her face flamed with embarrassment. "I'm sorry," she said. "It has been a long time since I have had anything much to eat. We last ate...I don't know when we last ate, a few days ago, I think, cold tubers and eggs."

"Do not be concerned, my dear," said Rodolph. "Please, sit and enjoy the refreshments the Wirliang have prepared for us."

"Thank you," she mumbled as she flopped down on a cushion and loaded a plate to overflowing. The first mouthful, an ecstasy of flavor. She closed her eyes, savoring it, as she swallowed. The bread, soft and freshly baked; the meats lightly spiced, and the vegetables pickled, tangy and sweet. She didn't speak as she ate her fill. As she ate, Rodolph poured her a large goblet of the red liquid.

"Thank you," said Elieana again as she took a sip of the most delicious wine she ever tasted. She leaned back with a sigh, letting out a tiny belch. Embarrassed she put her hand over her mouth. "I beg your pardon. Thank you, sir, we have travelled a very long way in very adverse conditions. It has been some time since any of us have had a decent meal." Suddenly she felt very guilty and hid her face, "My hunger made me forget all about Antonia and Darec," she whispered.

"Do not worry for your friends. When they have awakened from their rest they also will be fed," said Rodolph.

"I could not forgive myself if they missed out on this wonderful meal," said Elieana as she dabbed her mouth with a cloth napkin.

"There is naught to be worried about regarding your friends but there are more pressing concerns we must discuss. Jacq and Carlotte have come from the city of Pelagos. I understand that is where you also come from?"

"How would you know that?" responded Elieana rudely.

"Well, we..." replied Rodolph.

Before Rodolph could finish, Jacq interrupted him nervously. "I... we," motioning to Carlotte and himself, “know of you from the city. Your child is Nada and you are the healer.”

“Yes, and what of it?” replied Elieana. She sat up straighter on the cushion and put her fingers to her temples, massaging and pressing tightly. Her head hurt, thinking about Nada and worrying about her safety.

Jacq stammered on and proceeded to tell her everything that occurred, starting from the beginning. He told her of the sword and the dead soldier; of following Darec throughout the city when they removed the soldier’s body; he told her of her conversation with Darec when they stood in the doorway of her chamber.

An expression of mingled shock and anger spread across Elieana’s face, causing Jacq to lean away from her. He told of Girard and their kidnapping of Nada. Elieana grew so angry she wanted to jump across the table and strangle him. Jacq, seeing the threat she posed, scuttled back on his cushion to maximize the distance between them.

Elieana leaned forward, her hands on her knees, glaring at him. Tiny droplets of sweat ran down Jacq’s forehead. Carlotte moved closer to him, as if to protect him from Elieana’s threatening posture and at the same time passed him one of the napkins to wipe his face.

Jacq took it from her, nodding in thanks, and wiped the sweat from his brow, his hand shaking as he did so. The more Jacq told her the more a great weight lifted off his shoulders. He told her that he had wronged her and her child and very much wanted to repair the damage he had done.

The more Elieana heard, the more agitated she became. Her face grew red and her hands gripped her knees so tightly her knuckles turned white, skeletal, as the blood drained from them. She gritted her teeth and set her mouth in a sharp line.

At first Jacq thought her an attractive woman but now she looked demonic. When he told her that Girard locked Nada in a room and drugged her, Elieana shrieked then lunged across at him, upsetting the pitcher of wine. She grabbed the neck of his shirt, pulled him towards her, wrapped her fingers around his scrawny neck and squeezed.

Jacq looked directly into her face, making no attempt to push her away and in a choked voice squeaked out, "I'm sorry."

Shocked by Elieana's behaviour, Rodolph and Carlotte attempted to pull her off. Suddenly two Wirliang materialized. One of them reached over and gently squeezed Elieana's neck. Her arm numbed, she lost her grip on Jacq's throat, then she slumped down beside the table, bumped her head and slid onto the floor.

"Thank you," gasped Jacq as he massaged his throat. He nodded at the Wirliang who gurgled back at him in acknowledgement.

"Well, Rodolph, what shall we do now?" asked Carlotte as she helped Jacq to a sitting position and offered him a drink. "Her friend, Darec, he will be no easier to restrain," said Carlotte.

"Perhaps the two of you should let me take care of this myself," said Rodolph. "I think I know your story well enough to explain it to them. I will also tell them what is taking place and is going to take place on the surface, with the Sangan army. Go back to the lake and wait there for me. I will summon you when I am certain they will behave themselves."

Carlotte and Jacq left the room just as Elieana, confused and disoriented, pulled herself up off the floor. As they walked past her she reached out and grasped at Jacq's pant leg. He jumped aside and scurried out of the room as fast as he could go.

"So much like a ferret," she said as the door closed behind him. She looked angrily at Rodolph, her fury returning with a vengeance. "And how are you involved in this?" she demanded. Her eyes now tiny, fierce slits as she scowled at him and leaned forward, attempting to intimidate him.

"My dear, you have a very disagreeable temper," replied Rodolph calmly. "We may discuss this matter civilly or my friends here will again teach you some manners."

Elieana warily looked around the room, trying to see any disguised Wirliang. "There is no one else here," she said.

"Are you certain?" said Rodolph and he cocked his head to the side.

Elieana stared at Rodolph, her mind working on what he just said to her.

"Yes," she blurted out. "Perhaps my temper is disagreeable but look at what we have been through. Crawling through tunnels and escaping from huge monsters; being attacked by huge birds, what do you expect? That is totally aside from the fact I have just discovered my daughter was kidnapped." Elieana shook her head and spoke more to herself than to Rodolph. "I am responsible for this. They could not have kidnapped her if I remained, rather than leave on this ridiculous search for the missing papers. We found Nada's real mother and she is slightly crazy which just makes matters worse. What do you expect?" she said as she looked up at Rodolph with red rimmed eyes. She wanted to scream she felt so angry but thought better of it and slammed her fist into the cushion she sat on. Again, and again she punched the cushion until tears welled up in her eyes and she slumped down in misery.

"Perhaps I have...am being disagreeable but you just do not know what we have experienced since we left Pelagos." She thought about their journey, had it only been a few days since they left Pelagos, she wondered. It seemed much, much longer.

Rodolph nodded, "I am sure what you have been through has been very challenging for you, as it has been for Jacq and Carlotte. They were taken to the dungeon after they rescued your child. You did not let Jacq tell you that. Carlotte and Jacq, most assuredly, escaped with their very lives. What I must tell you though, there is more danger to come. You have seen only the beginning of the terror that will reign down on the land once the force of the Sangan army is released. The birds you saw on the mountain are the young being trained. The rest of the army is in Sangan across the mountains. They will swoop down across Pelagos and Baltica and devastate it with their power.

"I think perhaps your friends should be party to this discussion. You will be escorted back to the sleeping room and wake them. I will have the dishes replenished. I will invite

Jacq and Carlotte back into the room when I know your friends will act respectfully to them. Jacq and Carlotte are also the Wirliang's guests. I advise you, young lady, control your temper. Whatever the young man has done he has begged your forgiveness. He now wants to make amends for what he has done, and we must assist him until he proves himself unworthy of our assistance."

Rodolph motioned toward the door, where two Wirliang suddenly materialized.

Elieana rose without a word. One of the Wirliang opened the door for her. She walked down the hall behind the other Wirliang who led her back to the sleeping room. Darec looked much rested when Elieana entered the room but now seemed in a great deal of discomfort, his skin very pale and his cheeks bright red.

"Where have you been?" asked Darec, as he tried to push himself up into a sitting position.

"I have just met with Rodolph and the man with him when they found us in the cave. He has asked me to bring you to him, so you and Antonia can eat. He has some disturbing news to tell us."

Darec did not question her. He saw from her red nose and swollen, red eyes, that she had been crying. He rose from the pallet while Elieana woke Antonia. Elieana put her arm around Darec's waist and helped him walk down the hallway to the room where Rodolph waited for them, Antonia trotting along behind them.

No Wirliang were in sight, Elieana was thankful for that, certain if Antonia saw them her hysterical screaming would begin again. She did not want her to start screaming again and fought the urge to ask Antonia why she kept screaming. She realized she would just be antagonizing Antonia on purpose and shut her mouth firmly, clenching her teeth in aggravation. Rodolph's words about her temper sat heavily on her mind. She knew her temper could become foul, determined to show him she could control it, she held her tongue.

Elieana held the door open while Darec and Antonia entered. She followed them inside, leaving the door slightly ajar. Neither Darec nor Antonia noticed the door mysteriously close by itself, paying more attention to the abundance of food laid out before them. Antonia immediately plopped down on a cushion and reached out to take something to eat then snatched her hand back, realizing she had not been invited to partake of anything. She smiled apologetically to Rodolph who immediately motioned for her to help herself.

"I know you are hungry," said Rodolph as he passed a plate to Antonia, who took it, loaded it to overflowing, stuffing food in her mouth as she did so.

Darec reached out to take something but grimaced in pain from the wound in his shoulder and let his hand drop to his lap.

"Let me, Darec," said Elieana. "A bit of everything? It is all very delicious," she said, trying to keep her voice light.

Rodolph smiled at Elieana, acknowledging that she wanted to get along. He thought, most likely, it had more to do with the fact she knew the unseen Wirliang were present because she left the door open for them. Obviously, she understood they would do what was required to protect the safety of all in the room.

Elieana passed a plate of food to Darec and he placed it on his knees. He picked at the food, taking a few bites, then resting and breathing deeply as if he had just physically exerted himself. He leaned back on the couch as he chewed, as if he barely had the strength to sit up and eat.

Rodolph realized he had no need to be concerned with Darec becoming angry at Jacq, because of his weakened state. He rose from the couch, opened the door and spoke softly to someone. Darec opened his eyes half way and watched Rodolph. He could not see who Rodolph spoke to, which confused him, and he shook his head as if to shake cobwebs from his brain.

"I have summoned my friends, Carlotte and Jacq," said Rodolph, when he returned to the couch. "They have a lot to tell about what has occurred since you left Pelagos. Please, eat, it will take them a few moments to return from the lake."

Darec nodded at Rodolph, then he lay back on the cushions, struggling to eat the food Elieana had given him. Surreptitiously, Elieana watched him, her concern growing steadily at how much more feeble and weak he had become.

A short time later Jacq and Carlotte entered the room. Darec listlessly looked at Jacq, wondering where he had seen this little man before.

"I recognize you from Pelagos, do I not?" he mumbled.

"You may," replied Jacq nervously. I am seen about Pelagos, doing odd jobs, but mostly I am one of the gong farmers. You will never have seen me when I am working there."

"You are probably right. I do not normally travel under the city." He tried to laugh at his comment, but the sound came out as a breathy raising of his chest.

"What brings you here?" said Darec as he tried to sit up but couldn't and gave up, laying back awkwardly on the cushions.

Jacq warily regarded Elieana, a questioning expression on his face.

"Go ahead, Jacq, you are in no danger from me," said Elieana. She meant to reassure him, however it had the reverse effect, considering Darec did not know the details of what had transpired in Pelagos due to Jacq's greediness.

Rodolph squeezed Jacq's shoulder. "Start from the beginning, Jacq, if you please."

Jacq looked at Rodolph and nodded. He swallowed before he started to speak and Elieana watched the apple of his neck bobble as he did so. She stared so intently at him he became sweaty again. He wiped his forehead, he swallowed again and Elieana smiled as she watched him squirm. Rodolph frowned at her as he watched her silent attempt at intimidation.

Again, Jacq recited that Girard hired him to bring banned weapons into the city; how he accidently killed a man in his fear of being arrested; how he followed Darec and discovered Elieana and the identity of her daughter. He told of his fear of Girard and how he believed he could save himself by helping kidnap Elieana's daughter.

Jacq leaned closer to Carlotte, so their shoulders touched as he spoke, she moved towards him in support. He told of their escape from Mathilde's brothel over the rooftops of the city and how they went back to rescue Nada from Girard.

Carlotte told of the slide through the refuse chute and how she helped Nada and where they hid in the cave. Jacq started to quiver in fear, as he told of the attack from the sea beast. In the telling of their capture and arrest Carlotte seemed to change in her appearance. She grew intense and angry as she told of the dungeon and how they escaped and at the same time objects on the table started to rattle. Jacq patted her arm and held her hand tightly, calming her.

Jacq told of the murder of the farmer and how they promised to bring his body to Girona after he died. They ended with the discovery of the Wirliangs and their beautiful cavern. The only part Jacq left out of his recitation was the theft of the money bag from Girard's study.

Throughout the accounting of past events Darec watched both Carlotte and Jacq through his half-closed eyes. He didn't move a muscle but stared intently at them, not interrupting, letting them continue until they finished their story. During the recitation Elieana moved forward menacingly but Darec restrained her by placing a hand on her knee. Elieana's shoulders slumped and she moved back to her place, taking deep breaths to calm herself.

Throughout the recitation by Jacq and Carlotte, Antonia didn't pay any attention, an interesting story, but it did not appear to have anything to do with her. She sat quietly, nibbling at her food. It didn't occur to her they spoke of her daughter. Perhaps she didn't recall Elieana had told her Nada was her daughter, Silanne, and didn't link the two.

When Jacq finished, he gazed back and forth at Darec and Elieana. He nervously pulled at the collar of his shirt, feeling as if it had suddenly become too tight. He desperately wanted to leave the room. He reached up with his arm and wiped the beads of sweat off his forehead with his sleeve. His shirt was damp under his jerkin and he shivered uncontrollably although the room was very warm.

No one spoke, and an uneasy silence settled upon them. Suddenly Antonia piped up, "Could you not tell the King and have him bring his armies to meet the Sangans? Would this not give the element of surprise?"

All eyes turned to Antonia. Throughout their discussion, it seemed she had not been listening. In fact, they all thought she didn't understand, thinking her slightly touched in the head, but some things Antonia listened to very intently.

"You are right, m 'lady," replied Darec, "It is something I have considered since we left Vasilis' castle. It is imperative that we travel to Pelagos as soon as possible, to warn the King. We must have horses to do so. Are you up to the travel or do you prefer to remain here with our new friends?"

Antonia's eyes sprang wide at the suggestion she remain in the cavern and she blurted out, "I will travel with you. I will not stay underground. I am sorry, Rodolph, your hospitality has been most agreeable, but I find the Wirliang disturbing," and then she resumed eating, dabbing at the corners of her mouth with her napkin.

Rodolph nodded his head towards Antonia. He did not know who she was. He did notice Darec and Elieana treated her with deference, at times. Perhaps a well to do lady but how did they come to be on the mountain? Not his affair, he decided, and did not ask the question on the tip of his tongue. "I will help you in any way I can," said Rodolph, "As will the Wirliang. You may find it will be a much faster journey if you go to Girona and then by boat to Pelagos. You will not meet with any of Vasilis' soldiers, however, you must stay very close to the coastline, there are the water beasts to be wary of."

Jacq shuddered involuntarily and told them again, "One of those beasts attacked me when I escaped the city. Travel by land is much preferable."

"Although you are trying to make up for the errors in your ways you do not have a voice in this discussion," said Darec in barely a whisper. "You will come back to the city and stand before the tribunal for the death of the soldier you killed. I will state to the tribunal, however, what you have done to help Nada escape from Girard," said Darec as sternly as he could in his steadily weakening state.

Jacq's face paled and he slumped down as if his breath had been knocked out of him. "No matter what I do, no matter what I say, it always happens that I am punished. If I try to do good I am punished," he whined.

"You are punished for the error in your ways, not for the good you do. Continue on this new path and I will help you when you are presented to the tribunal," replied Darec.

Jacq looked at Carlotte as he rubbed the back of his neck and shoulders to ease the tension there, "I will try, for you, Carlotte."

"What of you, Darec, will you be able to travel?" asked Elieana.

"I will have to. If you can bind my shoulder tightly, I should be all right." He took a deep breath, closed his eyes and continued. "We will travel to Girona and then by boat to Pelagos, as Rodolph suggests. Perhaps we will be in time to warn the King before an invasion occurs."

"I will accompany you to Girona with two of my most trusted friends of the Wirliang, said Rodolph. "I believe now is the time for them to make the King aware of their presence. Perhaps if we all work together there will be some benefit for them, perhaps the King will reward their assistance with a place above ground where they will be able to raise their children and their race will again thrive."

"It is decided then," said Darec, "When can we be away?"

"In one day's time," replied Rodolph. "I will ask the Wirliang to prepare for our departure. In the meantime, Jacq and I must go to the surface and repair the damage done to the pool when the Sangan soldiers sealed you in. We must make it appear you escaped using a route off the mountain rather than going deep underground. We do not want the Sangans to discover this cavern as it will have dire consequences for the Wirliang.

"We will take our leave from you now. Perhaps, Carlotte, you will take our guests on a short tour of the cavern. You may then take your ease near the lake and return at your leisure to your sleeping room. One of the Wirliang will come to you later with your evening meal."

"I will stay here," said Darec, and he lay back on the cushions and closed his eyes.

Rodolph nodded his head towards the doorway, for the others to leave. "I will have someone watch over him while you are out," he said to Elieana. "Have no fear, he will be in good hands."

Elieana looked back at Darec, who had already fallen asleep. She picked up his plate of food, set it on the table, patted his arm and followed Jacq and Carlotte out of the room.

CHAPTER 13

Rodolph and Jacq climbed up to the laying pool, then followed the pathway along the stream to the surface. They removed a good portion of the rocks from the cave mouth, taking care not to stir up the water and cause more silt to be carried below and then peered outside to view the damage, e trampled and shredded plants and the pool cloudy with mud. No armed guards remained outside. Seeing none they removed the remaining boulders and exited the cave.

It was late in the day. The setting sun colored the sky a brilliant peach. Small white puff-ball clouds studded the sky, each one stained in brilliant yellow, pink and apricot. Rodolph breathed deeply of the fresh air, enjoying this most favorite time of the day. The fresh air tempted him to sit down and relax for just a moment, but they didn't have time to waste before the sun set. He instructed Jacq to move some of the rocks inside the cave to hide the tunnel leading to the cavern. He wanted to ensure the soldiers' search for the fugitives moved down the mountain and away from the cave.

Jacq set to work moving the rocks further into the tunnel. He piled them up on one side until there remained just a small space for them to squeeze through before sealing it up. Rodolph waded through the pool and picked some of the crushed plants, placing them in the pouch hanging from his belt. He thought it best to leave the banks of the pool as they were to avoid more silt flowing into the laying pool below. He also didn't want the soldiers to notice that someone had been there other than the fugitives escaping down the mountain. They could not risk them discovering the Wirliang settlement.

"Is there anything more I can help with, Rodolph?" asked Jacq as he exited the cave.

"Yes, Jacq, wet your feet and then we will both leave our footprints in the mud near the cave. You have smaller feet than I, so you must do this twice."

They ran towards the nearby bushes, leaving a conspicuous trail leading away from the pool.

"I hope they do not have any trackers to read the signs," said Rodolph as they walked through the bushes. They circled around in a large arc until they came to the edge of a cliff. From there they carefully picked their way back to the entrance to the cave.

Jacq soaked his feet again and ran off, following the previous trail. His footprints overlapping the ones they left before, making it look as if three people ran away into the bushes. The color of the sky had already faded to grey by the time Jacq reached the cliff, but he still had a few moments to enjoy the spectacular view of the mountains and valleys before him. Regretfully he turned his back on the sight and walked back to the cave while he still had enough light to see.

As he returned to the cave he saw, in the distance, a flock of birds, rising into the evening sky. He watched only for a moment then ran as fast as he could back to the cave and the safety of the tunnel. He ducked inside and hoped he hadn't been seen, he then peered out from the darkness of the cave to count how many birds flew. There were twenty-five already in the air and as he watched another group took flight, flying in his direction, all silhouetted against the fading bluish gray of the evening sky. He didn't wait to see if any others took flight but ran further back in the tunnel where he found Rodolph holding a small torch, waiting for him.

Out of breath and panting from his run, his heart raced at the thought of the huge birds flying closer each second. "Rodolph, you must dowse the light. There are birds flying this way. They will smell the smoke."

Rodolph smothered the torch in the gravelly sand at the edge of the stream. "Quickly now," Rodolph said, "We must fill in the final part of the tunnel before they arrive. Jacq nodded, his breath coming in ragged gasps. He guided Rodolph towards the narrow crack he left for them to return to the cave. Squeezing through the opening they piled up the rest of the rocks and moved as fast as they could back down to the cavern. From the opposite side, it looked like the stream ran down under the rocks, disappearing into the mountain.

"They were terrifying, but fascinating," Jacq told Elieana when they arrived back in the cavern.

“Yes, you are so right, Jacq,” replied Elieana, determined to be pleasant to him. “Terrifying to behold when they attacked us upon the mountain top.”

“The sheer size and number of those birds could devastate a city or an army,” said Jacq.

"If they are on the move now I think we should leave here as soon as possible," said Rodolph.

"I agree," replied Elieana. "I will let Darec sleep until we are ready to leave."

"We have a cart and dilhaa he can ride in," replied Rodolph. "He can rest and regain his strength as we travel."

Elieana nodded, thankful for the man's help and within a few hours they were ready to leave.

Carlotte did not want to leave, she had nowhere else in the world to go but as Jacq was leaving with Darec and Elieana she agreed to leave with him. Jacq told Carlotte, in private, after they met with Darec and Elieana that he needed to help them. He wanted to make his life right. He wanted to fix the things he had done wrong. She had her doubts that the honorable determination Jacq now had would reward him in any way. Carlotte was convinced the dungeon awaited him for the death of the soldier or, possibly, death for treason but as he had his mind made up she would go with him to help him in any way she could. After all, he had helped her escape from her life of servitude with Mathilde. She thought that one act extraordinary.

Although fearful of the consequences he faced upon returning to Pelagos, Jacq hoped he could do enough good that all charges against him would be forgiven. He didn’t tell

Carlotte, but, he was doing it for her. She already helped him more than she could know. If he faced only punishment but not death, then he planned to ask her to be his wife. He did not tell her this because if it happened he should be put to death he didn't want her to grieve for him as her husband. Jacq had another reason for wanting to go back, his self-respect. Girard and his men treated him like a worm. What better way to show he was not a worm, by showing his integrity?

Rodolph led the dilhaa and cart, now loaded with provisions and a thick mattress for Darec to rest upon, to the building where he rested. Although his injuries were not life threatening and the healing powers of the waters prevented further infection he remained weak and listless. The Wirliang confirmed Elieana's suspicion that poison covered the arrow tips, slowing the healing.

Assisted by Rodolph, Elieana spoke with the Wirliang's version of a healer. They exchanged remedies and discussed various plants and herbs, surprising Elieana that they used so many similar treatments. The Wirliang fascinated Elieana; their skin looked as if it had two layers; an outer, translucent covering and then a shimmering liquidity beneath. She wanted to learn more from them. She left their cavern full of regret but determined to return once they revealed this whole business of Antonia's kidnapping by Vasilis; returned Nada to her rightful place as the daughter to the King of Baltica; and averted any attack by the Sangans. It would be a great hardship for her to be parted from Nada but perhaps if she helped the Wirliang she could heal from the loss of her daughter.

A movement behind her interrupted Elieana's brooding thoughts. She turned around and saw Darec hobbling towards the cart, assisted by two Wirliang. He climbed aboard and lay down on the thick, soft mattress with a deep sigh of relief, as if he had not rested for a very long time. It pained her to see him so weak, Darec helped them so much with his strength and courage. He lay in the cart bed looking back at her, his face devoid of expression, causing Elieana to turn away so he could not see the concern on her face.

The Wirlean healer gave her some stone bottles full of the fresh, clean water from the laying pool. She told her of its very strong healing powers and instructed Elieana to cleanse Darec's wounds and make him drink it. The Wirlean healer told her Darec's recovery would take time because of the poison in his body.

Rodolph and gave Elieana a small packet of plants. "These are from the pool above. I collected them when Jacq and I went to seal the tunnel. You must crush them thoroughly, mixing them with the water from the pool then apply the paste to Darec's wounds. The leaves will draw any poison. You will see that by the time you reach Girona he will have reached near complete recovery."

Elieana nodded as she listened intently to what he said. She knew of herbs that produced rapid healing but not like what he claimed these herbs would produce.

"Why did the Wirlean healer not tell me of them?"

"They protect their knowledge and their healing from outsiders. They do not trust humans, which is the reason why they live as they do. It will take a very long time to gain their trust and their knowledge of these things. The healer told you only part of what she knows. Not until she is confident you are completely trustworthy will she impart all her knowledge to you."

"But what of the fact we know where they live and that they exist?" exclaimed Elieana, louder than she meant to speak. A few heads turned in their direction. Rodolph's mouth curved down in displeasure.

"I'm sorry, Rodolph, my enthusiasm sometimes gets the better of me," she said quietly. "If they trust us to know where they live is that not enough?"

"They have many places where they live underground. These mountains are riddled with caverns. If they feel their settlement is in danger of being discovered, they will leave. No trace of their presence would remain, as if they never existed. Remember, two of the Wirliang males are accompanying us to Girona. A message will be sent immediately to the settlement if there is danger.

"They do not want to share their knowledge with the outside world unless there is an agreement to allow them to live as they did in the past, on the surface and without fear of being persecuted or hunted for their female's skin. Their knowledge of healing far surpasses any known on the surface. They believe if they keep their knowledge safe then at least they have some bargaining tool. Now you must use the herb paste and apply it again to Darec's wounds when next you change his bandages."

Elieana nodded and tucked the package inside her jerkin. She reached out and squeezed Rodolph's arm. "I thank you, Rodolph, you have been very kind and most patient with a woman with a most disagreeable temper." She smiled at him and he returned it.

"Think nothing of it. Now come, we must leave shortly. I want to reach the surface before the moon rises. If the bird soldiers are on the move it is best for us to travel under the cover of darkness."

They paid their respects to the Wirliang assembled at the entrance to the cavern and then one by one they were swallowed up by the gaping tunnel. Two Wirliang accompanied the party, one at the front and one at the rear. Elieana looked back into the cavern before she entered the tunnel and waved to the group of Wirliang assembled there. She did not want to leave them. She now felt a strong sense of responsibility to these creatures and a huge sense of loss. Her heart clenched in her chest as she entered the tunnel to follow the wagon.

Carlotte perched on the seat of the wagon beside Jacq, Antonia on his other side. Rodolph walked ahead, leading the dilhaa. Elieana caught up to the cart and hopped into the wagon bed with Darec. His eyes were open, but he faced the side of the wagon as if he didn't want to talk so Elieana sat looking backwards towards the slowly shrinking opening to the cavern. She sat alone with her thoughts as they rode upward to the surface. She reached up to her pocket and patted the packet of leaves inside, hoping if she followed Rodolph's instructions Darec would soon regain his strength.

CHAPTER 14

Peter arrived at Jorian's house after taking a circuitous route through the city. He saw no one he knew, making him rest easy. As he approached Jorian's door he glanced around to ensure no one nearby watched, then he rapped softly. He heard a quick sound of footsteps inside then Jorian's wife, Mia, opened the door. Her small face was framed by a mass of short, dark, curly hair. Small of build and very thin she wore loose-fitting white trousers and a long blue tunic, giving the appearance of a much younger woman. A small boy, about five years of age, graced with his mother's looks, peeped around from behind her. She looked young and if one did not know they were mother and son they could have been mistaken for a much older sister and young brother.

"Come in Peter," she whispered as she peered outside into the street then grasped him by the arm and pulled him inside. Mia closed the door quietly. "We must keep our voices down," she whispered, "There are people in the next house who may hear. Jorian has told me what has happened at the castle and in the city. He has told me to go with you and stay away until he comes for me. We are ready but have only a small sack with some extra clothing. Will that be enough; do you think?"

"Yes, my dear," answered Peter as he patted the small boy on the head. "Do you have something warm in the sack for your young man? The sea may be cool at night."

"I have packed a water proof cape with a hood he can wear," replied Mia.

"Where are we going, mama?" asked Joel.

"We are going fishing with Peter. Won't that be fun?" replied Mia with joviality that seemed odd to Peter but then he thought perhaps she was just trying to reassure her young son.

She wrapped a scarf around her hair then picked up the sack with their clothing in it. "Jorian came just a little while ago. He told me you would explain once we get onto your boat. Please let us go quickly. What he has told me of the murders in the city have frightened me for the safety of our son," Mia whispered to Peter as she opened the door.

Peter squeezed her arm and nodded then he lifted Joel up onto his shoulders and they walked companionably through the side streets, hoping to avoid meeting any of the soldiers who knew them. Once they reached the main thoroughfare, leading towards the castle and in view of the city gate, Peter put Joel down and grasped his hand before he could run off into the crowd.

"Peter," said Mia, "I will walk a few steps ahead of you. If the soldiers stop me when I go through the gate, then hide in one of the alleys.

"Mama, where are you going?" asked Joel sounding worried that his mother would leave him.

"Shush now, Joel, you must be brave today. We cannot go onto the boat if you are not brave." She patted his cheek and kissed him. "I will see you in the fishing village. You go with Peter. Let him talk to the soldiers. You pretend you cannot speak, like the beggar on the corner of the market street. It will be our game. Do you think you can do that?"

Joel nodded his head excitedly for this game, his curls bouncing back and forth wildly. He wrapped his arms around his mother's neck and gave her a very large kiss on the cheek, making a loud smacking noise. "I will, mama. It will be a game, right? The one who does not speak for the longest time wins, right?"

"That's right, my sweet," said Mia as she wiped the spittle from Joel's kiss off her cheek. "Now, watch me go through the gate. I will see you in the village and when you get there we will look at all the big fat fish and guess which one we will have for dinner."

Joel smiled, nodding his head happily. The game had begun. Determined not to speak, because he surely wanted to win, he kept his lipped pressed tightly together. Joel watched his mother weave her way through the crowds at the gate. She stopped for a moment, looked back at Joel and Peter and then let herself be carried along with the throng passing through on their way to the village.

Peter and Joel followed behind the crowd gathered at the gate. One of the soldiers recognized Peter and nodded to him then waved him through. He did not question why Peter had the young boy with him.

When they passed through the gate Peter hoisted Joel onto his shoulders again. They wandered down the road, Peter amusing Joel by dipping and swerving around the other people walking towards the village. Passersby frowned at him and waved him away as he interfered with their passage on the roadway. No matter to Peter, he wanted to appear he had not a worry in the world, what better way than to amuse the young boy in his care. He would have preferred if Joel did not have the determination of his father. He didn't let out one squeal of delight. Instead he kept a very tight grip on Peter's hair and his mouth firmly closed, intent on winning the game. His stifled giggles as Peter swerved back and forth in the crowd, the only indication he was enjoying himself.

It occurred to Peter, when Jorian made his request, that a great many people would be on their way to the fish market, affording them very good cover for his plan of getting Nada, Mia and Joel to safety. Peter enjoyed the task, happy he could help. Spending time with lively young people certainly kept his mind off his own worries.

Peter spun Joel around as he walked, so he could see if anyone followed them. He thought, at one point, a short, fat man watched them but when he spun back a second time the man had melted into the crowd. Peter took a long, roundabout way to get to the main street in the village. When they arrived, he put Joel down and they walked together, stopping to look at all the dried fish hanging above the tables in the market and the various fresh ones laid out on display.

An enormous Nimrod fish lay across one table, its huge mouth gaping wide revealed rows of sharp, angular teeth. A smaller fish lay stuffed inside the Nimrod's mouth. Immediately Joel exclaimed loudly, "Oh, look," when he saw it. Surprised that he spoke aloud Joel clapped his hand over his mouth.

"Never fear, my young friend," said Peter, "It will be our secret."

Joel nodded, keeping his mouth clamped tightly shut, his eyes sparkling with joy at this game.

Such a happy child, Peter thought as they rounded a corner in the village, almost bumping into the fat man he saw earlier. The man was sweating profusely and mopping his face with a large, soiled handkerchief. He was unkempt, a day's scraggily stubble covered his chin. He surreptitiously looked over his shoulder and reached into his pocket. Peter stepped around the man and said, "Come, grandson, let us go visit grannie."

Joel tugged on Peter's arm as they walked past the man, but Peter pulled him along so that Joel had to run to keep up.

"But Peter, I am not your grandson," whispered Joel loudly.

"Yes, I know," whispered Peter.

"And you do not have a wife," Joel whispered.

"Yes, you are right, Joel," said Peter.

"Then why did you say that to me," said Joel.

Peter looked over his shoulder. The fat man had stepped around the corner of the building they just passed and peered back at them. Peter hoped he did not hear this exchange.

"Joel, there are bad men in the city these days. I did not want the man to speak to you."

"Oh," was all Joel said, and then he piped up. "Is that why my daddy went away with those men this morning?"

"What men were those, Joel?"

"Four of them, soldiers but not soldiers from the city. They wore green and black jerkins with an animal on one side. I asked my daddy who they were, and he shushed me and sent me to my room, then he left. It was just before you came to take me and mama away."

"I don't know who those men might be, Joel," Peter lied. "Perhaps they are from the city of Belisle, you know the King will be here for the wedding of his adopted son."

"What's 'dopted mean," asked Joel who suddenly clamped his lips tight, having forgotten they were still playing their game.

Peter pulled at the neck of his shirt, feeling quite warm and uncomfortable now. He glanced back and forth, nervously, certain the fat man still watched them. He bent down and looked directly into Joel's little face, holding gently onto his shoulders.

"Joel, do you know what my boat looks like?"

Joel nodded, sending his dark curls flopping loosely around his face.

"I think that fat man is a bad man. I want you to run to my boat as fast as you can. Do not talk to anyone. Do not stop until you get to the boat. Go inside and wait for me. There will be a girl there, her name is Nada. Can you do that for me?"

Joel vigorously nodded again.

"Then be off with you. Run now. Tell Nada and your mother I will be there shortly," Peter patted Joel on the head and gave him a little push in the direction he wanted him to go. As soon as he sent Joel on his way to the boat Peter walked back in the direction from which he had come. He saw no sign of the fat, sweaty man. With the throng of people in the fish market he doubted he would find the man if he didn't want to be found. He inquired at some of the stalls, but no one had noticed this stranger. Shrugging his shoulders Peter thought perhaps it was just his imagination. The man may have been looking for someone and wanted to ask directions. He shook his head in disgust and spoke in a whisper to himself, "You are just being suspicious, Peter, because of this errand."

Normally a helpful soul it was out of character for Peter to be suspicious and think ill of anyone. Convinced that coincidence brought the man across their path he walked back towards the end of the street where he moored his boat. He took his time, looking here and there, making small conversation with a few of his old friends. He purchased a few vegetables at one stall and a large stone bottle of ale from another along with a nice fat fish, a lovely feast for them, once they had the boat underway.

The boat gently rocked on its moorings when Peter arrived and neither Nada nor Joel were on the deck. He shrugged, thinking they were below. He lifted the hatch cover. No candle burned in the lamp hanging on the wall, leaving it completely dark. This seemed very odd but then Nada did not know her way around to find a flint. Mia had not arrived either so perhaps, he thought, Nada sat in darkness. This annoyed

Peter, an unusual feeling for him, but the situation seemed so strange he felt out of sorts and thought at least she could have lit one candle rather than sit there in the dark.

Peter started to climb down the ladder, his sack of purchases bumping against the rungs. Upon reaching the bottom rung he heard a shuffling noise but before he had time to turn around something hit him on the back of the head. Peter Bondar fell, coming to rest in a sprawled heap, knocked senseless.

The smell of sweat permeated the small landing at the bottom of the ladder. The fat man from the market dropped the belaying pin he hit Peter with. He mopped his face with his handkerchief then blew his nose then someone unceremoniously shoved him aside. Mia gave Peter a little nudge with her foot then she pulled the scarf off her head letting her black curls fall to her shoulders. "It's stifling hot down here. Find some rope to bind his hands," she said. Her tone matching the sneer she directed at the fat man.

"Well, Bela don't just stand there, find some rope." She mopped her face with the scarf while she watched Bela bind Peter's hands and feet. "Where is my son?" she demanded, suddenly remembering he should be with Peter.

"I saw him with Bondar in the market street. I thought they were still together," said Bela.

"Well, unfortunately we don't have time to wait, we must leave immediately. I am sure Jorian will be there to take care of him. Help me with this," she nudged Peter's inert body again with her toe. "Once we are out of sight of the village we will throw him overboard."

Mia pushed open a door to a closet and the two shoved Peter's body inside. After they finished Bela stood still for a moment, leaning on the wall and breathing heavily.

"Get us underway now before someone comes asking questions," said Mia angrily.

Bela scowled at her. Mia picked up the sack of food Peter dropped when he fell. She found the bottle of ale, cool and damp with condensation. She placed the cool bottle up against her face then opened it and took a long drink then she wiped her mouth with her scarf. Bela gazed longingly at the bottle, licking his lips.

"None for you until we are under way; we have a meeting with my father, and I do not want to be late," said Mia.

Bela's lips pursed angrily, puffing out his breath with a loud huff as he climbed up the ladder.

Mia pushed open the door to the boat's tiny cabin and looked down at Nada, tied hands and feet and laying on Peter's berth which was built into a nook in the wall. A mean looking smile stretched across Mia's once pleasant face. "My father will be very happy to see you," said Mia. "After all the searching throughout the city and here you are; fallen right into my lap like a nice, ripe apple."

"Who is your father, or do I really want to know?" replied Nada, trying very hard to keep calm.

"Why, Girard, of course," replied Mia contemptuously looking down her nose at Nada. "Did not Jorian ever tell anyone in the city my father is Girard?" she smiled insincerely at Nada and laughed.

Nada struggled to free herself. Mia laughed again, then kicked her leg. "Stop wiggling. You are not going anywhere."

"Why are you doing this?" said Nada angrily. "You are Jorian's wife. Why?" As soon as she asked the question she realized she sounded like a child whining. She shut her mouth tightly, determined not to say anything more.

"What? Did not Jorian tell you everything when you and he sat waiting for the tide? Did he not tell you my father, Girard, told him to take you?"

"Yes, he did but he told me he was wrong and that he would help get me to safety. He told Peter he wanted to get you and your son to safety as well," replied Nada now fearing that Jorian tricked her into trusting him and that her first thoughts were right when she saw him talking to the guards. Maybe he couldn't be trusted.

"Well of course he wanted us safe, there is to be an attack on the city," she sneered. "Of course, he wanted his son safe, but Joel never got on the boat with Peter and unfortunately we have to leave." Mia said this without a care or concern for her son. "We have no time to wait. Bela is getting the boat under way now."

"How can you leave without ensuring the safety of your son? What of all the innocent people in the city who will be hurt?" Nada exclaimed, astonished at Mia's callousness.

"Oh, please," replied Mia, her impatience showing very clearly.

Nada sat up abruptly, pulled herself forward and tried to stand up. "How do you know there is to be an attack? Who told you?" she demanded. "How can you leave your son?" she said.

"Oh, you stupid girl," Mia sneered, "I will not tell you everything?" Mia slapped Nada in the face, spun on her heel and stomped out of the cabin, slamming the door behind her.

Shortly after Mia left Nada heard a loud thump on the side of the boat and voices, men's voices. Jorian, she thought, disgusted, come to join his wife in safety while his comrades in arms fight against a new enemy. Anger grew in Nada's breast and she struggled harder to free herself. She must get away and warn the people in the city.

The discussion above stopped abruptly with the sound of a child crying. The crying became loud and insistent then stopped. Nada heard scuffling feet and at the same time the boat lurched, and she realized it was pulling away from the dock. Grimly Nada worked harder on the ropes binding her wrists. She scraped them against the rough wood of one of the supporting beams of the bed. Despair welled up inside her, what could she do to help the innocent people of the city? She knew the stories of war. Enemy soldiers gave no quarter.

The boat rocked and lurched then shuddered as the sails caught the wind and it leapt forward. Nada imagined what it must look like from the deck, the boat pulling past the other gaily colored boats as it headed out of the harbor. She remembered the first time she sailed on Peter's boat. Philen at the helm; the wind whipping their hair and laughing at the sight of the billowing sails and the speed with which the boat sailed out of the protected bay.

She was trapped with nowhere to go and was rapidly losing the opportunity to get off the boat before it got into deep water. The door opened a crack then, and a soldier stuck his head in. He nodded but didn't say anything to her then closed the door. Spurred on by her anger Nada rubbed the ropes even harder. How dare Jorian, she thought, tricking her into believing him? She blamed him for the injury to Aldred and all the other events that occurred in recent days. She blamed him for the loss of Darec and Elieana, for surely, she thought, they were lost having not returned. He even convinced some of his own men to help him in this plot, she thought and angrily kicked the wall.

The sound of the water rushing past the hull of the boat told her that her chance to jump off the boat and swim to the shore was nearly gone. Tied up and laying on the bed she could not see out of the tiny porthole above her head to see which way they headed. In any event the porthole was too small for her to squeeze through. Her only escape route, to climb up the ladder to the deck and jump overboard, if she could free herself in time. Determined to get off at her first opportunity she worked harder on breaking the rope tied around her wrists. After much scraping, the last strands snapped. She hurriedly untied the bindings on her ankles then stood up on the bed and peered outside. The porthole glass, filmed with dried salt, allowed her to see only shadowy images of land in the distance. At least now she knew they headed south towards Girona.

She knew Girona was a medium sized fishing town. She and Elieana had been there once but did not stay long. The people there did not welcome strangers. Well, they could do nothing about whether the people liked strangers or not and she didn't know if Mia and Jorian's plan was to go all the way to Girona or stop at some point along the coast. Whatever Mia and Jorian planned Nada had no intention of being a part of it. Becoming even more suspicious she wondered then about Peter's involvement. It angered her that Peter had spoken with Jorian and Jorian and Mia were now on the boat together. She realized from this tangled web of deceit and lies she could not really trust anyone.

She climbed off the bed, careful to make no noise, then quietly opened the door of the cabin. No one stood outside the door, so she pushed it open just wide enough to squeeze through then glanced up at the closed hatch above. Just as she started to climb the ladder she heard footsteps crossing the deck. The person stopped, and a faint line of light shone through as they opened the hatch. Nada lunged for a door across the small hallway and leapt inside. Something soft moved under her feet causing her stomach to flip sickeningly. She reached down and felt the rough wool of a sweater on someone's torso. She jumped back off the body and fell hard against the wall. Covering her mouth tightly she swallowed her scream before it burst out of her mouth. She moved her feet, so they straddled the body. The person moaned. She tried to calm herself, thankful the person was not dead. Suddenly, she felt very guilty, thinking it might be Peter, and for jumping to conclusions about the kindly man's intentions. Nada grasped the person's shoulders and shook them. "Peter, is it you?" she whispered.

The snuffling noise sounded again along with a low groan then the person sat up. “Yes, it’s me," whispered Peter groggily. "They hit me on the head, I have a terrible headache,” he moaned. “Nada, you must hide yourself. Crawl into the space behind me so they will not find you. Go now," he rasped out. "I hear someone coming down the ladder.”

Nada stepped over Peter and into the narrow space at the back of the closet. Her shoulders rubbed against the wall on each side. There was only enough room to crawl in the tiny space running parallel to the side of the boat. She knew the boat had a tank for storing Peter’s catch. Thinking perhaps she could find a way out, nearby the tank, she kept crawling until she came up to a wooden wall, sealed with pitch from the feel and smell of it. This must be the fish tank, she thought. The pitch waterproofed the tank, so water could be pumped in to keep the fish alive.

It was cool and very dark by the tank. She could hear the swishing of the water on the hull of the boat as it moved through the water. It was quiet. She couldn’t hear any water sloshing around inside the tank. It suddenly occurred to her she could hear no noise from above either. No one moved overhead; she could hear no sound of people talking or yelling. Bewildered she crawled around the outside of the tank to see if she could find a place to climb up and maybe hear what was taking place above. She found a small opening near the top of the tank and peered inside, expecting to see fish or at least water, but instead saw Bela and Mia sitting inside the dry tank. Both had their hands tied behind their backs, but their feet were free, and Mia was kicking Bela as hard as she could. Nada couldn't believe her eyes. She thought Jorian had been a part of Mia's plan to kidnap her. Hadn't Mia said so? Perhaps Jorian told the truth when he said he would take care of her and not betray her.

Suddenly she heard a loud shout and footsteps, running back towards the hatch leading below deck. A door slammed, and she heard more shouting announcing they had discovered Peter. She felt better for it, Peter needed help to get out of the small closet where they stuffed him. It also helped her feel a little less guilty for stepping on his chest.

She heard the tank lid slide back and Nada peeped through the crack again. Someone demanded the two captives tell them where they had hidden Nada. Mia spat at whoever spoke. The man shouted down at her that he certainly would not try to help the likes of her when they returned to Pelagos. It was hard to tell who spoke but then the man said something more, "By cracken," and she recognized Philen's voice. He always said that when he was angry but didn't want to say something foul.

Nada knew that Philen would never turn traitor; he must be there to help her. She scrambled around and crawled, as fast as she could, back to the door in the back of the closet. She pushed it open and crawled out, relieved to finally stand up. She stretched her back after being cramped up in the fish tank and then climbed up the ladder, pushed open the hatch and stepped up onto the deck.

The intense sunlight almost blinded her as she pulled herself up onto the broiling wooden deck of the boat. She hopped from foot to foot to keep the soles of her feet from burning then glanced towards the bow and saw Peter, Jorian and Philen staring at her. A large bandage, spotted with blood, covered most of Peter's head. He looked pale but appeared to be none the worse for wear. Peter motioned for her to join them. She slowly walked towards them, not entirely sure she could trust them not to grab her and throw her back down into the stuffy cabin below.

Philen took a blanket from a box on the deck and wrapped it around her shoulders, it smelled like fish and tar, but she welcomed its warmth. Despite the heat of the day it felt good to have something comforting to wrap around her body. Nada looked at the three men then said, "You must explain what has happened. I can't guess myself because, Jorian, I suspected you were deeply involved in this with Mia.

"Peter, I am sorry, I wasn't sure of your allegiance. When Mia grabbed me and threw me into the cabin. I thought for sure I had been tricked. So much has happened lately I am not sure who to trust."

Jorian ran his fingers through his hair and shook his head, new lines of worry beside his mouth marred his normally cheerful face. "These things that have happened, I blame myself for," said Jorian. "I must tell you how it is I met Mia. After a battle, weary, thirsty and hungry she brought us water and food. We moved out the next day and she followed along with the other camp followers. She had no one. She told me all her family had been slaughtered. We grew to be friends, good friends, lovers. Joel came along a year later so when the war ended we married and came to Pelagos.

"The day we found you on the beach with those two people I also discovered Mia's father lived. As I told you before we met him on the sea wall but later he came to our house, alone and very secretive. It didn't take long to discover he was the assassin behind many a killing. Darec and I have crossed his path many times, never catching him, always one step behind. I understood why we never caught him, after we met him. Mia knew her father lived and when she heard of any reference to our search for him she passed secret messages to him, helping him to always be one step ahead of us. This time, however, he threatened us both and our child, another game Girard and his daughter played. When I think on it now she has always been devious.

"Girard wanted me to surrender you to him. I was ready to do this, no matter the cost, for the sake of my son. You understand, do you not?" his voice held a pleading tone, his face showing his grief and guilt.

"Why did you change your mind, Jorian?" asked Nada quietly.

"Only last night, when we spoke, while we waited for the tide. So much has happened in such a short time." He shook his head in disbelief. "I realized I must do whatever I could to capture Girard and to keep you safe. Philen helped. He watched for the right moment. We knew you were on the boat, but we had to wait until everyone arrived because Peter and Joel separated. Bela followed them from the city, so Peter sent Joel on by himself. Joel stopped to look at the fish in the market and arrived after Peter."

"I think, if Bela had his way, he would have left me for dead in one of the alleyways," responded Peter. "I am a very fortunate man I have a very hard head."

"I am sorry, my friend, Peter, I mistrusted you," said Nada very quietly. "You knew of Jorian's plan?" she asked but it seemed more of a statement.

"No," replied Peter. "Jorian did not share his plans with me. A good thing too, I have difficulty keeping a secret. Surprised am I, to discover Mia has such a dark side to her."

"Where is Joel now?" asked Nada. "I heard him just before the boat left the dock. Is he not on board?"

"You heard him screeching in indignation, I am afraid," said Jorian. "He looked forward very much to sailing this ship, as he calls it. When I said, he must remain with Aldred he let me know, in no uncertain terms, he would not be put ashore. I believe he is below in the galley with a piece of fresh buttered bread in each hand. He is a very determined young boy and likes to get his way, often. From now on I must work hard on his temper."

Nada smiled at Jorian and then looked out towards the land slipping away. The brisk breeze filled their sails and carried them along in a southerly direction, leaving Pelagos behind. Nada looked around the boat and saw other soldiers on deck she hadn't noticed previously. She didn't know any of them, they looked to be of Jorian's age except for one who stood with his back to her. When the soldier turned around and looked across the deck at her, she recognized him. Liam, the soldier who carried her into the Palace of Justice. She smiled, then blushed and put her head down, wrapping the blanket tighter around her shoulders. "Where do we go now Jorian? Do we turn the boat around, go back to Pelagos?" asked Nada.

"No, we go to Girona," said Jorian. "It is not safe in the castle. Mia told us there is to be an attack."

"But we must warn the people."

Jorian's countenance grew dark and deep furrows seamed his brow. "I have warned those who would listen. I told Aldred of the secret passage you showed me and if she needs to escape she will do so. We first must deliver to Girard the prize his daughter has promised."

Abruptly Nada stood up and glared at him.

"No, Nada." He motioned for her to sit down. "What he won't be expecting is my surprise. Have no fear, I have no intention of handing you over to him. We will take Mia to him instead. They both have earned each other's company." A very disagreeable sneer spread across Jorian's face. He felt only contempt now when he spoke of Mia. She had endangered their son and betrayed Jorian to her father. She knew Jorian and Darec searched long and worked hard to capture Girard and Mia was the reason they were never successful.

"Tell me," said Nada. She hadn't meant this as a command, but it sounded like one.

"I have a little surprise for Girard. We proceed towards Girona. I sent a messenger to Girard that you will be at the rendezvous point."

"Me? You are going to take me to Girard?" she exclaimed, and her face burned with anger. She readied herself to run although she didn't know where to run except off the boat and at this point they were some distance from land and in deep water.

"No, no, not you, I will disguise Mia as you. She will go in your place. Do not worry, I will send the right person to Girard and it will not be you. The rendezvous point is a small chapel in the foothills, a few leagues from Girona. A trail leads to it from the coast and then continues into the mountains. Mia will be bound and gagged. She will not warn whoever comes to take their prize. Girard will get his daughter back. I believe he will send Arturo, his most trusted man, rather than go there himself. We cannot take the chance of being there when he discovers it is Mia and not you."

"But Jorian, how can you do this? Mia is your wife, the mother of your son," said Nada sadly.

"Mia has betrayed me many times. I have only just discovered the extent of that betrayal. When Girard arrived at my home she did not spare me the details of that betrayal. She is no longer my wife." His face looked like granite, hard, immovable. The love he once had for Mia quenched as a flame doused with water when she revealed the extent of her deceit. He would not change his mind. His life, as he knew it, had completely shattered.

Jorian had his son, and now he must always be on guard. Girard and Mia would search for the boy and take him. Jorian would have preferred Mia's death but this he could not do. He believed now, if it came to a choice between her father or himself, she would choose her father.

After Jorian told them of his plan he became silent and brooding. Nada pulled the blanket more snugly around her shoulders and lifted her face toward the sun. She closed her eyes and let the heat melt the chill she felt from Jorian's words, the heat seeping into her bones. As she relaxed some of her worries melted away. She remained silent but opened her eyes and watched the coastline change from flat lowland to rolling hills and then to craggy rock cliffs with tiny inlets along the way to give shelter in a storm. Sea birds, from time to time, came and hovered alongside the boat but seeing no sign of a meal they squawked loudly and flew off in their hunt for food.

They passed smaller boats, some operated only by a tiller at the back. The person at the tiller worked hard, especially when the wake of their much larger boat hit them. The occupants of the smaller boats, most of them children, waved and shouted out greetings. How brave or reckless they were to be out on the deep water in those rickety boats, knowing sea beasts swam below.

Nada daydreamed about how strange it would be to live your whole life upon a boat, to always have the rocking movement of the sea beneath your feet.

The sound of metal hitting the deck caught her attention. She opened her eyes and watched as the soldiers shed their weapons and any gear identifying them as soldiers. Peter moved to the stern to instruct them in the proper way to throw the nets. She overheard him say they should at least appear to be fishing so as not to raise suspicion, but also to pass the time as they traveled south, and if they caught anything it would add to their meager rations. The soldiers were very much out of their element as far as bringing in a catch. No matter, they could not store any fish as Bela and Mia still occupied the tank.

Philen, being the only one with some experience, besides Peter, took over the helm while Peter showed the soldiers how to pull in the nets. The soldiers hauled in a large assortment of small fish with a few large ones mixed in. As they sorted through the catch, saving the large ones and throwing the small ones back, Peter went below to the galley, calling over his shoulder, "When the fish are ready bring them to me and I will fry them up for our dinner." The men nodded to his receding back and turned to their work, sorting the fish. One of the men took out a large knife and busied himself at the stern, scraping off the scales, gutting the fish and throwing the entrails over the side of the boat.

“Is there a danger of the sea beasts in these waters, Philen?” asked Nada after she saw the soldier throw the offal into the sea.

“Yes, Nada, but don’t worry. We are only catching a small amount of fish. They will not be attracted by us,” replied Philen.

“What about the entrails of the fish the soldiers catch, if they are thrown into the sea?” she asked, moving closer to Philen.

Philen looked toward the stern. His face drained of color when he saw the soldier dumping the entrails over the side. He shouted for him to stop and immediately spun the wheel towards shore. The boat shuddered. The sails flapped as he turned the boat, then caught the wind again, turning the boat sharply.

Peter stuck his head up through the hatch, exclaiming loudly, "What are you doing that for? The galley is upside down."

Nada could see only his head stuck out of the hatch and she stifled a giggle as he looked like a small animal popping its head out of a hole. She covered her mouth and put her head down, not wanting Peter to see her laughing. The smile froze on her face when a loud warbling screech sounded behind the boat. As one, they all looked towards the stern as a long sinuous neck, streaming with water and writhing wildly, scooped up the entrails of the fish floating on the surface of the water.

"Oh! Be still," whispered Peter as loudly as he dared, putting a finger to his lips to get everyone to be quiet. No one moved a muscle or uttered a word as the monster curved its neck and ugly head in their direction.

Nada shook uncontrollably, remembering what Jacq told her and Carlotte about the monster that attacked him. Philen had crouched out of sight and was tying the wheel in place. They needed to stay still and out of sight, so the monster would not notice them and pluck them off the deck. The enormous sea beast swam close to the boat and looked over the side. It matched the speed of the boat, making it appear as if they sat still in the water.

The soldier at the stern and Nada were the only ones still out in the open, the soldier, closer to the beast, with Nada a few feet behind him. She wondered if the beast could smell their fear. Nada tried to imagine herself to be even smaller.

Peter's head popped up again and with a great heave he threw their catch over the side, then just as quickly he disappeared. Better the sea beast had their dinner than becoming dinner themselves. The fish hit the water with a splat attracting the beast's attention. It moved towards the floating fish and busied itself with gathering them up, giving the boat a few more seconds to move closer to shallow water.

Nada needed only seconds to conceal herself. She scrambled as fast as she could towards the hatch and threw herself down through the opening head first. She landed heavily, bumped her head on the ladder and wrenched her arm so hard her hand went numb. She lay on the floor where she landed, trying to gather her wits. Suddenly the boat shuddered, leaning hard to one side; a loud, blood curdling shriek sliced the silence then instantly stopped. A chill snaked down Nada's spine causing her hair to stand on end, knowing one soldier and Philen remained on the deck.

"Which one did it take?" she cried out in anguish.

Jorian came out of the galley and pulled her into his arms. He held her close and patted her back as he rocked her back and forth. Not more than a few seconds later, footsteps sounded on the deck, and Philen looked down at them through the open hatch, the expression on his face grim. Nada looked up at him, frightened to hear who the creature snatched from the deck. "Who?" she stuttered.

"Bela," replied Philen. "He somehow got loose and stuck his head out of the fish bin just as the creature came back for more fish. It saw him and pulled him out. I think we won't see the creature again, nor will we see Bela."

CHAPTER 15

Near nightfall Peter anchored his boat in a small, sheltered bay. The water, rippled by a slight breeze, sparkled with the colors of the setting sun. Nada sat on an overturned box, her chin resting on her folded arms on the railing. The heat of the day radiating from the deck and her grief for the loss of a life and Jorian's decision about his wife had sapped her energy.

She watched as the small jon boat with Jorian and a soldier at the oars rowed towards the shore. Mia, gagged, tied and wrapped in a blanket from head to toe lay at Jorian's feet. When they reached the shore the two men jumped out, pulling the jon boat out of the water. The pebble strewn beach made walking difficult. Jorian stumbled once when he picked up his burden. He nodded grimly to the soldier then walked towards the forest without looking back.

A tear slid down Nada's cheek as she watched Jorian and the soldier disappear into the forest. The soldier walked in front, carrying a torch, with Jorian behind him carrying his burden draped over his shoulder. They would not return before morning; they had a long walk to the chapel.

Nada's heart ached for Jorian. After he told her Mia would take her place he didn't smile. She gazed up into the evening sky and thanked the Goddess little Joel did not know his mother had boarded the boat, thanked her that he slept soundly, without a care in the world, in Peter's cabin.

CHAPTER 16

A shadowy figure climbed the steeply winding trail leading to the small chapel at the crest of the hill. The figure had not left the security of the trees at the base of the hill until he saw both men return from the chapel, empty handed of their squirming burden. He smirked when he thought of the huge reward waiting for Girard and for himself when they presented the Princess to her father. This would more than make up for the catastrophe in Pelagos not so many days previously.

The man chuckled as he climbed. Mia's plan had gone better than expected. To have her husband bring the girl to this chapel suited him. Arturo considered Jorian no better than a servant. He thought of Mia as a fine woman and her talents wasted on her credulous husband. He let himself wonder if he could win her for himself and felt confident he could, after this. Jorian could be threatened and then do exactly what she wanted him to do. She needed a strong man, someone who could lead and step into her father's shoes when he no longer could lead himself.

Arturo stopped to rest, when he reached the chapel. He leaned against the wall to catch his breath and pulled off the dark mask concealing his face. He smiled and breathed deeply, catching a whiff of smoke. Thinking perhaps a fire burned in the forest somewhere nearby and not wanting to get caught in an inferno he covered his face again then entered the tiny chapel to retrieve his prize.

In the dim light of the waxing moon he could see the bound form of the girl, completely concealed from head to toe. She squirmed and fought as he bent to pick her up. She didn't speak. Probably gagged her as well, he thought.

"Rest easy, Princess," he said with a sneer, "It is not long now; soon you shall see your father again."

The bundle kicked and bucked in his arms making it very difficult to pick her up and sling her over his shoulder. He set his captive back down on the floor of the chapel and took out a small vial from his coat pocket. Uncorking the vial, he upturned it onto a piece of cloth. He pulled back the hood covering the girl's face and roughly applied the cloth to her mouth and nose. Slowly her kicks and struggles subsided. He covered her face again, then hoisted her up onto his shoulder and picked his way carefully in the inky darkness to where he hobbled his horse and dilhaa.

CHAPTER 17

A soft, dark evening sky greeted the small party of humans and Wirliangs as they emerged from the tunnel. Trees sap scented the air with the coming of the cool night and the sound of small lizards chirping welcomed them back to the surface. Surprised, Elieana expected daylight, having lost track of the hours, even in the short time they stayed in the Wirliang's domain. She looked back once to try and get her bearings, related to where they entered the underground tunnels from the plateau above, but could not pinpoint where they entered in relation to where they stood now. She shook her head then thankfully turned her back on the mountain. It didn't matter where they entered, she had no intention of returning to that plateau.

As they wound their way down the mountain Elieana reflected on everything that took place after they left Pelagos. Something niggled at the back of her brain as she thought about Antonia and Nada. There was something different about Antonia, but she could not think of what it might be. The woman sometimes appeared to be slightly unhinged but at times cool and collected and in total control of her thoughts. Some of that behaviour could very much have to do with the fact she secluded herself in the tower for such a long time. It made no matter whether she self-inflicted the seclusion or not.

It seemed strange Vasilis kept her there in the castle. What harm could she have been to him? After leaving Belisle Antonia could not have reunited with her husband. The puzzle of Antonia remained shrouded in mystery, but Elieana believed Antonia would reveal herself to them eventually. Elieana hoped, for Nada's sake, they would not be too shocked when they discovered what lay hidden under Antonia's unusual demeanor.

Nada too, seemed different at times but not dangerous, not like Antonia. It might help to speak to Darec about it. He would have learned much about the royal family while he trained in Belisle. Perhaps the whole family had something about them that set them apart from the rest of the population. Elieana rubbed her face and rolled her eyes, what was she thinking? How could she think Nada and Antonia were different, or strange, or unusual? They were no different than anyone else. So much had taken place in the short time since leaving Pelagos her imagination ran wild, putting crazy thoughts in her head.

She looked up at the stars and tried to calm herself. She focused her attention on the tiny pin pricks of bright, twinkling light, now visible in the night sky. The moon, looked like liquid silver, a sharp and shining blade hanging in the sky. As she watched, a wispy cloud moved across it, obscuring it from view so that only silver light shone out from the edges of the cloud. She shivered at how ominous it appeared and turned away, drawing her cloak tighter around her shoulders and focused her attention on the direction they traveled.

The Wirliang's strength surprised the humans as they proceeded down the rocky trail. The Wirliang at the front moved large rocks out of the path of the cart and the one at the rear moved them back so the trail remained hidden after they passed. Now more carefully than ever before the Wirliangs hid the trail so it could not be visible from the air. Elieana realized now why they waited to leave the cavern until dark. In daylight, any bird soldiers flying overhead could have immediately spotted them as they traveled down the mountainside.

The journey to the forest remained uneventful until finally it seemed to rise like a huge wall in front of them. They could hear distant sounds of wild animals singing their night songs amongst the trees. They covered a lot of ground as they moved through the old forest. No shrubbery or undergrowth grew along the trail to impede their progress. Elieana promptly realized they followed a game trail and hoped what little food they carried would not attract any of the night hunting creatures.

The night was almost spent when they pulled off the trail and hid themselves well under the spreading branches of a gigantic tree. Its enormous branches gave shelter for all of them to curl up comfortably and take their rest, including room for the wagon and dilhaa. Darec remained in the cart, sleeping most of the way, only waking long enough for Elieana to apply a new poultice of herbs to his wound and to take sips of the purified water from the Wirliang cavern. The wound, still red and hot to the touch, seemed slightly better from the application of the herbs. Elieana gave him a drink of water, with a sleeping draught mixed in it, as well as some other medicines the Wirlean healer gave her before they left the cavern.

Glassy, blood-shot eyes stared up at Elieana. Darec started to sit up as she touched his face, burning with fever. Gently she pushed him back down. Keeping her expression blank so she would not alarm him with her concern. She intensely hoped for a break in the fever soon. Elieana smiled at him and smoothed back his hair as she placed a damp cloth on his forehead. She settled him comfortably then lay down beside him, so she could monitor his fever.

Darec slept fitfully, mumbling and at times whimpering. Elieana moved closer and wrapped her arms around him to comfort him. He eased somewhat and after a while they both slept. In the late afternoon, they awoke to a loud screeching noise in the forest, deafening and painful to the ears and then the loud squealing of a creature fighting for its life. No one spoke. They all sat and waited. What they waited for they didn't know until a whooshing sound of huge wings flapping passed overhead. Not a one of the humans in the party left the security of the overhanging branches of the trees to watch the birds pass by.

The Wirliangs silently moved forward and took on the color and texture of the branches as they touched them. The movement of the branches the only thing revealing them as they passed out from under the tree. When they had gone

Elieana laid her head down again but could not sleep, knowing that the bird soldiers were so near. A short time later she heard the Wirliang speaking rapidly to Rodolph in their gurgling language. Their movements no longer smooth and relaxed but agitated with quick jerks of their arms and heads.

Rodolph's face blanched as they spoke. He glanced at Elieana and Antonia, sitting in the wagon, waiting expectantly to be told what the Wirliang observed outside of the shelter of the tree. Rodolph approached the wagon to speak to them. "A great flock of the giant birds has just passed overhead. One of them carried a large beast in its talons, I think those were the squeals we heard when the bird took its prey. They are headed east, towards Girona."

"We must hurry," whispered Elieana. "What if they take the city before we get there? We must warn the townsfolk."

"I fear we may be too late, Elieana," replied Rodolph.

"But they make camp for the night, if we can pass by them we may have a chance of arriving in Girona before them. We must do what we can. There is not a moment to lose," replied Elieana stubbornly.

"We cannot travel until it is dark. They will see us from above. For that matter if they are in front of us, even if they do not go to Girona, we must be extra cautious we do not stumble onto their encampment. While we are moving at night, they will be camped. I am sure their birds, which are hunters, will hear us coming in the darkness," replied Rodolph.

Jacq piped up then, all eyes turning towards him as he spoke. This unnerved him a bit and he stuttered but then went on, "The Wirliang are hunters too. They can conceal themselves. They could scout forward as we move through the forest and guide us, so we do not accidentally walk into the encampment. We must follow Rodolph's guidance of traveling by darkness but perhaps we can get an earlier start if the Wirliang can determine which direction the birds went. If we travel a parallel path perhaps we will be able to out distance them."

"Yes, young Jacq," said Rodolph, "A good suggestion."

Rodolph spoke rapidly to the Wirliang who immediately left the shelter of the tree. "I suggest we all get some more sleep. If we are to travel a long distance tonight, we will need our strength." He walked over to the spot where he lay previously, wrapped his cloak around his body and immediately fell into a deep slumber.

Carlotte grasped Jacq's hand and squeezed, whispering quietly to him, "You did wonderfully, Jacq."

Jacq smiled back and put his forehead up against hers then kissed her gently on the cheek.

Surprised by this display of affection, Elieana averted her eyes, embarrassed. For some reason, she couldn't get the thought of the man being a gong farmer out of her mind. She walked back to the wagon where Darec slept and crawled in alongside him. It took her some time to fall asleep but eventually she fell into a deep, dreamless sleep.

Antonia curled up in a tiny ball under the wagon and shortly fell asleep herself. She slept until the Wirliang returned to the tree with a sack of small fruits and tubers. She lay there watching them as they moved about, preparing a spartan meal for the rest of the group. These creatures amazed and frightened her. She recalled stories of them from her childhood, but no one had ever seen one. She had thought they were fabrications, told to amuse small children.

Their skin shimmered in the waning light filtering through the branches of the trees. She wanted to reach out and touch one of them so that is exactly what she did. She rose from under the wagon, walked slowly over to the closest Wirliang, reached out and touched its arm. She felt it immediately, a stream of heat running up her arm and into her brain.

They spoke, the two of them. They locked eyes and spoke of things, ancient things. She heard the stories of their people in her mind. The horror of being driven out of their homeland to the underground caverns and the females hunted for their skin. She wanted to break this tie but could not. She screamed but knew she screamed only in her mind. She concentrated hard, willing her lips to move, she tried to call for someone to come to her rescue, but she could not. No more, no more, she cried silently, but they wanted her to know something more. She saw the tie between them and her people. She saw the future through their eyes. Death, destruction. A girl child. Her child. This child who would save them and unite the people. They must find her and rescue her from danger. They knew the child. She had the mark, a star shaped mark on the palm of her hand that only materialized with her coming of age. War but also peace would follow her when she returned the land to the Wirliang people.

Antonia sank to her knees. The Wirliang grasped her arms, helping her to lay down. She understood only some of what she saw in its mind. She also knew she must be strong and help them in this quest to find her daughter and stop the Sangans from taking control of these lands. If the Sangans triumphed, then the Wirliang people would slowly cease to exist. Antonia stayed where the Wirliang laid her down, she could not move her body. Her head hurt from all the information they crammed into her brain. She heard movement around her and the whisperings of the others in the group, preparing to leave the shelter of the trees. They finished their meal then gently lifted her into the wagon, where she now lay next to Darec. From a distance, she heard the woman, Elieana, speaking.

"I don't know what happened to her. She was awake when I lay down in the wagon, after we discussed our plan to get to Girona ahead of the bird soldiers."

Unable to speak or move Antonia lay in the wagon, staring up into the apex of the tree they sheltered under. All she could do was think and stare. She could not blink; she could not move a muscle. She started to panic as she wondered what the Wirliang did to her. Her heart pounded but she lay as if dead, her staring eyes looking up into the trees, the rise and fall of her chest the only indication she still breathed.

Carlotte and Jacq climbed up into the front of the wagon beside Rodolph. The Wirliang who remained with them walked in front of the wagon, guiding them on the trail they scouted out through the forest. The other Wirliang, who left the camp, continued to mark the trail for them so they could pass far enough away from the bird soldier encampment and not be discovered.

Elieana sat between Antonia and Darec. Darec's forehead seemed cooler to the touch. Under the poultice, he was healing well, the redness receding. She gave him a sip of water and herb tea. She decided it wouldn't hurt to give some to Antonia, so she lifted her head and gently tried to get her to drink but the liquid dribbled out of her mouth and onto the neck of her dress.

"Could this be a kind of fit or something," she said to no one in particular. Rodolph looked back at Antonia laying in the wagon bed. "No, it is not a fit. I have seen this once before when one from Baltica touched a Wirliang. There are some, who merely by touch, can communicate with the Wirliang. It is a wondrous gift. I have seen only one other person with the ability to communicate with them in this way, Vasilis. He is the brother of our Antonia here, is that not right?"

"Yes, she told us he was her brother, but why would touching a Wirliang and communicating with them in this way cause her to be in this state?" asked Elieana.

"I believe it is because it is such a shock to see the future and the past so vividly. We must let her rest. She will recover before we reach Girona," said Rodolph who turned forward again and slapped the reins lightly over the dilhaa's back.

Elieana looked down into Antonia's face. She couldn't quite decide which person she liked better, the crazy, unpredictable Antonia or the silent, staring one. Unnerved by her staring Elieana thought to cover her face, not just because Antonia's staring eyes disturbed her but because she wasn't blinking. Surely something from the trees might damage her eyes or they might become dry from being open for so long. She dampened a piece of cloth with some of the herbed water and gently placed it over Antonia's face.

Antonia breathed in deeply when she felt the cooling herb-soaked cloth placed on her face. She wished she could thank Elieana for that one small kindness. Her eyes ached from not blinking. She couldn't stop thinking of the many things that passed between her and the Wirliang. It frightened her as nothing ever had. She heard Rodolph tell Elieana about Vasilis. She knew this already. The Wirliang told her Vasilis became evil minded after he took up his acquaintance with Egesa. Vasilis was dangerous. She wondered how the Wirliang remained undiscovered, living so close to his castle. Surely, they were included in the destruction Vasilis and Egesa planned. Perhaps this would be revealed to her later but for now she thought only on what their future held.

The wagon bumped along under the forest canopy until they eventually met up with the Wirliang scouts. Rodolph informed them the birds were encamped some distance away on a rocky slope, bedded down for the night. The Wirliang scouts squatted down and conferred with the Wirliang who escorted the rest of the group. He drew a map on the ground and pointed out their route. He rested for a short time then left them, hurrying to the end of the trail to continue marking the route for the party to follow.

The night wore on and the sky lightened. At the break of dawn, they stood on the road leading into the town of Girona, there they parted from their Wirliang scouts, who silently walked back into the forest. They intended on returning immediately to the Wirliang cavern to inform them of the impending attack by the Sangan bird soldiers.

After traveling all night, the dilhaa was exhausted but with its first step onto the roadway it revived somewhat and plodded along towards Girona as if it knew there would be rest and food when it arrived.

Elieana jumped down out of the wagon, along with Carlotte and Jacq. They did not want to be caught out in the open. With the weight of the cart lessened considerably the dilhaa broke into a slow, joggling trot and let out the occasional bleat of greeting to other dilhaas in the fields as they passed.

On the outskirts of Girona Elieana and Rodolph jogged on ahead to the headman's house. They left Carlotte and Jacq in charge of finding an inn and getting Darec and Antonia safely inside. Rodolph told them the dilhaa belonged to them, a gift for returning the dead Wirliang to his people. Carlotte and Jacq took the cart to an inn nearby the waterfront. It seemed a happy place, small and clean, with a view of the harbor filled with gaily colored fishing boats rocking on their moorings. They helped Darec out of the wagon and to their surprise he could stand, although shakily, and make his way to the room they secured from the innkeeper. A door on the opposite side of the room led out into a small, walled courtyard, overgrown with flowering creeper vines. On the far side, a rusted iron gate led down to the harbor.

They carried Antonia inside and lay her down on a small cot. With Darec and Antonia settled comfortably, they left to find food, and to dispose of the cart and dilhaa. They had grown fond of the dilhaa and wanted to ensure it had a good home. The innkeeper told them of a farmer who was looking for one and would pay them a good price.

After Jacq and Carlotte left the inn, Darec stood up. His legs quivered as he moved around the tiny room, stretching his aching and cramped muscles. He felt like he hadn't moved for a long, long time. He pulled off the dressings covering his wounds and inspected them. He re-tied the bandage then lay down on the floor to rest, feeling as weak as a new born babe. Darec fell deeply asleep but awakened to a loud thump from above, then another and another. He heard screams coming from the street and the sound of trampling feet from the room above. He rose from the floor, using the furniture to balance himself and looked out the window. He saw boats gently bobbing up and down in the harbor and the sunlight sparkling blindingly upon the water. Another thump and this time the windowsill shook under his hands.

He staggered over to the door leading to the courtyard and peered out. Huge birds darkened the sky overhead as the riders dropped large rocks, about the size of a small piglet, upon Girona and its citizens. Their intention, to kill, and that is exactly what they were doing. A woman running across the street, her arms over her head to protect herself, fell in mid-stride from a rock which shattered her arm and fractured her skull.

The pungent smell of smoke alerted him to the other weapon the riders were using. Fire arrows rained down on the rooftops. Any houses roofed with thatch exploded into flames. He wondered what had become of Elieana, Rodolph, Carlotte and Jacq. In his weakened state, he wasn't sure he could lift

Antonia up and get her out of the building if it caught fire, for that matter where could he go to get away from the falling rocks raining down on Girona.

Suddenly Jacq hurtled himself through the gate in the courtyard, almost falling flat as he tripped on a creeper vine growing across the path. "Come, Darec. The roof is on fire. I have found a place for us to hide from the arrows and rocks. Carlotte is there now."

"What of Rodolph and Elieana?" said Darec.

"They went to the headman's house. We haven't seen them since then, but we have no time to wait. We must leave before the bird soldiers catch sight of us."

The two men lifted Antonia up between them. Darec, still very weak, lost his grip and he dropped her. Jacq said not a word and just nodded to him to try again. Darec lifted her again and they both carried her out into the courtyard.

A wave of birds flew past overhead, away from the water. They did not see the three people escape from the rear of the inn and run down the pathway leading to the harbor, stumbling many times, before they came out at the much wider sea wall below. Jacq and Darec both realized the soldier's only plan of attack was to fire the buildings and kill the people as they ran for safety.

The harbor was built up with a stone sea wall along the water front to prevent erosion. Steps led down to a walkway, built just above the high-water mark. The walkway led to the pier further down and had alcoves built into the wall, for storage of small boats, nets and other equipment.

"Here," Jacq nodded with his head at the first alcove. "Help me lift Antonia up."

Darec helped Jacq hoist Antonia into the alcove then Jacq pulled Darec up. A few people peeked out from behind an overturned boat, some fishermen and children along with Carlotte, who sat on top of a pile of wooden boxes. Her face beamed at them when they climbed inside, then transformed to a look of horror. In unison Darec and Jacq looked towards the opening of the alcove to see what frightened her. A flock of riders had just flown overhead and were setting fire to the fishing boats.

"What if they see us," she whispered loudly.

"Move as far back as you can. Get behind those boats, conceal yourselves," whispered Jacq fiercely.

The occupants of the alcove shuffled quietly back into the shadows, all realizing if the riders spotted them and fired an arrow into the alcove, with no way of escape, they would be burned to death. One man suddenly screamed and ran out from behind the shelter of a boat leaning against the wall and jumped into the water. The riders spotted him and flew towards the alcove to investigate.

"No one move," hissed Jacq. He held tight to Carlotte and a small boy beside him who quivered in fear.

"Not a sound, do you hear me?" he whispered to the little boy who looked up at him with huge, fear filled eyes and nodded.

Everyone in the alcove nodded their heads, looking to Jacq for direction; no one moved a muscle or spoke. They could hear the man splashing and screaming in the water and the flap of the bird's wings as it hovered above him. The riders were using the man for sport. The soldiers showed no compassion for the man in the water. With a sudden deafening screech from one of the birds and the man's piercing scream, those left in the alcove surmised correctly, the bird plucked the man out of the water. The man screamed and screamed then fell silent.

The sound of the soldier's laughter echoed against the stone walls as they flew away, their sport finished for a time. They never thought to look for more escapees hiding in the alcove. Perhaps because they knew easier sport could be found with the fleeing citizens of Girona.

CHAPTER 18

Elieana and Rodolph spoke to the headman of Girona, who laughed at them and their story, of birds with riders upon their backs attacking from the air. He treated them with disdain and told them to leave his house, heckling them as they walked away, but it wasn't long before the smile faded from his face.

"Do you see the dark cloud in the distance, headman?" Rodolph called back over his shoulder. "If you look closely you will see it does not move in the same direction as the other clouds in the sky. What could it be, I wonder?" He met the headman's gaze then called out loudly for all nearby to hear. "Citizens of Girona, take cover. Run for your lives. There comes an attack from the sky you would never in your wildest imagination have thought possible. Look to the south, do you see it? If you look closely you will see the sun reflecting off the armor the riders wear. They will stop at nothing. They will kill all in their path. Do not waste time to gather your belongings, save yourselves."

The citizens nearby gazed in the direction Rodolph pointed and gawked at the approaching bird army. Some pointed at the dark cloud undulating and moving as if it were being buffeted by the wind, but there was no wind, not even the slightest breeze. Some edged away to seek shelter from the approaching dark cloud, too strange to ignore. Some watched with fascination as it slowly approached from the south.

A man pointed and shouted excitedly, "I see something. I see something shiny, bright, like fire. Do you see it? There is fire in that cloud." He looked in Rodolph's direction. For just a moment the man did not say anything then said, "I know you. You are Rodolph. You are from this place. Are you here to warn us of this danger? You do not jest?"

Rodolph shook his head, "They will be upon us in the blink of an eye. They come fast and will kill. You must save yourselves," he shouted.

The man who spoke to Rodolph then raised his voice, "I know this man, and he would not lie. Run, save yourselves," he screamed as he ran away down the street, grabbing at people as he passed. "Run, save yourselves," he shouted. The man ran towards the outskirts of the city. He didn't stop to see if anyone followed. A few followed his example, others just stood in the overhanging shelter of the buildings and watched the approaching birds.

At first it seemed they were close by and not so large. They often saw large flocks of birds, especially at harvest time when plenty of food lay in the fields but this was not harvest time. Some looked toward the approaching flock and laughed at the man who ran away, commenting on how he was craven, had always been craven.

A hush spread through the crowd as someone shouted out, the awe apparent in his voice, "Those are not small birds.

Look, there are riders, do you not see?" He spun around and sprinted down the street in the same direction the first man ran.

Fear took hold on the observers remaining in the street. They pushed and shoved, as they ran, knocking people down as they passed by; some took shelter in doorways; others ran into their homes and slammed their doors, the sound of bolts clanging to. Still others stood watching, in disbelief, the ominous approach of the birds flying towards them.

Elieana stood riveted in one place, fearfully watching the approaching birds, their bright colors visible and their riders sitting atop them, decked out in shining breast plates and helmets. Some carried lanterns, which burned brightly, as they flew towards them.

Rodolph grasped Elieana by the arm and guided her towards the harbor. As they jogged away she kept looking back over her shoulder, unable to break the spell of seeing the huge flock of birds.

When the bird soldiers reached the outskirts of the city they dropped their lanterns onto the roofs of the buildings. The flames licked and danced momentarily then burst into a roaring inferno as the fire devoured the thatch. The occupants of the burning buildings escaped out into the street only to fall from the volley of arrows raining down on them. Plumes of black, acrid smoke rose above the city, the screams of the frightened people rising with it. The carnage the soldiers wrought on the people of Girona was quick and deadly.

Rodolph and Elieana ran until their lungs burst. When they reached the harbor, they saw soldiers dropping huge rocks onto the smaller boats, which immediately started taking on water. They dropped lanterns down onto the larger boats, igniting the sails in a burst of flame. Soon every boat in the harbor burned like a huge, floating bonfire. A ripple of fear clutched at Elieana's stomach and she stumbled against a wall.

A scream to their right attracted their attention and they saw a man jump from the sea wall into the water. One of the soldiers engaged in burning the boats flew his bird to where the man desperately swam away from shore. The bird swooped down close to the water and with a great flapping of wings rose back up, the man grasped in its talons. They rose higher and higher and then the bird dropped its catch and the man plummeted back down into the sea, only to be picked up by another bird. Horrorstricken, Elieana watched, she could not look away. The man struggled and flailed but to no avail.

Suddenly the bird clenched its feet tighter and the screams died instantly. The man's body hung limply from the bird's talons and then the bird dropped him into the sea. Rodolph pulled Elieana away from the sight.

"Rodolph, why?" was all she could say as he led her away, into the shelter of a stone archway.

"They are Sangans or they are the henchmen of Sangans. They are blood crazed and will not stop until they have killed everyone. Come, we cannot help anyone now, we must save ourselves," said Rodolph.

They scrambled down a covered, stone stairwell, its steps well-worn from the feet of fishermen who had taken this route to the harbor for centuries. At the bottom, it opened to a lower sea wall, leading onto the docks. The cold, dampness of the stairwell smelled of salt and fish and piss, but it was welcome protection from the attack taking place overhead.

Elieana clenched her fists tightly by her sides. She couldn't tell if she was in shock or this feeling was anger. Never during the previous war had she seen anything like this, an attack, without warning. Usually talks and warnings and posturing came before an attack, but she knew of no warning of Vasilis' or the Sangan's intentions. Pelagonia and Baltica had agreed to sign a treaty to end their war and there had been no fight with the Sangans for many years.

"What was it Vasilis agreed to with the Sangans?" she said. "To raise this army of bird soldiers must have taken a very long time. Rodolph, they gave no warning."

"Yes, Elieana, there were many warnings, but no one listened. The Wirliang met with your leaders many years ago, but no one believed them. That is why the Wirliang have been watching the events taking place in the cities of Pelagos and Belisle with great interest.

It was only a matter of time before something happened. You see the King of Baltica has no heir. His line has died and so he has agreed to adopt Vasilis' son, Michael. Baltica will pass on to him when the king dies and Pelagonia will be within his grasp when Michael marries Princess Verenase of Pelagonia. He will have much power. I think though..." and he paused, a look of amazement on his face. "I think Vasilis has been betrayed." His brow furrowed, and his eyebrows knit together in a tight frown. "I believe the Sangans were to control the territory near the mountains, leaving the rest for

Vasilis and his son. I think this attack may not be in Vasilis' plans. I think he did not intend to kill all the people, but if the Sangans want to take control, they will kill everyone to have all the lands north of the Barbicon Mountains."

Elieana could not see his expression, but she could tell from his voice, the information he gleaned in his work for the Wirliang was sufficient to give him insight in the ever-changing politics of the region.

Suddenly a huge shadow passed by, blocking out the bit of sunlight that shone brightly at the bottom of the stairwell. A shiver of dread ran up Elieana's spine. "Rodolph, where are we to hide?" said Elieana.

"We will wait until dusk. I think perhaps these soldiers will take their birds to a place of safety, away from the city. They must tether them and feed them soon. Even if they feed on the livestock from the farms on the outskirts of the city, they will still have to find a place where they can tether them and be far enough away they cannot be attacked at night." He sat down then and patted the stair beside him, motioning for Elieana to sit. "We will wait, there is nothing we can do now."

Elieana sat alongside Rodolph, watching the little patch of sunshine that seemed to beckon her into its warmth as it moved across the bottom of the stairwell. From time to time a shadow passed, but only for a moment.

They sat in the cool, musty darkness of the stairwell for hours. Both dozed off from time to time but awoke upon hearing a random scream or screech of a bird. They held onto each other tightly as they sat waiting for someone to discover their shelter and drag them out into the bright light of day.

Thankfully no one came. The patch of sunlight faded until it no longer radiated any warmth at all and lingered as a patch of dull light causing them to shiver in the damp, clammy stairwell.

After a long while it seemed as if the sounds of destruction had slowed. Rodolph got up and stretched his stiff, cramped muscles. Keeping his voice low, he whispered to Elieana, "Stay here, I will look to see if it is safe to leave."

Nodding, Elieana stayed where she was, exhausted and deeply overwhelmed by the death and destruction, she didn't think she could even stand.

Apprehensively Rodolph climbed the steps and looked outside. The fire in the city burned fiercely, blocking their escape. He descended to the bottom of the stairway, leading to the harbor, and motioned for Elieana to follow him. The last rays of the setting sun sparkled on the sea, painting it gold and pink. The water, unusually calm, reflected fluffy clouds overhead. It didn't seem right to stand and watch the glory of the sun's descent below the horizon, knowing blood ran red in the streets of the city.

Elieana paused, not wanting to leave their shelter but Rodolph grasped her hand and pulled her gently from the stairwell. The city was deathly quiet except for the crackling of the fire as it consumed the buildings. The boats in the harbor burned brightly on their moorings, no one there to douse the flames. They walked along the seawall scanning the harbor for any boats left undamaged but there were none. They knew by the deafening silence the soldiers had vacated the city.

At another stairway, Rodolph put his fingers to his lips and motioned for Elieana to stay at the bottom. He climbed the stairway, keeping low. He peered over the edge of the wall and the carnage he saw made the bile rise in his throat. He had to swallow and take a few deep breaths before he moved again.

Atop one of the unburnt buildings perched a solitary bird, its colors enhanced in the light of the setting sun. Its rider sat precariously, on the rooftree beside it. Surely, thought Rodolph, there must be more soldiers, but he did not wait to find out. With a heavy heart, he descended the steps to where Elieana waited for him. He raised a finger to his lips for her to be silent and proceeded back along the seawall until they came to an alcove large enough for the storage of small boats and nets. They sat down on some old fishing nets and discussed what to do next.

"I saw one soldier and his bird perched on top of one of the buildings," said Rodolph. "Let us go back the way we came to see if there are more soldiers at the other end of the street. They may have all left but for the one."

Elieana nodded, her brow wrinkled in concern for their friends, but before she could say anything a noise from the back of the alcove interrupted them. They peered back into the gloom and saw Jacq's face pop up from behind an overturned boat, then Carlotte, Darec and lastly Antonia, all pale faced and bedraggled but so overjoyed they broke out into laughter. Rodolph immediately ran his hand across his neck and pointed upwards. They instantly stopped and gawked at him, wide-eyed.

Darec pushed himself up to a standing position and stumbled around the end of the boat. He clenched his jaw with concentration as his face turned a pasty white. They greeted each other with relieved hugs then looked to Rodolph for direction. "Rodolph, you know this city well. You will be our leader," whispered Darec. "I cannot defend any of you while I am as weak as a newborn babe."

Rodolph nodded his head and quietly replied, "We will go into the city, if it is safe, and bring back food and drink, if there is any to be found. Darec and Elieana, will you stay with Antonia and these others?" He pointed with his chin towards the other people who moved tentatively from behind the overturned boat. Darec nodded and Elieana, realizing Darec might not have the strength to help yet quietly whispered, "Yes," to his request.

Rodolph clapped Darec on his injured shoulder, making him wince in pain. He knew it would be difficult, for a strong man such as Darec, to be left in charge of women and children, but he read gratitude in Darec's eyes for recognizing his inability to move around with agility yet.

"I will take Carlotte and Jacq," said Rodolph. "Carlotte, you know this city do you not?"

She nodded and whispered a quiet, Yes.

Carlotte, Jacq and Rodolph left the alcove. They circled around through the back lanes of the city, keeping out of sight. Many dead lay in the streets and in the laneways, lying where they had fallen from rock and arrow. No one remained to fight the flames. Citizens had either fled into the nearby fields or hidden inside their homes and shops. Why the soldier sat with his huge bird on the rooftop they couldn't tell. They circled in behind the building where the huge bird perched and saw no other riders. He seemed to be the only one remaining.

"Rodolph, if there is only one soldier, perhaps we can kill him and his bird," whispered Jacq.

"I think that is a good idea," said Rodolph. "It will certainly help the citizens of Girona. They, at least, will be able to come back and salvage what is left of their possessions, before everything is burnt. We will find some weapons we can use against the creature; it will not be easy to kill. We passed a stable earlier, let us go back there to see what we can find to use as a weapon."

They retraced their steps to the stable, finding it full of feed for the owner's animals. The feed would burst into flames when the steadily growing fire reached it. No animal remained, each stall door gaped wide. Their search turned up some large grappling hooks and some strong rope they could use in hopes of taking down the huge bird. They would have to kill the bird first and then deal with the soldier. None of them wanted to have the bird attacking them. Elieana told them about the tie between the birds and their riders and how they protected them with their lives.

Carlotte searched on the other side of the building and called out to them when they were ready to leave. "Jacq, Rodolph, I have found some food. Just give me one moment to put it in a sack and I will bring it along." She rummaged around for a sack then filled it with the meal someone had left uneaten, in their haste to escape. As she walked out of the room something black screeched and landed on her shoulder. She screamed loudly, bringing Jacq and Rodolph running from the stable. They found Carlotte leaning against the wall, her hand to her throat, trying to calm herself by taking deep, slow breaths. At her feet sat a tiny black and white kitten staring up at her.

"What is it?" demanded Jacq. "Why did you scream?"

Carlotte only pointed to the floor and Jacq rolled his eyes.

"He jumped on my back when I was leaving the room," she exclaimed.

"Well, he must fend for himself," replied Jacq without a second look at the kitten. "We cannot take him with us."

"Yes," Carlotte said, nodding her head. Still startled from the encounter, she scooped up the kitten and put it inside the pocket of her skirt, then ran to catch up with Jacq.

They left the stable and ran back through the narrow, twisting laneways towards the house where the soldier and his bird kept watch on the city. They arrived at the back of the house, which was surrounded by a high stone wall, and let themselves through a tiny gate. Litter lay strewn across the small yard and it struck Carlotte as funny that the laundry, still wet from the wash, hung unattended on the line. The wash pot bubbled merrily away over the still burning fire. Whoever lived in this house abandoned it in haste. The back door hung ajar as if the owner just stepped away for a moment.

They pushed the door open further, thankful the hinges didn't squeak and alert the soldier on the roof and crept quietly towards the front of the house, their boots crunching on the remains of the front window, smashed by one of the falling rocks. They stayed on the main floor to discuss their plan before they ascended the stairs.

The house was dark, lit only by the flickering light of the flames from the huge fire burning at the end of the street. It lent an eerie atmosphere to the room, making Carlotte troubled and nervous. Something familiar about this place bothered her but she couldn't recall what it might be. She gazed slowly around the room and realized she had been here long ago. Her aunt and uncle lived here years before. When her parents died her aunt and uncle moved, with their family, into Carlotte's family home, leaving this one for the use of their eldest son.

Carlotte left the men as they discussed their plan. She wandered throughout the rooms on the main floor and then climbed the stairs to the second level. A shuffling noise startled her as she reached the top step. Difficult to see in the darkened hallway she whispered, "Is there someone there?"

The shuffling noise sounded again. By this time her eyes had grown accustomed to the dim light and there in front of her stood a fat, black rat, attempting to get away from her by scratching at the crack under the door at the end of the hall. Completely on edge now every little sound startled her. She glared at the rat and stamped her foot causing it to run towards her and scamper into one of the open rooms.

Carlotte tiptoed down the hallway and peered into the rooms as she passed, wondering if one of her relatives still resided in the house before the attack came. Whoever lived in the house may have escaped the destruction, she hoped they had. They must have listened to the warnings to take cover and leave Girona. In each room drawers hung open, clothes scattered on the floor marking the swiftness with which they left.

The door to the last room she opened carefully and peered inside. A huge bed stood on one side of the room which she recognized as belonging to her aunt. Much finer furnishings had filled her dead sister's house and she had left the bed for her son. Anger stirred in Carlotte's heart at the thought of her aunt. She entered the room and touched the ornaments sitting on a tiny dresser. She opened the wardrobe, clothing still hung neatly inside. She searched more thoroughly but found nothing to indicate who lived here now.

Dirt and sticks from the thatch of the roof littered the floor and the bed. The rafters above groaned as if the roof beams held too much weight. Immediately Carlotte realized the giant bird was perched on the roof directly above this room. She gazed up and saw more dust and thatch filter from above.

Carlotte pictured in her mind the bird sitting on the rooftree, its talons grasping onto the thick rooftree and thatch. The soldier leaned against the chimney, the chimney for the fireplace in the room she stood in. She imagined herself standing on the roof of the house opposite this one and pictured the scene in her mind as if she looked directly at it from across the street.

Two windows in the room faced out onto the street. They could throw the grappling hooks up on the roof and hopefully snag the man or the bird and pull them down off the roof. They could then easily dispatch the bird, especially if it struggled and became tangled in the trailing ropes. "That will fix them," she whispered to herself and silently tiptoed out of the room and back down the stairs.

Carlotte quickly descended the stairs to where Jacq and Rodolph waited for her. "I know exactly where the bird and the soldier are on the roof of this house, come upstairs," she said.

The two men followed her as she ran up the steps on her toes, careful to make no sound, energized now, knowing they could attack the soldier before he realized enemies were in the room below.

Jacq and Rodolph reached the top of the stairs where Carlotte waited for them, excited about her discovery. She raised her finger to her lips for them to be very quiet then led them to the room at the end of the hallway. Carlotte pointed to the roof and the two men looked up at the rooftree where the bird's giant talons had pierced the thatch of the ceiling. Jacq looked at the huge talons and immediately had misgivings. He doubted they could stop the bird with the grappling hook thrown up from the tiny window as Carlotte suggested. They would have only one chance and if they missed it would be their end.

As he stared up at the bird's talons he instantly had another plan. He pulled Rodolph out into the hallway and explained what he meant to do. When Jacq went back into the room he quietly hooked two of the grappling hooks securely to the farthest edge of the fireplace hearthstone. He signaled to Rodolph to help him move the huge wooden wardrobe into the middle of the room. They carefully lifted it up and moved it over without making a sound. Jacq climbed on top of it, signaling for Rodolph to do the same.

Jacq now stood on the wardrobe, bent over beneath the rooftree. He carefully reached up through the damaged thatch to loop the rope around the bird's leg. The bird lifted its great foot up, pulling the loop of rope off before they could tie it securely. It put its foot back down and again the talons sunk through the thatch and Jacq started again. This time more slowly, so the bird would not again lift its foot. Rodolph reached up through the thatch and grasped the rope as Jacq looped it around the bird's leg. Sweating profusely, Jacq's sodden shirt stuck to his back, droplets streamed down his arms making his fingers slippery, so he had difficulty tying the knots.

Carlotte stood, wide-eyed, watching them wrap the rope around the bird's leg, realizing if the bird grasped either man the sharp talons would pierce them through.

As soon as they secured the ropes both men yanked hard and all the knots tightened at the same time. The bird immediately lifted its huge foot, its talons sliding out of the thatch. Both Rodolph and Jacq leapt to the floor. The knots held fast and as the bird lifted its foot it pulled the ropes through the thatch, ripping clumps of the roof away and revealing the cloudy sky above. Alarmed, the bird tried to move around upon the roof, raining thatch and vermin down on the heads of Rodolph, Carlotte and Jacq.

Mesmerized, Carlotte watched the gigantic bird, which she could see distinctly through the hole in the roof. A slight breeze ruffled the top knot of feathers on its head. The soldier patted his bird to calm it, unable to see what caused its restlessness.

"Hear now, Abbas, stay, stay," the soldier crooned, "It must be the fire, let us be off," he said as he climbed up into the saddle on the bird's back. "No one from this city will return, the fire burns much too fast and much too hot," said the soldier as he urged the bird upwards.

The bird rose off the rooftop and one of the ropes attached to the hearthstone became taut then snapped, throwing the bird off balance. The bird rose higher and the second grappling hook came loose from the hearthstone and zipped up through the hole in the roof, narrowly missing Rodolph, before becoming fixed fast into the rooftree. They heard a loud scream as the soldier fell out of the saddle and landed with a sickening thud on the cobbles below.

As soon as the soldier hit the ground the bird let out an ear-piercing screech then suddenly the room started to shake. More thatch and debris fell in on them. The rooftree broke away from the walls and hung from the bird's foot, swinging crazily. The swinging of the beam became more and more erratic as the bird tried to fly. The beam crashed back into the side of the house smashing part of the wall away.

Spurred into action, Carlotte, Jacq and Rodolph ran from the room to avoid being buried under the falling debris. They hadn't expected the power of this huge creature. Another crash and the building shuddered, causing them to stumble into each other as they reached the bottom steps. Fearing the house would tumble down on top of them, they ran out into the street.

"I think the bird is not leaving because he doesn't want to leave his master," whispered Rodolph.

Jacq ran over to the soldier and saw that the man's neck had snapped from the fall. He grasped one arm and the bird shrieked. "Rodolph, take his other arm. We will lead the bird towards the fire, perhaps it will follow."

Together they dragged the body down the street, the head lolling at an obscene angle. The bird followed overhead, the beam, still attached to its leg crashed back and forth between the buildings, causing glass and debris to rain down upon them.

At the end of the street they turned the corner leaving Carlotte alone, riveted in place, and watching with horror at the beam swinging perilously back and forth. She feared the rope would not hold and the beam would fall, crushing Rodolph and Jacq.

When Carlotte realized she was alone in the darkened street amongst the debris and the dead she let out a little whimper, hiked up her skirts and ran after them as fast as she could go. When she got to the end of the street she could see Jacq and Rodolph in the middle of the square, their bodies framed by the light of the flames. Carlotte could feel the intense heat burning her face from where she stood.

Jacq and Rodolph took the soldier's body as close to the fire as they could. The bird still hovered overhead and when Jacq and Rodolph ran away it landed beside the man's body, gently moving it with its beak. It let out another cry, not as before, but a lament. The bird tenderly picked up the body in its talons but then a gust blew a spark onto the bird's back and its feathers burst into flame. It screeched in fear and pain and flew into the air. The wind from its wings fanned the flames as it flew higher and higher and away from the city.

Carlotte watched the bird as it flew away to its death. She felt a choking feeling in her throat as she watched this beautiful creature being consumed by the flames. The dam to her emotions burst and she stood there sobbing, the tears leaving streaks in the soot covering her face.

CHAPTER 19

After running a short distance away from where they dropped the body of the soldier, Jacq and Rodolph watched the bird as it tried to awaken its dead master, nudging him with its beak.

"I have never seen such a bond between man and beast," whispered Rodolph.

"Yes," replied Jacq, "Imagine if that bond could be used for good."

They watched in amazement at the gentleness the bird displayed towards its master and both felt regret this majestic creature would die. They watched the flames catch in its feathers as it flew up into the air, with the man's body clutched in its talons. The beam still hung from the bird's leg and as it tried to fly the beam threw it off balance causing it to fly erratically. The rope burned until it broke, and the beam fell with a crash into the flames sending showers of sparks into the air. The bird flew towards the forest and Rodolph said a silent prayer to his God that it would perish before it reached the trees.

"Do you think it will survive the flight back to where the rest of the bird army has gone for the night?" asked Jacq.

"I do not fear that as much as I fear it landing in the forest and catching fire to the trees. What will happen to the Wirliangs then? I think they will surely perish if there is no forest for them."

They watched for a moment longer and then just before it reached the forest the bird plummeted to the ground and landed in the middle of a wide-open field in a burst of sparks and flame.

Rodolph put a hand on Jacq's shoulder, "Come, my friend, let us find Carlotte. We left her behind and I am sure she will be frightened, alone in this empty place."

Both men retraced their route and found Carlotte collapsed at the end of the street, her face streaked with tears and soot. She held the tiny kitten nestled close to her neck, where it tried to burrow under her hair. Her grief was palpable. She looked up at them and their hearts clenched with sadness for her.

Jacq realized, by the expression on her face, that she must have seen what happened to the bird. He reached down and helped her to her feet then put his arm around her and they walked back towards the docks where they had left the rest of their friends. "Don't talk, Carlotte, just rest your head on my shoulder," he said softly and gently hugged her close.

Carlotte allowed Jacq to support her as they walked together back to the docks. She sniffled and hiccupped then reached down and pulled the hem of her skirt up, using it to wipe her face and nose. "Please excuse me, Jacq, I don't have a handkerchief," said Carlotte, embarrassed for using her hem to wipe her nose.

"After all we have been through, Carlotte, do you think it matters right now?" Jacq asked and gave her a little squeeze. "You brought the kitten, I see."

She smiled up at him through a haze of tears. "Yes, I couldn't leave him behind in the fire. Jacq, did you see the bird?" she asked, her voice quivering.

Nodding Jacq looked down at her fondly.

"It was so horrible. The bird tried to get the soldier to stand, it tried to wake him up," she said.

"I think we did not know the strength of the bond between these riders and their birds," replied Rodolph. "If that is the case then perhaps this will be an advantage when or if it comes to war. The birds will be hard to kill with arrows but if the man could be killed then this may be a way to win a war with this flying army. I must discuss this with Darec. I am sure he will be very interested to hear about the events of this night."

More tears flooded Carlotte's eyes as she listened to Rodolph speak about killing the majestic birds. She tucked the kitten back into her pocket then held onto Jacq tighter as they walked through the gruesome scene of the dying city of Girona. The fire crackled as it consumed the thatched roof of another building and roared with the sound of the walls of another building crashing down. Carlotte tried to be brave but could not and hid her face against Jacq's shoulder.

"Jacq," she mumbled, "Thank you. I don't think I can look at another dead body. There are so many here. It seems as if the whole city is lying in the street. They killed everyone, man, woman and child." She choked back her tears, her voice quivering with emotion as she spoke.

Jacq hugged her close, "Don't look, Carlotte, close your eyes, I will guide you."

Carlotte nodded and closed her eyes so she would not see the staring eyes of the dead as they picked their way through the carnage.

"What do you think, Rodolph, will it be like this in every village, town and city along the coast? Do you think this is the first of many?" said Jacq.

"I do not know, Jacq. I can only imagine. It is incomprehensible even why they have done this. Is it Vasilis or the Sangans or is it someone else? I do not know." He shook his grizzled head which hung low, grief etched across his face. "If only we had arrived sooner, if only we could have saved them."

As they rounded the corner into the last street leading to the docks the fire light revealed a fishing boat tied at the very end of the dock. They quickened their steps, looking at each other in surprise.

"They sank all the boats before we left, did they not, Jacq?" said Rodolph.

"They did. This is a newcomer for certain," replied Jacq. "From the decoration on the hull it comes from Pelagos."

Carlotte opened her eyes then and stared down the dock at this welcome sight. As they got closer she broke from Jacq's protective arms and ran towards the boat, towards someone who had just stepped onto the quay.

"It's Nada," she exclaimed. "Nada, Nada," she shouted as she ran towards the boat.

Nada looked up when she heard someone call her name. Her mouth opened in surprise.

"Carlotte, what are you doing here? What happened here?"

Carlotte cupped Nada's face in her hands then wrapped her arms around her and hugged her as tightly as she could. She held her back again at arm's length and searched her face but before she could say anything Nada hugged her again.

"Carlotte, I am so sorry they took you to the dungeon, but how did you get out? How long did you have to stay there? Where is Jacq?"

"Oh, Nada, I am so happy you have forgiven us," but then she paused, tilting her head slightly in question, "Did you forgive Jacq?"

Nada could see from the look on Carlotte's face this was very important to her. She looked intensely at Nada, trying to see her face in the dim lantern light from the boat. "I hold no anger for either of you," replied Nada. "But you must loosen your grip on my arm Carlotte before it loses all feeling."

Jacq, who had walked up and stood behind Carlotte, shifted uncomfortably, not meeting Nada's eyes.

Nada smiled at Jacq. "After they took me to the castle, Princess Verenase held me captive in a room. It is difficult to know in these times who is a friend and who is an enemy."

"I am your friend, Nada, or perhaps like a big sister," said Carlotte. "I have no family now," she said as she made a sweeping gesture towards the destruction behind them.

"Well," replied Nada, "It appears I have no family either. Elieana left me and did not return. I am the daughter of the King of Baltica, but I do not know him, and I have no mother." As she spoke a hard lump grew in her throat.

Carlotte's face brightened then and a huge grin spread across her face. Nada looked at her angrily, taking a step back from her. "Why do you smile?" she questioned Carlotte. The tone in her voice now hard-edged and angry.

"You do not know," exclaimed Carlotte excitedly, "Elieana is here. We were on our way to meet them when we saw your boat."

Nada looked behind them along the dock, searching. "Where is she? Is Darec with her?"

"Darec is with her, and someone else you may want to meet."

"Who? I do not know anyone here in Girona."

While they spoke, the men from Peter's boat came forward to stand behind Nada and listened with interest to their conversation.

Carlotte recognized one of the soldiers standing directly behind Nada. She stepped back, bumping into Jacq. The soldier had questioned her and Jacq after their arrest. "We will not go back to Pelagos with these soldiers. Jacq will not be taken away," said Carlotte. She could feel her anger surging just below the surface. She moved closer to Jacq and pulled his arm around her waist, holding tightly so he could not move away.

They were distracted by a loud, rumbling, crash behind them, and they all watched as another building collapsed in upon itself, sending sparks flying high up into the air. The flames mesmerized as they flickered and licked at the thatch of the next building, seeming alive and hungry.

"We cannot stay here," said Peter as he walked up behind them. "If the sparks land on the boat it will burn to a cinder." He gently pulled at Nada's arm, trying to get her to follow him back to the boat.

She pulled her arm away and started to walk forward, towards the sea wall, then stopped as she noticed a small group of people walking slowly towards the dock. Nada watched them coming and recognized Elieana, walking with an elderly man and supporting Darec between them. Darec looked weak and stumbled a few times as he slowly trudged towards them.

She saw a woman she didn't know walking behind them. She was light of build with very long hair, hanging to the backs of her legs. The woman gazed at the flickering flames engulfing the city as she walked. Suddenly she stopped, as if she knew Nada watched her and then she met Nada's eyes. A chill ran down Nada's spine, the hairs raised on her arms and the back of her neck in a ripple of goose flesh. The woman's face seemed very familiar. Despite the heat, she started to shiver then quietly, almost too soft to hear, she said, "Mama?" "Mama," she said again louder this time.

The woman stopped walking, she stood riveted on the spot then slowly her face drained of color and she slumped down onto the flagstones in a dead faint.

Elieana saw Nada standing on the dock, overjoyed at the sight of her. Her happiness spread across her face but then she heard Nada call out to her mother. Elieana's heart clenched and she felt as if it would break but then Nada looked at her, her face lit up and she ran to Elieana, jumping up and wrapping her arms around her neck. Elieana stepped back with the force of Nada jumping up to hug her and momentarily lost her grip on Darec's arm.

"Elieana," Nada whispered into her ear, "I've been so afraid for you and Darec. I thought for sure something terrible had happened to you." She fiercely hugged Elieana again then stepped back and looked at Darec's haggard face. "Oh, Darec, I didn't notice..." she stumbled over her words. He looked nothing like the man who came to see her the day she injured her foot.

"Just an inconvenience," replied Darec lightly, "Nothing more."

Elieana looked at him, a queer expression on her face but said nothing.

Suddenly a flare of light brightened the sky again as the thatch roof of another building caught fire and was devoured by the flames.

"Come, my friends," called Peter, very agitated now. "We must move away from the dock, the flames are coming too close, the boat may catch fire."

Two of the soldiers rushed to pick up Antonia who remained where she had collapsed. Peter then ushered the rest of the group onto the boat. "Come, come," he waved to a small cluster of people who stood nearby where Antonia fell. "There is room for you. Come, we must be away."

The remainder of the townsfolk, who hid in the alcove, tentatively walked down the dock towards Peter's boat. Peter welcomed them as if he was asking them to enter his small house. He patted them on the shoulder or the back or a child's head as they climbed aboard. "We will see you safe, my friends. Sit down over there," he pointed to the stern.

"Raise the sails, men. Cast us off, Philen," Peter shouted in a voice surprising all who didn't know him. The boat slowly moved away from the dock and out of danger of the sparks flying up as the town of Girona died.

After Peter sailed his boat out of the harbor the few people from Girona on board approached him. "Please, can you take us to shore, sir?" Their spokesman asked. "There must be some of our people left alive. Some who ran to the forest when the birds approached, I am sure of it. We must find those who remain. We cannot desert them." The man hung his head in despair and fiddled with his cap, twisting it around and around in his hands as he stood waiting for Peter's reply. "If we find none alive, perhaps then we can bury those who have not been burned in the fire," he whispered, almost too quietly to be heard.

Peter clasped the man's sagging, thin shoulders and tried to insert cheerfulness in his voice to encourage him. "Yes, we will do that for you, my friend. Do you know of a place that will be safe to go in close to shore?"

The man looked up into Peter's face, his eyes brightening just a little, "There is a small bay to the south of Girona. It has deep water and a small dock. The fishermen visit a shrine to the Goddess of the Sea there. If you take us there we will find our way back to Girona."

"At first light, we will take you there, but for now, we will stay where we are. I do not want to risk damage or monsters of the deep."

The man nodded. Without a word, he clapped his battered cap back onto his head, nodded again and moved back to his place near the stern.

The soldiers, now accustomed to work on the boat, anchored it some way off shore from Girona, still in the shallows, but far enough out to be free from smoke and ash and any random sparks shooting up into the night sky. Fortunately, only a light breeze blew across the water and it remained calm. The refugees from Girona huddled down on the deck, their hollow eyes staring back at what remained of their homes.

Jorian sat at the bow of the boat, the furthest away he could get from everyone. Little Joel lay beside him, curled up in a tight little ball, sound asleep. Jorian cuddled his son protectively, absently patting his back whenever he moved in his sleep. It saddened him to think of his life and many other's lives torn apart so cruelly. How could he have been so blind about Mia? He listened to the stories the townspeople told them, or those remaining of the townspeople. The huge birds attacking the town. It sounded so unbelievable. Although he had not seen them he imagined the awesome sight as they flew through the sky in such numbers. Eventually even Jorian dropped off to sleep, with his arms wrapped protectively around his son.

Sometime during the night, the sky opened, sending a deluge of rain to drench the occupants of the boat. Not a breeze blew, the huge drops fell straight down, bouncing off the deck. A heavy mist hovered over the water and dark, ominous clouds hung low overhead. The stench of smoke, heavy in the air, made it seem as if they had sailed to the edge of the underworld. From what they could see of Girona nothing remained except blackened walls of stone reaching to the sky, a wet, stinking, smoldering ruin. No one spoke, no one dared break the gloomy silence.

CHAPTER 20

Peter's boat bumped up against a narrow quay constructed of stones like the sea wall in Girona. Although the fiery destruction of Girona was complete, the citizens of Girona, a bedraggled bunch of humanity, clustered at the bow of Peter's boat, anxious to go back and find anyone who may have survived the attack.

At the end of the quay stood a small stone chapel and a statue of the sea goddess, revered by all fisher folk. Peter whispered a small prayer for these people of Girona. He watched them as they climbed from the boat onto the quay, carrying all their worldly possessions. They walked towards the chapel and a narrow path leading up the hill and into the forest. A few of them paused to wave but others, so full of grief, trudged up the pathway, never looking back.

Carlotte started to climb off the boat, Jacq following closely behind her, but Darec reached out and grasped Jacq's coat and pulled him back. Jacq stumbled backwards, falling against Darec's chest and in Darec's weakened state they almost toppled over. "You will not take him, Darec," said Carlotte as she grabbed Jacq's arm and pulled him towards her. Her voice sounded venomous, her face turned red and it seemed as if her hair rose like a mane, making her look formidable. There was no softness about her and as she stared back at Darec small objects on the boat started to rattle and bounce crazily across the deck.

Jacq leaned towards Carlotte and put his hand gently on her cheek. He gazed lovingly into her eyes. "Be still, Carlotte, this I must do myself." Jacq straightened his shoulders and turned to face Darec.

"I committed a grievous crime in my desire to have a better life. I did not think about anyone but myself. Many people have been hurt because of what I did that night in Pelagos. I will live with that my whole life. I did not set out to kill the soldier. I struck out in fear. I am ready to face what charges and punishment are waiting for me, but I ask you to consider what I can do for the survivors of Girona. Let me help them. In doing so I will help myself. I am asking for a truce. Let me help these people. If I do not, then in one year I will submit myself to the punishment I deserve."

Darec moved towards Jacq, his face an emotionless mask. He towered over Jacq and stood close to him, endeavoring to unnerve him. Jacq wanted to take a step back but didn't. He stood up as tall as he could and faced Darec, waiting for his reply.

"It is a poor man's truce, Jacq," said Darec. I do not trust you, but you have worked towards regaining your humanity in helping the Wirliangs and the people of Girona. Go."

Jacq put out his hand to seal the bargain and Darec took it, pulling him close. Darec whispered in his ear so only Jacq could hear. "If our paths cross again and I hear you have not kept your word to help these people I will bury you in a hole like you did my man."

Jacq took a quick breath, upon hearing Darec's threat, the only display of emotion he showed but after all he had been through he knew he would keep his word. He nodded and then with his arm around Carlotte's waist they both stepped off the boat onto the quay. They walked hand in hand towards the trial but then Jacq stopped. He spoke to Carlotte quietly then turned back.

"You have changed your mind, Jacq? You want to return to Pelagos and face your fate?" Darec growled at him.

Jacq walked right up to Darec and, overcoming his fear of the man, stood close and looked directly into his eyes. "I have a book I think you will enjoy reading," said Jacq. He pulled the tiny book he carried with him from Pelagos and tapped it against Darec's chest. "It is not mine to give away, but it will assist you in your attempts to capture a man you have been searching for." Jacq's heart pounded but he felt strength well up inside him and glanced back at Carlotte who stood very still, her eyes closed tightly, concentrating. Jacq believed the confidence he felt came from her.

"One other thing, Darec," Jacq swallowed, the apple of his neck wobbling as he did so. "I took a bag of money from Girard the night I escaped from Pelagos. You will find it hidden in the little cave nearby where your soldiers found us that morning. I intended on keeping it to make a new life for myself, but I no longer want or need it."

Darec looked down at Jacq, intending on belittling him, but he couldn't. His mouth opened but no words came.

Jacq nodded, spun on his heel and without looking back walked towards Carlotte. He took her hand and they followed the last of the people into the forest.

Made in the USA
Middletown, DE
21 April 2018